THE MEMORY MAN

THE MEMORY MAN

Steven Savile

severn House

This first world edition published 2018
in Great Britain and 2019 in the USA by
SEVERN HOUSE PUBLISHERS LTD of
Eardley House, 4 Uxbridge Street, London W8 7SY.
Trade paperback edition first published
in Great Britain and the USA 2019 by
SEVERN HOUSE PUBLISHERS LTD.

British Library Cataloguing in Publication Data
A CIP catalogue record for this title is available from the British Library.

ISBN-13: 978-0-7278-8842-6 (cased)
ISBN-13: 978-1-84751-965-8 (trade paper)
ISBN-13: 978-1-4483-0175-1 (e-book)

All Severn House titles are printed on acid-free paper.

Severn House Publishers support the Forest Stewardship Council™ [FSC™],
the leading international forest certification organisation.
All our titles that are printed on FSC certified paper carry the FSC logo.

MIX
Paper from
responsible sources
FSC   FSC® C013056
www.fsc.org

Typeset by Palimpsest Book Production Ltd.,
Falkirk, Stirlingshire, Scotland.
Printed and bound in Great Britain by
TJ International, Padstow, Cornwall.

ONE

D arkness and light.
Shadows and pain.
They were inextricably linked, feeding off each other, enhancing each other.

Darkness and light.

Shadows and pain.

All it ever took was a single spark to banish the absolute black, but in that moment the two came together to give life to something new. The shadows. Everyone knew that the real monsters hid in the shadows, not in the dark. No amount of light could make them less monstrous. All it ever succeeded in doing was changing the face of their evil into the more familiar masks they wore every day as they moved among us. But then that was the essence of evil, wasn't it? Looking normal. Some mornings it wore your neighbour's face, some afternoons it looked like your best friend, some evenings it masqueraded as your lover and late at night your father confessor. It came dressed in familiar skin, and for a while there you even welcomed it.

For a while.

A narrow slash of yellow underscored the ancient oak door that imprisoned the man. The jaundiced light only lived for an inch before the darkness overwhelmed it. He'd lost track of how long he had been in there. It couldn't be anywhere near as long as it felt. He'd woken naked and cold with a fierce thirst and a tongue that didn't feel like it belonged in his mouth. He had a shit-smeared blanket for warmth. At first, he'd sworn he'd rather freeze, but that stubborn resolve had weakened. Now he clutched the blanket around his shoulders and shivered as he tried to ignore the crust and the smell.

He'd given up shouting and hammering at the door. No one came. He'd made bargains with the darkness, promising not to prosecute them if they just opened the door. He'd even wait long enough for them to slip away. No one ever needed to know who they were. Being a public figure brought all kinds of unexpected trouble, and being a politician meant there was always someone who hated him. Every policy decision transformed him into someone's own personal Antichrist, no matter how well-meaning it was. He wrapped the blanket tighter around himself. There was nothing he could do but wait it out.

He struggled to piece together what had happened. The memories were fragmented and confused, a side-effect of the drugs they'd pumped into his system. There had been an invitation. He remembered that much. It had been nicely written on a small white card. There had been a time and a place, beneath a cryptic message that urged him to *Remember Bonn*.

No, not remember, it was something else, a foreign word. Latin? *Memini*. Remember Bonn. Bonn. Was this about the climate conference? It was hard to believe anything he'd done there could have warranted this. He tried to think. Everything was dulled with the lingering fog of the sedatives. There had been a lot of back-channel negotiations, plenty of incentives changing hands, nothing unusual. He'd done things he shouldn't, including one diplomatic gift that was barely legal. Was that it? How could the shadow know about that?

He heard movement on the other side of the door. Gaoler or rescuer?

He stumbled to his feet, the blanket hanging on his shoulders, and hammered on the door until his knuckles were raw.

More movement, and then they were gone and silence reigned supreme. He slumped down against the wall, hunger tearing away at his gut, confusion soaking his thoughts. The plates of his skull threatened to pull apart on their biological fault lines.

Somewhere in the darkness hope died.

It wasn't a prank. There was nothing harmless about it.

He was lost.

When the bolt finally ratcheted back he had no voice left to beg with. When the key turned in the lock and the door opened he had no tears to soften the pain as he blinked desperately against the light. The air was filled with the smell of his own urine.

'*Please*,' was the only word he could muster, and even that was barely a whisper. The bare bulb hanging from the ceiling behind him turned the figure in the doorway into a shadow.

'I hope you've made your peace with God,' the shadow said.

'What do you want?' Four words. Now, at least, he could find the words if not the strength to deliver them.

'What makes you think I *want* anything?'

'Everyone wants something,' he said, ever the politician looking to make a deal.

'I want nothing from you.'

That threw him. It had to be a lie. He needed it to be a lie.

'Then why am I here?'

'You must undergo a trial. If you succeed, I will allow you to confess your sins.'

'I don't understand.'

'A test of faith. Don't tell me you have forgotten everything?'

He shook his head. It might have been denial. It might have been disbelief. 'You disappoint me.'

'I need water, please. A drink.' As he reached out the blanket fell away from his shoulders to expose a ripe belly matted with a wire of greying hair and flaccid cock that had shrivelled up to the size of his thumb and was all but lost in the tangle of more hair. 'Please.'

The shadow held something out to him. It took him a moment to realize what it was: a plastic water bottle.

'Is this what you want?'

He nodded.

'Good. That should make the trial interesting at least. It's always better if there is a genuine dilemma,' the shadow said. 'Resist the temptation to drink from this bottle for the next twenty-four hours and I will hear your confession. I will cleanse your body and your mind and you will find your release.' The shadow placed the bottle on the floor and kicked it, sending it skittering away into one of the dark corners.

He scrambled on his hands and knees, clutching at the darkness as he reached for the bottle.

The door slammed, the key turned in the lock, and the bolt slid back into place.

This time there was no light.

He fumbled around frantically, his hands finding only empty darkness as he crawled on all fours. All he could think about was the water and his overwhelming need. His hand came down in something wet and his heart sank. He lowered his face to the dirty stone slabs ready to lap at the water like a dog until the astringent reek of his own piss had him recoiling and laughing at himself in disgust and relief.

He kept on searching the darkness until he found the bottle. He crawled back into the far corner and pressed his back up against the wall. He clutched the bottle to his chest.

Twenty-four hours.

There was no way he could go that long without breaking the seal on the bottle cap. It already felt like days since he'd last had a drink. It wasn't a trial, it was torture. Just one sip. Not even a swallow. Just the feel of the cool refreshing wetness on his tongue. He didn't have to swallow, just savour it. He could dip his finger into it and run the tip across his cracked lips. That wasn't drinking, was it? The shadow had said resist the temptation to drink. He hadn't said don't open the bottle. Don't wet your lips. Don't drink. That was specific. He convinced himself there was a loophole, a way to save himself from the hell of his trial, or at least lessen the torment.

He was weak.

He had always been weak.

He knew who he was. He didn't hide from his weaknesses.

The thirst was all he could think about.

It was the devil inside his head, whispering its need over and over until his fingers fumbled with the plastic cap.

He pushed his finger down into the neck, then tried to moisten his lips, but that was never going to be enough. It only served to make the craving more intense and without realizing what he was doing he put the bottle to his lips and took a swig. One mouthful was nowhere near enough to slake his thirst. He took another swallow. Another mouthful. And then another.

The cold water burned his raw throat as he guzzled it greedily down. He didn't stop swallowing that one endless mouthful until the water spilled back out of his mouth and dribbled down his chin and chest. He'd drunk maybe half of it and spilled another precious quarter. As much as he wanted to just drink the rest and be damned, he struggled with putting the cap back into place and promised himself he was saving the rest for later. He had twenty-four hours to get through. He needed to ration the last sips out to keep his strength up if he was going to have a hope of overwhelming the shadow when he returned. He wasn't going to die here, he promised himself, even as the bottle slipped from his fingers and he started to slump against the brickwork. The last thing he felt before he blacked out was the cold kiss of stone where his face hit the floor.

And then there was nothing.

When he came around he was sitting upright, strapped into a too-small wooden chair, hands bound behind his back, the blanket draped over his legs to hide his modesty. There was an unholy war raging inside his skull, and he was on the losing side of it. It looked like the same dank cell. The door was wide open. The bare bulb from the other room cast everything into sharp relief. It was so bright it burned to look at, like the sun. With no way to shield his eyes, all he could do was blink and turn his head, trying to look away.

It took him a moment to realize he wasn't alone; the sound of breathing betrayed his tormentor's presence.

'You disappoint me,' the shadow said, behind him. 'All you had to do was show some restraint. You knew the reward that awaited you. Release. But you surrendered to temptation. Not easy, is it?'

'You were never going to release me,' he said, finding courage in the certainty that he was already dead, and this was hell.

His own personal devil came around to face him, leaning in close enough that he could taste the sulphur on his breath. With the stark light behind him it was impossible to make out any features. And yet there was something about the voice that seemed hauntingly familiar; a long-forgotten sound that stirred a distant memory. *Remember Bonn.*

'You didn't speak out when you had the chance,' the shadow said, pronouncing judgement on him. 'You could have made it stop. All you had to do was speak out. But you chose silence. You chose complicity. You could have prevented so much harm . . .'

And again, he couldn't find the words, this time to save himself. In truth he didn't know what to say. Denials wouldn't save him. Confession wouldn't cleanse his soul. Nothing he said now would make the slightest difference. It was too late. So, for the second time in his life, he chose silence.

A strong hand clamped around his jaw. The pressure was relentless as the shadow man's fingers forced his teeth apart and his mouth open. He tried to scream, but before the sound could take on any real shape his torturer caught a hold of his tongue.

The more he fought against it, the fiercer the vicelike grip became.

The shadows finally gave way to pain.

'You should have spoken out,' the shadow man said, and then the world was reduced to searing pain and blood as the blade sliced through the meat of his tongue.

He tried to scream but was already choking on his own blood.

TWO

Peter Ash stood in the shadow of River House, the nickname of the massive old Ministry of Defence building, looking along the river.

It was a view that he knew better than he knew himself. The circus of the city was there for all to see in splash after splash of vibrant colour and designer labels, reflected in the sunglasses. The crush of bodies filed along the South Bank towards the Tate Modern and the big wheel. An amusement park had been set up, spilling into the already narrow street making it so much more stressful for the tourists to file past the London Dungeon and the Festival Hall and turned that stretch of the Embankment into a pickpocket's heaven. Every cloud, Pete thought, glad to be on the other side of the water.

He'd walked passed the entrance three times already, but had kept going, unable to face whatever fresh hell waited for him inside. It'd been more than a week since he'd last braved the office, which was a fancy name for the broom cupboard that he'd been assigned – a genuine broom cupboard that been converted for him. No windows, no ventilation, and no space. He could touch all four walls without having to leave his seat. The European Crime Division was a fancy name for a cross-border investigative team that spanned the entire Eurozone, their prime directive to cover sensitive crimes that crossed member-state borders. It was great in theory. It was also a bureaucratic nightmare in practice, and only getting worse since the Brexit vote had thrown everything up in the air in terms of British involvement. No one had a clue what would happen once the whole ugly divorce was over. There'd be fallout. How could there not be? But plenty of the suits higher up the chain seemed to think someone somewhere would pull off some kind of deal to keep the whole cooperation thing alive. Ash wasn't holding his breath. Since Mitch's death the one thing he could say for certain was that there were no certainties in life.

When he had been seconded onto the project back in 2012, Ash had convinced himself that it was going to be a dream gig. And for a while it had looked like it was, but it hadn't taken long for the various national agencies to decide they wanted nothing to do with the Division's intrusions. It quickly degenerated into jurisdictional pissing contests and endless red tape, and that was when they were cooperating. When they decided to be deliberately obstructive the whole thing became positively Dantean. The Greeks didn't want Turkish detectives meddling in their shit. The French weren't exactly fond of the Brits hopping on the Eurostar and trampling all over their lovely walkways with the size-nine Doc Martens. Not that Her Majesty's boys in blue were any happier with the idea of Germans in their jackboots making a mess in their green and pleasant Broken Britain. And with the crap going on in Catalonia the Spaniards didn't want anyone coming over, full stop. It wasn't new. It had been going on ever since MI5 decided that they wanted to get involved in anything that caught their eye. That was the logic behind Division locating them in a Secret Intelligence Service broom cupboard. Like it or not, even on home turf they were outsiders.

They.

It had been three. Now it was two, so it was still a they, just. No decision had been made about whether Mitch would be replaced, so for now it was just Ash and Laura Byrne, who somehow kept the office functional while he chased shadows. It had to be a lonely existence for her; late thirties, no children, and a bitter divorce in the rear-view that still burned. She was his only friend in the world these days. He wasn't sure what that said about him. Or her.

He still hadn't made the few short steps up to the glass doors when he sensed rather than saw someone walk up behind him.

'Thought you might need this.' Laura offered him one of the two over-sized paper coffee cups she was carrying. 'Any reason you keep walking away?' She nodded towards the door.

He took the cup from her. The heat coming through the paper made it too hot to hold comfortably. 'You must have asbestos fingers,' he said, changing his grip. She smiled at him. She looked tired. It was hardly surprising. Grief wasn't exactly conducive to sleep. It didn't take a degree in psychology to realize she missed

Mitch every bit as much as he did. If anything, she'd probably spent more time with his partner in crime than he had. The two of them were rarely in the office at the same time, but Laura was part of the furniture. She never went anywhere. 'I'm good,' he lied. It wasn't even a good lie. 'It should have been me, Law,' he said, looking up at the blind windows of the new building.

'What?'

'It should have been me. I should have been in Marseilles, not him. I should have been shot,' meaning not Mitch. 'He shouldn't have been there. And now he's dead.'

Laura shook her head. 'That's not how it works, Pete. It's not your fault. I'm serious. Mitch was a big boy. He knew what he signed up for. And we both know he'll haunt you if you keep this shit up.'

'He was scheduled for down time, but he insisted on being a gent. It's not like I had anything better to do.'

'Look at me, Pete. I'm only going to say this once, and if you ever quote me on it, I'll deny it, OK?' His own smile was sad, but they could share that sadness for a moment without worrying about hiding it. 'You're awesome. Mitch loved you like a brother. And was just as protective of you. There's no way he'd let you put yourself in the crossfire just because he was due a week of R&R. You got that? Besides, it's not like you didn't have enough crap going on. So, if you want to blame someone, there's a bean-counter up there who decided we could only spare two cops as our contribution to the initiative. Two cops. Blame the government. Blame the morons who voted for Brexit if you want. Blame the Russians and their fake-news interference. Blame intolerance and fear and protectionism if you must, but most of all blame the prick who pulled the trigger, because he's the one who deserves it. Not you. And you dying in Mitch's place is the absolute last thing our boy would have wanted. Got it?'

She was right, and he knew it, but that didn't make it any easier. He didn't want Mitch Greer haunting him for the rest of his natural life.

'You're a wise woman, Law.'

'Damn right I am, that's why they pay me the big bucks to wrangle you boys.'

She said boys. Plural. He didn't correct her.

When the Division was created, there was an understanding that they'd be able to call on the assistance of local forces if there was a crime being committed partly on British soil, but if the trail led or originated overseas then Ash and Mitch were on their own. Unsurprisingly, it hadn't taken long for the workload to outstrip the manpower, but no amount of begging released more funds, and the Brexit vote had effectively ended any hope of money or shared resources coming from the Continent. The 23 June 2016 vote was like a stone that had been thrown into the English Channel and what should have been a small splash before it was swallowed whole promised to become a tidal wave of unintended consequences. Right now Ash felt like he was a lone watcher keeping a vigil on those famous white cliffs facing down the oncoming storm. With luck he'd get swept away.

'Got it?' she asked again.

He nodded.

'Anything interesting on the docket?' he asked, looking to change the subject. The job was the only thing they had in common, so work it was.

'Depends on how you define interesting.'

'In other words, no.'

'In other words, nothing that won't wait. You coming inside?'

'Why not,' he said. 'Have to face it sooner or later.'

'That's the spirit.'

There was a moment as he opened the door to the broom cupboard and saw the reflected glow of Mitch's workstation on the wall when he thought his mate wasn't dead, that it had all been some shitty mistake and Mitch had just gone to get a cup of that godawful machine coffee from the kitchen. That moment was the best and the worst moment of the last ten days.

His own terminal was on, waiting for him to sign into the system.

One of the advantages of being inside River House with SIS was the digital fortress the intelligence boys had built up around them. It went beyond firewalls into a world he didn't understand. That didn't matter. You didn't need to know how to make lemon drizzle cake to know it tasted damned fine. Sometimes it was just enough to eat it and remember to lick the icing off your fingers. It didn't hurt that SIS had access to all manner of information he wouldn't have had a prayer of getting his hands on if he was outside River House, either.

Ten minutes later Ash had read through most of the group messages and checked the current active list of investigations across the Division. It made for pretty grim reading, but most of them had been in play before Mitch . . . he shunted that train of thought off to one side before it could derail him. As far as he could see there were only a handful of new cases on the docket; a suspected sarangas plot foiled in Berlin, at least two of the suspects still in the wild; agitators infiltrating the demonstrations in Spain over Catalonian independence; a politician marked as missing in Stockholm, suspected kidnapping; but most of the other items seemed fairly trivial. There were flags against each entry to indicate which countries were involved with the investigation; some had two but several had four or five. Ash hated the flags. Mitch had always said they were a nice graphical justification of why Division existed. He wasn't wrong in that. There was nothing like a line of the Eurozone's brightest and boldest colours lined up to say this shit's widespread, it's insidious and invidious and any other word we can't think of that means serious. See, it's got six flags, it's got to be important. Even with all those flags there was nothing on there that demanded his immediate attention.

Mitch's name had already been deleted from the system.

He picked up the phone.

If coming back into the building had been difficult, then making the call to Division was nigh on impossible. He stared at the line of speed dials. All he had to do was press one button, technology would do the rest.

'I'll leave you to it,' Laura said, picking up her bag and heading for the door.

Working in such a small office meant that there could be no privacy, no secrets. It was good of her to give him some space. She didn't have to. But she was smart, she knew it wasn't going to be an easy conversation. The one benefit of doing it over the phone rather than in person was that Control couldn't see the state he was in.

All he had to do was keep it together for a couple of minutes and hope his voice didn't sell him out.

THREE

Monsignor Jacques Tournard looked out through his office window at what had to be one of the most humbling views in the world; the Cathédrale Notre-Dame de Paris. Without doubt the single most beautiful building in the whole of France. He could have made an argument for it being the most incredible architectural feat in the whole of Europe if not the world, and he was blessed with it as the view from his chambers. He might not have been as young as some of his counterparts within the Church, but they had nothing he wanted, not even their youth. That was a punishment best served on the young.

Tournard had visited the office many times across the last three decades, but this was the first time he had entered the chamber as its rightful occupant, and that made today the greatest day of his life. Even so, he tried not to think of it in terms of personal gain. From here he could do so much good. He could make a difference. He had feared that age had overtaken his deeds and would deny him the office, but the Church was unlike other professions. As a carpenter or builder or in any other honest job he would have retired long ago, incapable of keeping up with the physical demands. As a book-keeper or banker his failing vision would have put paid to any long-term advancement, but not in the Church. Age was a benefit. It conferred wisdom. He was a man of learning. A man of faith.

The gentle tap on the chamber door pulled him back from his thoughts.

'Enter,' he said, knowing that it could only be his secretary, Henri Blanc. Tournard did not know him well, that would come with time, but everyone he had spoken to smiled and said never was a man better named than Blanc. He truly was whiter than white. Blanc was his buffer between the real world and his sanctuary with a view. No one reached his door without passing Blanc first, and that went for the Reverend Monsignor himself. Tournard smiled at the thought of their Little Father being kept waiting because Blanc was such a stickler for propriety.

'Monsignor,' Blanc said as he entered. Everything about the stick insect of a man was tentative as he approached. He came bearing a small package. 'Forgive the intrusion. I have dealt with the day's correspondence, but this came for you.' He held out the package. 'It's marked *personal* so I thought it best I hand-deliver. Your predecessor required that I deal with everything, including all mail marked private and confidential, unless of course it was coming directly from the Holy See. As we have yet to discuss how you wish to handle such arrangements I thought it best to deliver it.'

'Very good, Henri,' Tournard said. 'I think perhaps it is best we follow the old ways, don't you? The fewer changes we make, the smoother things will proceed.'

'Monsignor,' Blanc nodded.

'Leave it on the desk.'

'Very well. Security have examined the parcel, but if you would rather they opened it I can call them?'

'That won't be necessary, Henri.'

'Alas, we cannot be too cautious in the current climate, you understand?'

'I hardly think someone will send me a bomb as a welcoming gift,' Tournard said with a wry smile. 'I would like to think I am not *that* unpopular yet.'

'You can judge a man by the calibre of his enemies,' Blanc said, offering a wry smile of his own.

'I think we're going to get along just fine, Henri.'

'Was there anything else, Monsignor?'

'Not for the moment,' Tournard said, but the man showed no sign of leaving. 'Was there something you needed?'

The secretary shook his head and left the chamber without turning his back to the Monsignor. Tournard returned to his contemplation of the view, but the moment had been spoiled. He turned his attention to the package on his desk. It wasn't particularly large and was wrapped in plain brown paper and secured with brown string. His assumption was that it was some kind of gift from a well-wisher, congratulating him on his elevation, though it was too small for a bottle of brandy. Truffles perhaps?

He settled himself into the supple calfskin leather of his new chair and pulled the wrapped cube towards him.

The address label had been printed on a computer, including the payment receipt for the parcel delivery service. There was no indication of any return address. Indeed, there was nothing to help determine who might have sent it.

Tournard took an ivory-hilted letter-opener with a gold blade and used it to slice through the string, which frayed and snapped on the third draw of the blade and teased away the tape sealing the wax-paper wrap. The box inside wasn't an expense brandy bottle casket, or a cuff-links case, or any of the more exclusive branded boxes he might have hoped. It wasn't a Patek Phillipe watch and it wasn't heavy enough to be a paperweight. There was a single sheet of white paper wrapped around what appeared to be a plastic takeaway carton.

He removed the page without reading the short message written neatly on it, appalled by the contents of the box. At first glance it looked like a piece of meat, liver, going brown as it turned, sitting in a slick of blood.

Why would anyone send him something like that? He reflexively made the sign of the cross.

This was no piece of liver. It was tongue, though what animal it belonged to he had no idea. It was too small to have been harvested from a cow.

He pushed the carton away from him without replacing the lid and picked up the piece of paper that had accompanied it.

He read the note.

There was an address for a cafe he was familiar with, and a time that was less than an hour away. Beneath those was a simple two-word message that shook the foundation of his oh so comfortable world. *Memini Bonn.* Remember Bonn.

Tournard's hand trembled as he folded the paper and pushed it beneath the blotter.

He didn't register the soft sound of Blanc knocking on the chamber door. The door opened anyway. Tournard reached for the open container, but his secretary caught sight of the contents before he could close the lid.

'What in the name of all things holy is *that*?' Henri Blanc asked, and answered himself before Tournard could. 'Is that a *tongue*?'

'It can't be real,' Tournard said, 'I fear I have attracted a better-calibre enemy than I initially suspected.'

But the other man wasn't convinced, and with good reason. It was hard to deny the evidence of his own eyes. 'Would you like me to call security? Or should I contact the police directly?'

'Neither,' Tournard said, thinking of the paper beneath the blotter. The last thing he wanted was attention. 'I need to go out for a while. I will take care of this when I return. I do not need to tell you I expect your full discretion, Henri. Not a word about this to anyone outside of this chamber. Do I make myself understood?'

'Monsignor,' Blanc nodded. 'Should I put it into the refrigerator?' It was a practical suggestion, to preserve the integrity of what would become evidence. Tournard could hardly object to that.

'That is a good idea, Henri.'

The Monsignor carefully replaced the plastic lid back onto the box as if he half-expected the tongue to strike up at him like some sort of serpent. Out of sight it was almost out of mind. He excused his man, who retreated with the boxed body part.

There were so many things going through his head; so many memories that he had thought he had long since escaped brought back with the implicit threat of those two damned words. And he wasn't labouring under any misapprehensions. It was a threat. You didn't send a piece of offal through the mail as a friendly reminder. But after all this time, who else would remember Bonn? Who else had been there to remember? He had plenty of time to worry over it as he rushed towards the cafe. He nodded to Blanc as he left his chambers and swept down through ornately decorated corridors with their gilt plaster details and warm, rich colours, his footsteps echoing an air of desperation as he rushed too quickly through this ancient place to the street below.

The spectre of Notre-Dame loomed over him as he hurried away.

FOUR

'You going to answer that, Frankie?'

Francesca Varg looked away from the computer screen that she had been staring half-blindly at for the last thirteen minutes. She was precise like that. Others might round up or down or sacrifice precision for the skin-crawling 'about'. Not Frankie. If something took thirteen minutes, it took thirteen minutes.

She had been so wrapped up in the words she hadn't registered the phone.

Lasse Henriksen stared, waiting for the penny to drop. It took another full ring cycle. The office was finely balanced on the line between the Scandinavian functionality that encased them in one of the ugliest buildings in the otherwise beautiful city and the chaos of ever-evolving threats. There were new directives coming in every day demanding a new way of working. More than anything, she just wished the pen-pushers and pencil-necks would let her get on with it. It didn't have to be meeting after meeting and this forced liaison with idiots. She had no time for fools, and yet Division seemed intent to force them upon her.

She didn't recognize the number.

Expecting another damned robocall trying to sell her a new mobile-phone package, she answered it with one word, 'Varg.'

'Miss Varg?'

'I know who I am,' she said. Her words were clipped, not bothering to mask her irritation at the distraction. 'How about you fill in the blanks, starting with who you are?'

'My name is Henrik Frys. My apologies for the intrusion. I was given your number by the Prime Minister. I must say he speaks rather highly of you.'

Even as the man spoke Frankie typed his name into the police index, a massive fully customizable database that worked around the personal number system that underpinned the entire structure of the nation. The name sounded vaguely familiar, not a politician, someone who worked in the background getting things done.

Frys. It meant Freezer. That was where she knew it from, he was Head of Security over at the Riksdag. Never had Durkheim's labelling theory been more aptly proven than by Henrik Frys's parents because he was one cold son of a bitch.

'I can't imagine why,' she said. 'How may I help?' The computer came back empty. Any info on Frys was well above her pay grade.

'Does the name Jonas Anglemark mean anything to you?' He waited for her to fill in the silence. Of course it meant something to her. The country's first openly gay cabinet minister, and a one-time rising star of the political right, and still a political force to be reckoned with at seventy-seven, you would have needed to be living under a rock for decades not to recognize the missing politician's name. That and the fact that his face had been plastered all over *Dagens Nyheter* and *Svenska Dagbladet* for a week and filled every single slot on the twenty-four-hour news cycle, even with nothing new to report. It was impossible to get away from him. People didn't just disappear. Not high-profile people. There was an air of dreaded expectancy about it all. The country's memory was long. Anglemark's disappearance was only a hop and a skip removed from the fates of Anna Lindh, stabbed to death in a department store, and Olaf Palme, murdered on his way home from the cinema. No one was saying it, but everyone was thinking it: *not again.*

Anglemark's disappearance had already been flagged up on Eurocrime's intranet, which lead to the obvious conclusion that it wasn't some mentally unstable opportunist like Mijailović, Lindh's killer, or some drug-addicted petty criminal like Christer Pettersson, who fourteen years after his death remained the best suspect in the unsolved Palme assassination. It was organized, and international. That escalated it to another level.

She didn't say anything, knowing the other man would eventually fill the silence.

'The Prime Minister has asked if you would personally take over the investigation.'

'I'm not sure I am in a position to do that.'

'As I said, he speaks very highly of you, and assures me that your discretion can be relied on. Sadly, the same cannot be said for certain elements within SAPO.'

The Security Service had five main jurisdictions: counter-espionage, counter-terrorism, counter-subversion, protective security and dignitary protection. This was their remit, not hers, no matter what the Prime Minister might want. There were protocols in place for a reason. And with a hundred and thirty officers assigned to protection, they had the manpower that Frankie didn't. And they most certainly weren't cursed with loose lips. The entire service was formed around the old promise *En Svensk Tiger*, which had a double meaning as tiger not only meant the strength of the animal, but because of the verb form also meant *A Swede Keeps Silent*. The inference that someone within SAPO threatened the integrity of the investigation was unnerving to say the least. So for now at least she chose to ignore it.

The obvious first question was: why her?

She shouldn't have even been on his radar, never mind the whole thing about speaking highly of her. That made zero sense. Frankie didn't like it when there was no logical explanation for something. She much preferred an empirical world. Nothing was random. Chance and coincidence just meant you'd not paid attention to the inciting factors that got the ball rolling. That she could accept. People were essentially blind, even with social media bullying them to open their eyes and see the truth. Those bullies were just different liars in different cities pretending to be people they weren't.

What she didn't hear in his voice was any intimation of impropriety or a personal relationship with the PM, but the direct request from on high came loaded with so many presuppositions Frys had to be wondering the same thing, surely?

She'd only met the Prime Minister once to her knowledge, and that was hardly an eventful meeting, a few words of encouragement from him, a nod from her, and he'd moved on down the line. It wasn't the kind of meeting that left any sort of meaningful impression on anyone, let alone the most powerful man in the country.

She'd come across a piece of information that, in the wrong hands, could have been used as leverage against him, and in the days before that brief exchange had made sure he both knew it was in the ether and that she had no intention of using it for her own gain. That had been before he was elected, back in 2012. She'd still expected the secret to resurface. Things like that didn't stay buried for ever. But six years on there was no sign that anyone had put two and two together. So, was that what this was? A delayed reward? A high-profile case as thanks for her not ending his career when she'd had the chance?

'SAPO are better placed to find Anglemark,' she assured him.

'He's already been found,' Frys interrupted. 'Or rather most of him has.'

'When? Where?' Two key questions reduced by economy of phrase to two words. The how and why would come.

'His corpse was fished out of the Riddarfjärden an hour ago.' The Knight's Firth was the main lake that turned the city into the Venice of the North, emptying out into the Baltic. It encompassed all the landmarks of the city, including the main island that housed the parliament building. 'A taxi driver saw something in the water.'

That still didn't explain why the Prime Minister had thought of her; but she could hazard a guess, at least, given that the rainbow flag flew from more flagpoles along that stretch of the islands than the blue and gold did.

'Significant or random?'

'As I said, Miss Varg, the Prime Minister wants someone who will operate with discretion.' Which translated to damage control. Anglemark was an openly gay politician, the first. As an old man now he didn't feel the need to hide who he was. He had been a trailblazer. Even in a country as enlightened as Sweden there had to be a first, and thirty years ago when he came out, it was front-page news. Now, with the rise of the *Sverige Demokraterna* there were still plenty of bigots who hated him for who he was, and the murder of a high-profile politician because of his sexual proclivities was a scandal no matter how you carved it up, even if it wasn't the slice of orange in the mouth and plastic bag over the head of auto-asphyxiation that was often used to discredit men like Anglemark.

Frankie said nothing.

That the PM was intimately familiar with people who cruised those streets remained unspoken.

'I can have everything sent over,' Frys said. 'SAPO have agreed to hand the case over to you.'

Now *that* surprised her.

'They have?' There was no legitimate reason they'd simply

cede control of such a high-profile case, unless, she reasoned, they already knew something that would lay it squarely at her door, even with pressure from the PM's office. The murder of a sitting MP was a crime against the nation. She still remembered the outpouring of grief back in 2003 with the streets around Hamngatan closed off for mourners and the hundreds of thousands of red roses and grave candles piled up outside the door of *Nordiska Kompaniet*. 'Why me?'

'We have reason to believe that this case crosses international boundaries,' Frys told her.

'What reason?'

'A note was found with his possessions. We believe it was related to his disappearance. I'd rather not give any more details over an unsecure line, Miss Varg. I have made arrangements for a copy of the note to be sent to you along with everything else we have on the disappearance.'

'You're assuming I'm not going to refuse you?'

'I know you won't,' Frys said matter-of-factly.

Frankie breathed in deeply. 'If we're going to work together it's Frankie,' she said. 'I'll need to advise Control that I'm taking the case.'

'I took the liberty,' Frys said. Which explained why Anglemark's disappearance had already been flagged in the system.

'I'll take a look at the file, but no promises.'

That seemed to be enough for the man. 'The post-mortem is scheduled for tomorrow morning.'

'Not really my idea of fun,' she said.

'Given his tongue has been cut out, I think it might prove useful to observe.'

With one statement a torrent of questions filled her head, but Frankie held a silent phone to her ear. The other man had killed the connection, no goodbyes.

The murder of the first openly gay cabinet member promised to be much more interesting than the tax-fraud operation she'd been contemplating. And who was she to argue with the Prime Minister?

FIVE

It wasn't unusual for Henri Blanc to find himself at his desk long before the Monsignor left his private apartment. Blanc's work ethic was second to none. Every aspect of his life was devoted to making the Reverend Monsignor's life as comfortable as possible. He had a gift for organization and efficiency, more often than not appearing to have discovered a missing hour in every working day that allowed everything he did to appear effortless.

He had his morning rituals, with much of every morning dedicated to the same tasks.

The Monsignor had failed to return to chambers after leaving for lunch yesterday, though that in itself was nothing to be concerned over. There were no appointments in the diary, and it was always going to be a daunting proposition finding his feet in this new role. Blanc could rationalize it a thousand different ways, but none of them made the plastic container and the tongue it contained go away.

His first duty of the day was to ensure that yesterday's delivery was still in the small wine cooler he kept in his office. It was, so he turned his attention to the day's correspondence.

He was not a superstitious man, but a devout and practical one. Yet when the grandfather clock in the corner chimed ten times he felt the hairs on the back of his neck prickle and knew deep down in his bones something was wrong.

It was unlikely that the Monsignor had overslept, and assuming he had attended morning mass in the cathedral he should still have reached his chambers more than half an hour ago, even with people pressing the flesh and wishing him well in his new position.

Blanc tried to call through to the Monsignor's apartment, but there was no reply. That did little to settle his unease.

Thirty minutes later, Monsignor Tournard had still not appeared and Blanc was convinced he was in trouble. He looked again at the tongue in the cooler and wondered what had possessed him not to report it the day before. The threat it represented was obvious, and the Monsignor's insistence the police not be involved only made it more so. But before he took matters into his own hands, Blanc needed to be sure Tournard was not merely sleeping under the influence of some heavy sedatives or suffering from illness. Or worse. His predecessor had, after all, died in that very bed less than three weeks ago. It was an inevitability in some regards, but one did not like to imagine death would come so soon given that Tournard himself was still a relatively young man for the position. Blanc put the thought from his mind, retrieved the spare set of keys from his desk drawer, and bustled through the labyrinthine corridors toward the Monsignor's quarters.

He knew every twist and turn of the ancient building well enough to walk them blind. Every passageway possessed its own unique echoes and silences, shaped by the thickness of the walls and the various stained- and plain-glass panels that offered a glimpse of the godless world outside. The walkway between the chambers and the Monsignor's quarters was lined with marble busts of his predecessors going all the way back to the fourteenth century. The wisdom and piety in those carved white eyes was both humbling and calming, suggesting that as it had been, so it would be, regardless of the passing of time. This world he found himself in was eternal.

Blanc paused at the door, the key in hand, and knocked twice, sharply, waiting for a response from within. When none came he took a deep breath and opened the door.

'Monsignor?' he called out tentatively as he stepped inside.

There was no reply.

There was nothing that immediately struck him as out of place, and no sign that housekeeping had made their daily visit yet. He moved toward the bedroom, calling out again. There was a simple elegance to the apartment's decor, but that did not mean it was lacking. The vast canvas of an Italian master dominated one of the feature walls, seeming to draw the light out of the day. There were plush divans and ornate gilt statuettes and figurines, but more in keeping with the man himself there was a comfortable leather armchair and an Anglepoise reading lamp beside it.

There was an open copy of the complete plays of Marlowe on the small mahogany table, well-thumbed and well loved.

The white double doors to the bedroom were closed.

He knocked again before opening the doors.

The bed hadn't been slept in.

He didn't have a choice; he couldn't wilfully ignore the Monsignor's absence or the tongue in the cooler any more. He needed to report.

He made the call from the Monsignor's quarters, dialling through to the switchboard. There was only one person to contact in times like these. 'This is Blanc, put me through to Donatti.' Ernesto Donatti served as a Vatican envoy, a title that covered a multitude of sins. If anyone would know what to do, it was Donatti.

Within a minute of making the call, the voice on the other end of the line took control of the situation, calmly instructing Blanc, 'Do nothing until I get there.'

'And the tongue?' Blanc asked.

'Leave it. Do not under any circumstances mention it to anyone else, do you understand?'

'Yes,' Blanc assured him, his head nodding faster than he could form the word, even though there was no one to see him do it.

'I will be with you this afternoon.'

'Should I see to it that chambers are made available?'

'That won't be necessary. If the Monsignor returns though please call my offices. If there is no one to take the call it redirects to my cellular phone. And I cannot stress this enough, Henri, not a word to *anyone*. Discretion is imperative. As far as the world is concerned it is business as usual. Should the Monsignor make contact, or anyone who claims to know his whereabouts, I would be grateful if you refrained from mentioning my involvement. Do not dispose of the tongue.'

'I will remain in chambers until your arrival and should anyone ask I shall merely inform them that the Reverend Monsignor is indisposed.'

A problem shared had just become a problem doubled.

SIX

Jacques Tournard woke in a makeshift cell.

The only light came through a dirty glass transom window above the locked door. It allowed enough of the dim glow to leak into the cramped room to banish the deepest of the shadows.

His head burned, the blood vessels stretched to the point of bursting.

There were gaps in his memory.

He remembered leaving his chambers and the hurried walk to the cafe to confront the mystery gift-giver. He arrived first and ordered an espresso. He didn't drink it. He waited, the hustle and bustle of Parisian life all around him. Mothers, babies in pushchairs, shoppers with straining bags branded like mobile advertising hoardings, and those wizened old men with their stubby Gauloises dangling from their lips as they contemplated the philosophies on the pages before them. He hadn't recognized the stranger who joined him at his table, but the man obviously knew who he was, as he negotiated the crowded room to join him without needing to scan the faces of the drinkers. Tournard was well enough known in his own circles to be recognized by some, but he was hardly movie-star familiar.

He remembered too, sipping at the bitter espresso waiting for the man to come to the point, after all they weren't old friends looking to reminisce. One of them had sent a tongue and a threat to the other. As much as he wanted to know about the tongue, there were more pressing matters at hand: *Remember Bonn.*

He had told the man up front he had no interest in raking over the past. What was done was done. It had not shaped him then and he would not allow it to shape him now. The man had seemed content if not pleased to let sleeping dogs lie, and when he began to feel unwell graciously offered to help him into a town car to return him to chambers. That hand on his shoulder as he lowered himself into the back seat was the last thing Tournard could remember.

He should have exercised greater caution. He had wrongly assumed the stranger was a journalist who believed he had stumbled upon some deep dark secret in the Monsignor's past. *Remember Bonn.* He had been wrong. The stranger had somehow drugged his espresso, and bundled him into the waiting car, and now he was here. And he was in trouble.

Tournard fell to his knees beside the bed, his instinct to pray.

The floor was hard on his knees. He had no idea what might lie ahead, but he felt the need for communion.

The door opened before he could clear his thoughts.

He eased himself up with the aid of the bed, but the sudden wave of nausea that accompanied the movement was enough to prove the drug was still working away in his system. He felt a moment of confusion and had no choice but to drop onto the bed rather than risk falling back to the floor.

'You know why you're here,' the stranger said, looking down at him. There was no pity in his eyes. He should know him. It made no sense that he did not.

'There is a price to pay for my soul to be cleansed,' he said, offering no denials or claims of innocence. He knew there was no point. 'But what gives you the right to claim it? What is your part in all this?'

'My role here is merely that of father confessor. I offer you the opportunity to show your contrition, to test your faith, and should you prove worthy, to confess your sins. No more than that.'

'I am not a guinea pig,' he said, but there was no fire in his belly. A younger man would have demanded his release, even knowing what he had done, or failed to do, yet that ceased to matter as his mind drowned beneath long-suppressed memories.

'You understand that the penitent man must confirm his faith if he is to be granted forgiveness, no?' He didn't wait for an answer. 'It is not enough to be sorry. Without faith anything you say is no more than hollow testimony, empty words. What is the value of such a promise? I will tell you. It is worthless, Jacques. And yet we live in a world where empty promises are traded like gold every single day, and it has ever been thus.'

'And if I fail? Do you intend to kill me?'

'I will not stand in the way of a true believer who makes his peace with the Almighty,' the stranger said. It wasn't an answer.

'You presume to act as His vessel? To take my confession?'

'He already knows. He has already seen. Is that not so?' It was a rhetorical question. 'You need to say the words, Jacques. That is all. Not for my benefit, for your own. What happens once you have admitted your sin is on your conscience.'

'You seem to know me, so tell me, what do you think I have to confess? What laws have I broken?'

'You know as well as I do. Your sin is silence. Your guilt is complicity. You saw but said nothing. That is on you.'

'Hence the tongue?'

'You could have prevented it. All you had to do was speak out. I am giving you a second chance.'

'Who would listen? The police? Is that what you want? After all this time? If I offer my confession as a truly penitent soul and receive God's forgiveness isn't that enough?'

'You must live with your choices, Jacques. Others may speak out even if you do not.'

'I'm not the only one? Of course I'm not,' he answered himself. 'Whose tongue was it?'

But his would-be father confessor didn't answer him. Instead he retreated from the makeshift cell and closed the door, locking Tournard once more in the half-dark. Until that moment he hadn't really believed his captor was a killer; he had no such doubts now. He clasped his hands in prayer, though thought better of sinking from the stinking mattress to the hard floor, and instead bowed his head, looking for guidance. His mumbled entreaties fell upon deaf ears.

God was not listening to him.

SEVEN

Ernesto Donatti was glad to be off the plane. He was not a good flier. The flight from Rome had taken a little over two hours, which in the cramped confines of the discount airline compression chamber in the sky was more than long enough. By choice he was a train man. There was an elegance to that form of travel, though the journey to Paris would have taken closer to eleven hours, passing through spectacular country-side, including the mountains of northern Italy, which were proof if any were ever needed of God's great design. If time had not been so pressing he would have welcomed the solitude of the journey as an excuse to be alone with his thoughts and perhaps work a little. Instead, he walked through the arrivals gate, diplomatic papers in hand, and straight through the customs control without so much as a backwards glace.

With the wonders of on-board WiFi he had been able to procure both a hire car and a hotel room from thirty thousand feet, which was truly a miracle of the new gods of this modern world. He could, of course, have left the task to one of the secretaries, but he rather enjoyed browsing the listings and looking for something a little bit different from the run-of-the-mill tourist fare, though he was never extravagant in his choices. He had paid in advance for three days and trusted he would need neither the car nor the room for longer than that.

During the flight he had familiarized himself with Monsignor Tournard, his iPad another of the joys of the modern world. There was plenty to read, but nothing to really make the man stand out from any of his brethren. He was unremarkable in many ways. Perhaps the most interesting thing about him was that he had only taken up his position in the last forty-eight hours. It was more than likely their paths had crossed more than once in the Holy See, but Donatti did not recall ever having spoken directly with him. Tournard's rise had been slow and steady; he was well liked and respected without ever being considered a rising star, and was well into his sixties before being appointed cardinal. This latest position, although prestigious, was more about him returning to the city of his childhood as a reward for years of faithful service than anything else.

There were, he realized, gaps in his history.

It was not uncommon to come across missing months. It often signified the occurrence of some event or scandal the Church preferred to remain secret and thus excised from history as though it never happened. It was less common now in this age of accountability, but forty years ago, fifty, it was no great difficulty to make time disappear. Which made Jacques Tournard infinitely more interesting.

He scrolled back quickly to the front of the file and noted the redaction code he'd missed first time. Access to everything the Vatican had on the Monsignor would need special authorization, and without a very good reason for the request he wasn't going to get it. In so many regards his employers were arcane, preferring to gather all shreds of evidence to some uncomfortable truth to themselves and hide them away in the deepest darkest vaults where they would never see the light of day again. In other words, if the truth was uncomfortable enough they'd want it to stay buried, and the fact that Tournard was missing wouldn't be considered a pressing enough need to grant access to whatever happened during those missing months.

And more likely than not, whatever they were hiding almost certainly bore little or no relation to the man's disappearance. It was a long time ago.

Even so, why send him a tongue? What was the significance? Because it had to mean something, surely? The Monsignor's man, Blanc, was convinced it was human in origin. Donatti wasn't familiar enough with his animal anatomy to know which other creatures possessed tongues of the same relative weight and form that they might be mistaken for human, a dog seemed unlikely, but perhaps a sheep?

His best hope was that the Monsignor turned up alive and well, dishevelled perhaps, disorientated after his adventure, and perhaps suffering from the lingering effects of an episode, dementia, Alzheimer's, there were credible reasons he might not have returned to work after all, but with every passing hour they became less and less likely, and coupled with the tongue the fact that it was a full twenty-four hours since anyone had seen Tournard was the prime motivation behind his hasty journey from Rome.

It was mid-afternoon before he was behind the wheel of the hire car; a small Citroën with a boot space that barely held his overnight bag. It would suffice. He keyed the address into the sat nav and drove slowly out of the airport into the endless jam of Parisian traffic. It took another hour from leaving Charles de Gaulle before he made the left on Rue de la Cité and pulled up in front of the building opposite the grand cathedral. He showed his identification to the security guard who approached the window, ready to move him on. Recognizing the seal of the Holy See, the man retreated to the warmth of his booth, leaving Donatti to find his own way.

Henri Blanc did not cut an imposing figure; indeed, he was utterly unremarkable. He was a skittish little man who didn't seem to know how to occupy his hands whilst he waited for Donatti. He had no doubt worn a smooth path in the plush pile of the carpet with his endless pacing back and forth since their brief telephone conversation.

He met Donatti at the door to the receiving room and led him through to the Monsignor's chambers. Beyond an initial hand-shake and an exchange of names he said nothing until they were behind closed doors, where he struggled to frame the question.

'Would you like to see the . . .?'

'The tongue. Yes. Along with all packaging and anything that might have come with it.'

'I shall return presently,' Blanc assured him, and returned to his own office.

Donatti took the opportunity to acquaint himself with the room. The cleaner had already taken care of the waste-paper basket, which didn't bode well for the fate of the package's wrapping material. He sat behind the Monsignor's desk, running his fingers across the thick white paper lining the blotter. There were no obvious indentations from the pressure of writing.

He looked up to see Blanc carrying a small plastic container in one hand and a sheet of brown waxed wrapping paper in the other. He placed both on the desk and took a step back.

'No note?'

He was obviously about to say no but caught himself in the middle of shaking his head and said instead, 'The Monsignor pushed something beneath the blotter as I first entered chambers. I had completely forgotten . . .'

'Understandable,' Donatti said, lifting the leather blotter. 'It isn't every day you open the mail on something like that. You did well calling me.' There was a single folded sheet of paper lying on top of the desk's green leather inlay.

Donatti picked it up by one corner and teased it open, careful not to smother what might prove to be key evidence with his own greasy fingerprints. It was one thing to claim the authority of the Papacy within the Holy See, but quite another to pretend at any sort of jurisdiction out here in the real world. Assuming the worst, he was going to need the cooperation of the gendarmerie. Backs needed to be scratched, it was just a fact of life. In Rome, he had contacts with law enforcement. There were people he knew and trusted to be both discreet and relentless in their investigation, and those same people knew and trusted him. This was half a world away. Here he was a stranger, and there was no denying Paris was a strange land. Trust the wrong man and every salacious detail would end up in the tabloids.

Pulling the cuff of his shirt down over the heel of his hand, Donatti smoothed out the paper well enough to read the words written on it. The address meant nothing to him, but that didn't matter. It wouldn't be too difficult to discover whether the sender expected Tournard to find it.

'You know this place?'

Blanc nodded. 'Yes, I do. It is a little way from here, but very much walking distance. It is one of the older cafes in the city. There is a wonderful chocolatier next door. You really must indulge . . .' Blanc broke off, remembering the purpose of the other man's visit. 'Forgive me. I can show you, if you like?'

'That would be helpful.'

Blanc waited for a moment then left the Monsignor's chambers and returned a moment later with a gaudy tourist map with oversized cartoonish drawings of all the major landmarks. Donatti studied the simple two-word message below the address: *Memini Bonn. Remember Bonn.* Those words were enough to send a shiver step by step down the ladder of his spine. He carefully folded the piece of paper and slipped it inside his pocket, turning his attention to the waxed paper the parcel had come wrapped in. There was no blue *par avion* sticker, meaning the sender had been inside France when they mailed it, and although the franking across the stamps was blurred it was possible to distinguish the city of origin. Calais. Which, Donatti reasoned, made sense in terms of flight, either to the United Kingdom on the ferry, or into the landmass of Europe across the unpatrolled borders. There were thousands of miles of unprotected borders across mainland Europe. He'd once travelled from Verona to Oslo, taking in both Vienna and Prague along the way, without having to produce any form of identification. It was a decent place from which to disappear.

Or to come closer, hiding in plain sight. That possibility could never be discounted.

Henri Blanc unfolded the street map and laid it out on the desk.

'The cafe is here,' he said, drawing a circle to mark its location, 'and we are here,' he jabbed a finger at where the cathedral was unmistakably marked. It promised to be a circuitous route at best, an hour or more trapped in the rat's maze of Parisian back alleys at worst.

'Would the Monsignor have known where to go?'

'Yes. Remember, he grew up in the city and this cafe is amongst the oldest.'

'Popular with the tourists?'

Blanc shook his head. 'Not particularly. It is rather off the beaten track. I would suggest it is more the kind of place where the young scholars drawn to Paris can pretend to be in touch with the thinkers of the city's past.' For a city that had harboured some of the most creative souls of centuries gone by in her literary salons it was no surprise the young students would be drawn to her cafes in the hopes of capturing some of that spent magic.

Donatti nodded. In the sender's place he would have chosen somewhere public to lure Tournard, but more likely a tourist-friendly place that would be used to seeing hundreds of guests pass through its doors every day rather than the kind of place that thrived on a returning clientele. You didn't want to go somewhere you'd be remembered. He took the choice of venue to mean the sender knew the city. Plenty of people knew Paris, of course, it wasn't exactly an exclusive club, but it was a first background trait on the profile he was slowly constructing.

He picked up the container, peeling back the plastic lid to look at the tongue inside. If he had been a gambling man Donatti would have put good money on it being a man's tongue. A man with a rich diet and relatively poor dental hygiene. There was a white furring around the edges that was almost certainly thrush, and some damage to the taste buds where the webbing had been carved away to cut the meat from the hyoid bone. He was no expert, but Donatti knew that while anyone could exhibit the symptoms, thrush occurred mainly in the mouths of the young or the elderly, or those on immuno-suppressants. He closed the lid and gave it back to Blanc.

The other man took it reluctantly, holding it at arm's length as though he expected it to move.

'Put it back in the refrigerator. I shall have someone collect it, but they won't be able to do anything until tomorrow morning, now. When you've done that I want you to go home. I will meet you back here in the morning.'

Blanc nodded, looked like he was about to ask another question, then thought the better of it, and retreated.

Donatti waited until he had closed the door behind him before he called in a favour.

EIGHT

Familiarity bred contempt. The first time Peter Ash had travelled on the Eurostar it had been the most marvellous thing, a train hurtling through a tunnel carved into the bedrock of the English Channel. It was a feat of engineering unlike anything else he'd ever experienced. There was a palpable sense of billions of tonnes of water pressing down on them. The weight was just *there*. He'd even smiled as they hit the exact halfway and all the electronic signs shifted language. Now it was just a train. It was funny how quickly incredible things became ordinary.

Like a phone call from the Vatican, or at least a representative of the tiny state. Strictly speaking the Holy See was outside his jurisdiction despite being in the heart of Rome. Ash had crossed paths with Ernesto Donatti before, but would hardly have called him a friend. He was a good man, a clever man with a sharp mind and a healthy grasp of irony, but his loyalties were such that he'd have to be a fool to trust him. The Catholic Church was the be-all and end-all of Donatti's world, and he would move heaven and earth to protect it. Still, Ash couldn't help but like the man, so when he called asking for a second pair of eyes he booked himself on the next train out of St Pancras.

Donatti hadn't given much away during their brief conversation, but the simple act of asking for his help meant he was into something *big*.

A missing person fell outside Ash's normal remit, even a missing priest.

'I'm not seeing what makes this an international matter,' he said. 'The gendarmerie are going to be better placed to hunt for your missing Monsignor.'

'It needs to be someone I trust,' Donatti said. 'And there are very few people who have earned my trust, Peter. Very few.'

'OK, no need to get mushy, mate. What have you got?'

'Tournard disappeared yesterday afternoon, first day in the job.

Just after receiving a gift in the post. There was a short note that included an address and two words: *Memini Bonn.*'

'*Memini Bonn*?'

'"Remember Bonn." Latin.'

'Bonn as in Germany?'

'Are there any others? Hence my thought that this might stir some interest with your people,' Donatti said. 'As far as I can ascertain, the Monsignor's career hasn't taken him to Germany.'

'You want me to run immigration checks to see if he has visited there for any other reason?'

'I was hoping you would.'

'Assuming he arrived by air it's easy enough, but frictionless borders make it just about impossible to know for sure.'

'You can only do what you can,' Donatti assured him. 'I'm the one in the business of miracles.'

Ash laughed at that. It summed the other man up perfectly. 'So, what about this gift? I take it it wasn't socks.'

'It's best we save that until you get here.'

Ash didn't press the point. 'OK. I'll need to make a call,' he said. 'Just to let people know I'm not actually deserting. I'll be with you in the morning.'

'Tonight would be better.'

'That bad?'

'Could be.'

'OK. Book me a room. I'll be there as soon as I can.'

'Already taken care of,' the other man said. 'What can I say? I knew you couldn't resist. I'll text you the details.'

'Thanks. I think.'

The call to Control was straightforward enough. They'd asked if he was ready and took his yes at face value.

He had checked the Division's intranet before heading out, updating the system to show that he was en route to Paris and creating a case file for Monsignor Tournard, with the alert *missing person* tagged onto it. He wasn't the only missing person on the list. The missing Swedish politician had moved up from an item of interest to an active part of their caseload with Frankie Varg as the officer assigned to the case.

He'd never met his Swedish counterpart, but he'd heard plenty about her from Mitch after they'd worked a case together last year. His chosen adjective when Ash asked what she was like was 'fearsome'. It was hardly surprising given her background; she'd been assigned to the Division after a decade in the military police. In a world of men, ranks, and discipline, she more than held her own. Mitch had told him stories of his time up in Stockholm. The one that stuck in his mind was a wilderness chase out in the forests somewhere. Middle of winter, knee-deep snow, minus ten temperatures not factoring in the wind chill, and Mitch dressed like it was the middle of spring freezing his tits off as he slipped and slid on the ice – not realizing the huge expanse of white he was running across was actually a frozen lake until the first deep crack resonated and he felt the entire ground shift beneath his feet. He'd heard Varg yelling at him to get off the ice, the only problem was she was yelling in what amounted to a rush of syllables that crashed together into a single nonsensical word that sounded like: *gawvizon*. The guy he'd been chasing had gone under within thirty seconds, a huge plate of ice tearing away and very nearly taking Mitch with him into the black water. She hadn't hesitated. She'd fallen to her knees, brushed away huge sweeps of soft snow with her arms until she could see the face of the man pressed up against the ice desperately clawing at it as he tried to breathe, and put a dozen bullets into the ice around him to break off a huge block, then she'd gone in after him. She'd saved the man's life, despite everything she knew about him. The pair of them had nearly died of hypothermia on the way back to the car.

His crime? He'd been using the refugee crisis to smuggle girls from the Eastern Bloc into Scandinavia, hiding them with legitimate asylum seekers, and once they were over the border stripping them of the vital papers they needed for legitimate work and forcing them to live like cattle in a hostel he'd turned into a brothel in one of the most expensive streets in the city. If any of the girls refused to work they ended up as a newspaper headline, no second chances. They were replaceable. When Division had raided the house on Strandvägen they'd liberated thirty-two girls, some as young as fifteen, none older than twenty-two. The oldest of them had been there for three years. It was a mess that would take a lot of cleaning up, but Frankie had made sure the son of a bitch running the gig would stand trial for what he'd done to

those kids even if letting him die would have been the expedient
option. That spoke volumes about the woman.

Mitch had nicknamed her the Wolf, a literal translation of her
surname, and given the stories, it was easy to imagine Frankie
Varg in that role.

He opened the case file.

The politician, Jonas Anglemark, was no longer categorized
as missing. He'd been marked as deceased. His body had been
found floating naked in the water. A second notation on the file
caught his eye: Anglemark's tongue had been taken by his killer.

Thinking about wolves and tongues, Ash looked out at the line
of lights that appeared to strobe across the length of the train's
windows as it hurtled on. The porter pushed a trolley cart with
unappetizing sandwiches and overpriced drinks on it down the
aisle. He didn't feel much like eating but waved the man over.

'Une bière, s'il vous plaît.'

NINE

Tournard's prayers went unanswered.

There had been a time when he was sure God had at least heard his prayers. Receiving an answer had never been essential to his belief. It was enough to know the Almighty was listening. But that had changed. He blamed himself, thinking his prayers had lost their conviction. Lacking conviction, he had begun to doubt his own faith. Doubting something so essential to his self, he had struggled. He had found a compromise; even if his belief in the Lord had wavered, the Church was everything. It did not matter if he no longer saw God in it.

The lock rattled with the key, drawing his eyes to the door as it opened again.

The man stepped inside, carrying a small tray with a chunk of bread and a glass of water on it. Was this to be his test? A deprivation of the luxuries he had grown used to? He ate well every day, it was true. He enjoyed the finer things in life, including a nice sherry after his meal, perhaps a brandy snifter before sleep. But going without did not mean someone else would eat, only that the food would go to waste. He understood the modern world well enough to know that privation did not make the slightest difference.

'How long?' he asked.

'How long?'

'How long do I have to live on bread and water?'

'How long do you think would be a true test of your faith? A week? Two? Forty days and forty nights? Do you think that would be long enough?'

'Perhaps,' Tournard said, though he doubted he would last half that time on a subsistence diet of bread and water. He was an old man, and though far from frail, he lacked the will to starve himself merely to amuse his captor. 'I didn't know,' he said, meeting the man's eye. 'You have to believe me.'

'I don't,' the man said. He picked up the tray and left Tournard with nothing to eat or drink, which the priest couldn't help but think was the most he deserved.

Tournard paced the room. It was a frustrating nine and a half steps long, a little less than five wide, thanks to the bed. The only other furniture was a small cabinet which, like a cheap hotel room, contained a Bible. He sat with the good book, turning to familiar passages for comfort. There was barely enough light to read by, but the words were so very familiar he didn't need to see them for them to come alive in his mind.

It wasn't until he took the book over to the narrow slash of light coming in through the transom window that he realized it wasn't in French, and neither was it in Latin. He was a well-read man, versed in Italian and English, with a basic understanding of German and Spanish, but his knowledge of other languages was limited to little more than hello and goodbye and even then he could not be sure he had them in the right order. Still, with the familiarity of memory to guide him, he tried to read. He could fathom out the rudiments of the language without knowing which country it belonged to. There were roots that ran from language to language, and with a basic understanding of one Germanic and one Romance language it wasn't unreasonable to think some element of sense could be deciphered, given time. At the moment time was something he could only hope he had plenty of. But then again, perhaps he didn't. Only his captor knew his intentions. Perhaps he was destined to suffer the same fate as the man who had gone before him, his own tongue or some other organ sent on to the next unfortunate on his captor's revenge list.

It didn't take long to discern the extra letters that marked it as a Scandinavian language, but rather than the Danish and Norwegian Ø it was the Swedish Ö he saw repeated in the text. Not that it helped him much to know that slight difference, as one was much like another when you couldn't read it properly. There was enough similarity to the base German that he could decipher a few words in the opening sentences even if he couldn't work out the full extent of the text.

He tried to sound some out, stumbling over the peculiar place-ment of vowel sounds and the seemingly endless consonants that butted up against them. He tried to convince himself that this holy book was his best way of finding his route back to God and clung on to that idea even as the words he stared at lost all meaning.

Telling himself he wasn't giving up, merely resting for a moment to conserve his strength, Tournard set the book down on the bedside cabinet and lay on the bed. He closed his eyes.

It was as though his tormentor had eyes in the room, because no sooner had he settled than the door opened again. This time when he entered, the man carried a small gas lamp, which he set down beside the Bible. The flickering blue flame was no brighter than the light streaming in through the open door.

'It should be enough to read by,' he said. He returned to the door and knelt to retrieve the tray with the hunk of dry bread and the small glass of water.

'Bless you,' Tournard said, as the man set the tray down on the bed.

His tormentor said nothing, leaving him alone again.

Tournard drank down the water greedily, then tore off a chunk of bread and swallowed it, barely chewing in his hunger. That was enough to bring a surge of appetites he couldn't resist. In less than a minute both the bread and the little that had remained of the water were gone.

Tournard was still unsure what exactly was required of him, but perhaps it was as simple as truly believing he could once more connect with his Lord?

The light was barely enough to read by, and then only if the book was held close to the blue flame. He felt the urge to remain where he was for a moment longer and simply rest his eyes. He hadn't understood how very, very tired he was.

Tournard eased himself up off the bed, his left knee threatening to betray him as he struggled into the kneeling position. He focused on his need to pass this test of faith, his mouth drier than it had been even a few moments ago, and tried to find the words to say to his God, to forgive him his silences and deliver him from this evil, for His truly was the Kingdom, the Power, and the Glory.

The words were a comforting ritual. They were part of the process of cleansing his mind, communing with the divine. But this time the memories would not be held back.

Hoping that the concentration trying to decipher more of the book demanded might be enough to silence them, he returned to his task.

'God give me strength,' he implored, as another wave of tiredness swept over his old bones. Sleep was such a temptation. The warmth of it irresistible.

This wasn't right.

He shouldn't have been so tired, but with each passing moment it became harder and harder to resist the lure of unconscious oblivion.

All he wanted was to close his eyes.

He leaned forward, resting his head on his arms, the pages of the Bible creasing beneath his cheek as he promised himself no more than a moment's rest, but sleep soon overtook him and with it came the fear that he had already failed.

TEN

It was gone eight at night by the time Ash stepped off the train in Paris.

Almost as soon as the Eurostar had left the tunnel Donatti's text had come through with details of the hotel.

A second text offered a pick up at Gare du Nord, but Ash had texted back that he'd meet him at the hotel and they could grab a bite while Donatti filled him in on the Monsignor's disappearance.

Despite his basic secondary school level French, he wasn't worried about the taxi driver treating him like a tourist. He had a way of making sure he didn't end up going on any scenic tours of the city. He wrote the name and address of the hotel on a slip of paper and tucked it into the wallet beside his warrant card. He walked up to the first taxi in the rank and made sure the driver saw the card as well as the address before he clambered into the passenger seat. The driver nodded but made no attempt at small talk. With his overnight bag on the floor by his feet, Ash settled in to enjoy the ride.

The city looked as if it was in the middle of a shift change. The office workers were gone, even the most determined shoppers were flagging, the tourists heading to restaurants in search of food. The taxi driver avoided most of that, taking them through narrow back streets to find the fastest if not the shortest route to the hotel.

He paid cash, tipping the man well as they pulled up outside the art deco portico.

He double-checked the name of the hotel against the one on his phone. It was the right place. First impressions, the grandeur might have faded, but once upon a time it must have been quite luxurious with its grand ballroom, crystal chandeliers, and sweeping marble staircases.

'Hi there,' he said to the smiling receptionist as she looked up at him. The teeth behind the smile were a little too white, the lip gloss a little too shiny, the smile itself a little too forced, but that was probably in her job description.

'Good evening, sir,' she responded instantly in English, her French accent thick, like a well-smoked Gitanes. 'How can I help you?'

'You should have a room reserved for me? Peter Ash.'

'Ah yes, Mr Ash,' she said. She quickly checked him in and leaned back to take an oversized key with an oval brass tag stamped 229 from the rack behind her. There was a folded note in the box beneath the key. She put both of them on the counter.

'You need me to sign anything?'

'All taken care of, Mr Ash.' She pushed the key and the note towards him. 'Monsieur Donatti has made sure everything is covered. The elevator's down that corridor.' She indicated a passageway across the foyer's mosaic floor, second on the left.'

He opened the slip of paper.

Call by my room when you've dropped off your luggage, Room 301.

It only took five minutes to dump his luggage and splash some water on his face. The room was spacious, with high vaulted ceilings and a king-sized bed. The en-suite was a wet room. The minibar was generously stocked with a variety of chilled beers and a half-bottle of red, as well as snacks. He was tempted to crack open a bottle, but work had to come first. He pocketed his key and made his way to Donatti's room.

He gave the two sharp raps on the door.

It swung open.

'Peter, good man. Come in, sit. We have a lot to talk about.'

The room was similar to his own, though as a corner room, it had two windows on adjacent walls. It overlooked both the main road and a side street lined with tall plastic bins. There was an orange glow from the streetlights. Two armchairs were set either side of a cast-iron fire grate. Coals smouldered in the grate. Two tumblers of single malt waited on a low table, one cube of ice in each.

'I thought you might be ready for one,' Donatti said.

'Like you wouldn't believe, my friend,' Ash said, sinking into the chair. He lifted the glass to his nose and breathed in the sweet wood-smoke fragrance. It was like a hit of ambrosia. Donatti was right, he was ready for it. He stretched out his feet in front of him. Donatti sat down across from him, his posture upright, more intense, more precise as he leaned forward and reached for his own glass.

'Thank you so much for coming at such short notice.'

'Anything for a decent Scotch and a few moments of peace,' Ash said.

Donatti raised his glass in salute. 'Well then, here's to a few moments of peace before we have to ruin it with work.'

'I can drink to that.' He took a mouthful, savouring the flavour, then nursed the glass for a full minute before he asked, 'So, how about you bring me up to speed?'

Donatti put down his glass and produced a sheet of brown waxed wrapping paper. 'Monsignor Tournard received this yesterday morning. There was a note inside. I have been careful not to touch the inside of the paper on the off-chance the sender was careless.'

'Always possible,' Ash agreed. He pulled a small tobacco-tin sized package from his pocket and rolled it open on the table. He wasn't a forensics expert, but he carried some of the basics with him. He slipped on a pair of latex gloves and pulled a pair of tweezers from the roll.

'My first thought was to see if any of the staff remembered seeing Tournard and whoever had gone there to meet with him, but the cafe was already closed when I arrived. They open again at seven. Fancy an early breakfast?'

'Sounds good to me. So, Tournard? No obvious health problems?'

'That was my first thought when his man called, but he wouldn't have been given the position if he was suffering from dementia.'

'Dementia? How old are we talking?'

'Seventy.'

That raised an eyebrow. 'Isn't that a little long in the tooth to be offered a big job like this one?'

'The reward for long and loyal service to the Church,' Donatti explained.

'Is that how it works? The Church, not the congregation?'

'The Church is the people, my friend,' he replied. It was a well-practised answer that tripped off his tongue without much thought. Ash resisted the urge to laugh. He'd seen the reach of the Church first hand, and it was hard to believe its actions were always in the best interests of the people it supposedly served.

'So, what was in the package?'

'I need your assurance that what I tell you stays between us.'

'You know I can't do that, not if a crime has been committed. That's not how it works.'

'At least until we are sure we know what has become of Tournard?'

'I'm not promising anything. I can't help with one hand tied behind my back. For one, we're going to need help running any prints from the wrapper.'

'If you must.'

Donatti rose from his chair and walked to the small refrigerated minibar and opened it. A shelf had been cleared to make room for a plastic container.

Donatti put the box on the table.

A dark liquid had settled around the bottom of the container, but it wasn't thick enough to hide the darker stain of something heavy swimming in it.

Ash peeled back the lid to reveal its grotesque contents.

'It's a tongue,' he said, stating the obvious.

'You think it's human?'

'I know you do or you wouldn't have called me in.'

Donatti nodded.

'And it just so happens I think I know whose it is.'

'How is that possible?'

'A little wolf told me.'

'I'm not following?'

ELEVEN

It was late, but then it always seemed to be late by the time Frankie found herself wandering down the supermarket's aisles. She wasn't big on domesticity. There was a Pot Noodle in her cupboard that had been there for nine years. She wasn't about to eat it, but it was part of the furniture now, so it wasn't going in the bin, either. She preferred to order in two or three times a week, but even then was adult enough to know a kitchen needed a certain amount of supplies, so as infrequently as possible she made the pilgrimage to the huge all-under-one-roof supermarket out towards Fitja. It wasn't a great area. She wasn't prejudiced, but it was undeniable that there was a heavy Syrian contingent in the region, and problems had increased over the last couple of years, especially with kids stealing cars and torching them.

The only other souls she encountered were the staff restocking shelves.

She was only after the bare essentials: coffee, milk, bread, cheese, a couple of frozen pizzas, maybe some fresh fruit and veg if she was feeling ambitious.

She used the self-service checkout and bagged her meagre purchases in a reusable cotton 'earth' bag and went out into the cold night.

The weather was turning. Give it a few weeks and it would still be light at this hour.

There were a dozen other cars in the car park. They were clustered around the entrance.

She noticed a solitary car parked at the far side of the car park, maybe three hundred metres away. It was caught between the pools of light cast by the overhead lights.

It could have been a police lure, set to catch car thieves in action.

She loaded her groceries into the car, remembering too late that she had forgotten the milk.

She wasn't going back to get it.

She got in and headed towards the exit.

All she wanted to do was get home, take a bath, have a glass of wine, and maybe delight in the ping of the microwave as one of those pizzas was served up.

She caught sight of someone running across the path of her headlights and hit the brakes, hard. The back end slewed away from her, but mercifully she didn't hit them.

She didn't see where they went.

A moment later, the car she had thought was a lure erupted in flames.

She pushed the car back into gear and pressed on the accelerator, the wheels screaming as they failed to find enough grip before speeding away in the direction the figure had run.

It took a second for the headlights to pick up the runner. He'd made it to the far end of the car park.

She floored the accelerator, closing the gap between them fast, but had to slam on the brakes before she hit the verge, and slid sideways barely stopping before she hit the concrete dividing wall that separated the German DIY store from the supermarket.

Frankie was out of the car and running.

Her quarry was sprinting away up the grass bank. There was woodland back there. If he reached the trees she'd never find him.

'Police!' Frankie shouted, though she knew it was technically a lie.

She had zero jurisdiction when it came to something like this, but the guy didn't know that. Not that he slowed down. He didn't break his stride. He ran, head down, arms and legs pumping furiously, and didn't look back.

She shouted again, warning that she was armed and prepared to shoot.

That only spurred him on, with the trees opening up to engulf him in their endless shadows and secret places.

Frankie gave it everything she had got, driving herself on.

An instant later an engine roared into life and she knew that she had lost the race; the man had hidden a cross-country motorbike in the shelter of the trees. The roar of the engine grew more and more distant as he surged away, weaving between the trees until he was so far away it was nothing more than a mosquito buzz.

She couldn't chase him into the trees.

Frankie walked back to her car, the burning vehicle now a blaze bright enough to light the entire car park.

The roar of the raging blaze was caught up with the sound of the scream. One of the check-out women stood, backlit by the flames, staring at the burning car.

'There's someone inside!'

Frankie ran to the car, but the heat was so intense she couldn't get close to it. She took off her jacket and tried to use it as a shield, running at the car, but it was useless. The fire tore through the cab, consuming everything with its voracious hunger. Even so she tried again, getting to within arm's reach of the passenger door, but the tell-tale *crump* of warning had her scrambling backwards as the petrol tank exploded, the shockwaves of the detonation fierce enough to punch her from her feet.

TWELVE

Patrick Dooley flattened the card out on his desk.
When he had first read it, he'd screwed it up and thrown it at the wastepaper basket, missing the shot. Ten minutes later he'd retrieved it.

He heard the rattle of her key in the lock of the front door and hurriedly pushed the note into the pocket of his dressing gown.

Two days.

It was two days since the package had arrived.

Two whole days with that thing sitting in his desk.

The housekeeper knocked politely on his study door, already opening it before he called for her to come in.

Dooley pushed the plastic box to the back of his writing desk, pulled down the roll top, and locked it as she entered the room.

'Morning, Father,' she said, breezily. 'Not dressed yet? Or are you planning on going back to bed? I'll have your breakfast ready in a jiffy. Scrambled eggs sound good?'

'I'm not hungry,' he said.

He had already let a cup of tea get cold without taking a sip.

'Nonsense. We all have to eat. I'll whip up a bite, just how you like them.'

'I really—' he started to protest, but the housekeeper silenced him with a dismissive wave of her hand and a soft, 'Whist.' That was all it took.

'All right, scrambled eggs, plenty of pepper, nice bit of farm-house toast, and a fresh pot of tea.'

Dooley knew better than to argue.

The woman didn't understand the meaning of the word 'no', which was one of the things he loved about her normally. But today wasn't a normal day. At least by giving up she'd get on with her household chores and leave him to stew on the delivery in peace.

'Let me get washed and dressed first,' he told her. 'I think I will take an early morning constitutional, too. Perhaps a walk to the church is in order.'

'That will be nice for you,' she smiled that 'I'm not really listening' smile she'd perfected over the years. The old church was the only place he felt able to find peace these days, mercifully out of earshot of her vacuum cleaner.

Thankfully, his replacement was more than happy to allow him solitude once he took up his seat in the pews. There was always plenty for him to do for the parish, which allowed them to dispense with conversation. And today he didn't even feel like talking to God.

Patrick Dooley needed to be alone with his thoughts.

The problem was all that he could think about was the contents of the plastic box locked away in his roll-top desk and the card that accompanied it.

THIRTEEN

B reakfast was already on the table by the time Dooley returned from his ablutions. That woman could cook. Plain and simple food, but it tasted heavenly. And she kept the house polished to within an inch of its life.

'There you go, Father,' she said as he pulled back the chair at the kitchen table. She poured a cup of Darjeeling for him, dropping a slice of lemon into the tea. It was a routine; almost a ritual.

Coexistence was a delicate balancing act, and they knew each other so well now it was almost easy. But things were about to change.

Looking down at the plate, he felt more hunger than he'd expected, but then there was nothing like Mrs Moore's scrambled eggs. Carefully he cut away a corner and piled the farmhouse bread high with peppered eggs, but mid-swallow he was reminded of the thing in the plastic box and his appetite fled.

He felt the bile in the back of his throat and took a too-big sip of the piping hot tea and choked it down so that she couldn't see his reaction.

He pushed the egg around the plate, mainly eating the bread, managing to secrete much of the yellow eggs into a wad of tissues which he slipped into the pocket of his jacket, which hung on the back of his chair.

At this time of the day there was a fair chance he would find the new priest's black Labrador lounging in the porch of the church. The dog was more than a little fond of Mrs Moore's scrambled eggs. He wasn't a dog man himself, but the parishioners adored the animal, and anything that helped his flock was more than fine by the old priest. More often than not he'd find someone sitting beside the dog, offering a few words of their own confession before leaving – sometimes without going inside. If talking to the dog served the same purpose as talking to God, well, he was fine with that, too, because the Lord was always listening, not just in his house of stone.

Dooley sought out the old dog.

The black Lab struggled to his feet, shaking itself off as Dooley walked through the lychgate and made his way along the path towards the church. The grass verge, he noticed, was a little unkempt. Weeds grew through the cracks in the old flagstone path. Most of the stones themselves had been worn smooth by the passage of countless penitents and pilgrims over the years. The stone church itself was Norman in construction, one of the first to be built after the invasion, and had stood in various forms for nigh on a thousand years. The construction was, Dooley felt, testimony to those old masons and their unwavering faith. That they were capable of such craftsmanship when other aspects of civilization had been so backward. He smiled, seeing again the faint lettering on his favourite grave. It was its very own little tragedy, for Lily, Who Sleeps, killed by a cart going at the ungodly speed of four miles an hour. Oh, how the world had changed, and not all for the good.

'Ah, morning, Tolstoy,' Dooley said as the dog sidled up beside him. The old dog sniffed at his jacket pocket. 'You can smell that, can you, boy?'

He smiled as he retrieved the wad of tissue from his pocket. Tolstoy's tail wagged faster and faster, and for just a moment he might have been a young pup again, not the worldly old soul he was. Like they both were. Without a word the dog sat and looked up at him, waiting patiently while Dooley tipped the egg onto a patch of stone for him to lap up. In a matter of seconds there was no trace of Mrs Moore's scrambled eggs left. He ruffled the old dog's fur. 'There's a good boy.'

'Are you leading him astray again, Patrick?'

Dooley looked up to see his replacement standing in the open doorway, a shock of white hair against the semi-darkness of the church's interior. Michael O'Hare was barely into his forties, but the good Lord had gifted him with the gravitas of a much older man. Dooley would never admit it, but he'd had his doubts about the man when the bishop had appointed him as his successor, but Michael had more than proven himself to be a good man and shown his commitment to the parish time and time again. In this day and age Dooley had, he felt, reasonably worried that the young man was some kind of career cleric, keen to progress through the ranks of the Church without a genuine affection for his parishioners. But nothing could have been further from the truth. Young Father Michael, as everyone called him behind his back, had fallen in love with the place, and it in turn had fallen in love with him. Given a choice, Dooley doubted his replacement would ever leave. He might not have a choice.

'Caught in flagrante,' Dooley said, with a wry grin. He screwed up the tissue again and buried it in his pocket. 'How about we keep this our little secret? Just you, me, and Tolstoy here? There's no need for Mrs Moore to know, is there?'

'How much is it worth to you?' the other man asked with a wink.

'Father O'Hare, are you soliciting a bribe? Tsk, tsk.'

'I wouldn't dream of it, Father Dooley. Rest assured, your secret is safe with me.'

For the long silence between heartbeats Dooley thought the other man *knew* and felt sick. But of course he didn't. This place was his refuge. The problem was that now the memories were uncorked they insisted on flooding back, and there was nowhere to hide from them. Not here. Not even in this sanctuary. He breathed deeply of the hypocrisy that was the foundation of his faith and wished with all the fervour of a zealot that the damned package had never arrived. He could have died happily without reading the two-word message on the card. How could he forget?

His fingers felt for the card in his trouser pocket. He thought about requesting the sanctity of the confessional to unburden himself but that wasn't fair on the other man; it wouldn't change anything, and realistically just meant someone else had to bear his shame.

'I appreciate that.'

'I'm just heading back to the vicarage for a cuppa.' He nodded towards the sandstone house that had been Dooley's home before his retirement had seen him move into the cottage down the way, which admittedly was better suited to his needs, even if it still didn't feel like home. 'Can I tempt you?'

'Not this morning,' Dooley said. 'I was rather hoping for a little quiet time.'

'Need a chat with the boss?' O'Hare lifted his gaze skyward.

'Something like that.'

'Make yourself at home,' O'Hare said, stepping aside. 'Come over when you're done, if you like. Bring Tolstoy back with you.'

The man placed a hand on Dooley's upper arm and gave it the lightest of squeezes before heading off towards the road.

The Labrador looked up at Dooley but showed no sign of going after its master. It understood.

'Just you and me then, fella. I guess you'd better come in.' Without hesitation, the old dog walked straight to the back of the vestry and curled up on a piece of carpet that had been placed there for that very purpose. Dooley took a moment to just drink in the calm of his old church. He had spent so much of his life within these walls. He could only delay it for so long; it was time to make his peace with God. Then, and only then, could he come to terms with what he must do next.

He walked slowly towards the altar and knelt slowly, lowering himself to his knees in front of it. He closed his eyes, hoping to feel the familiar presence of the Almighty, but there was nothing, no matter how fervently he prayed, not even the slightest sign that anyone was listening. This was not his sin to confess. His failure was simply one of inaction. He should have done something. But it was all so very, very long ago now. He had lived with that guilt for most of his life.

That package had undone everything about this fragile life he had built for himself. Now all he felt was sadness. He wasn't the man he had always believed himself to be.

Dooley rose unsteadily to his feet, his knees complaining as he did so, and with effort took a seat in the front row of pews. He sat for a full minute in silence, not in prayer, before he pulled the card out of his pocket.

He had lost count of the number of times he had read it. It didn't matter how many, to be fair, he hadn't misread or misunderstood the message. There was no room for interpretation or mistakes.

He knew what it meant.

The message was simple, '*Memini Bonn.*' Today's date had followed those two words along with a time and destination; the coffee bar in a quaint little cafe down in Epsom itself.

It was too late for him to make the journey now, meaning he would have to face whatever consequences the anonymous sender intended.

It had taken him a moment to realize what the object was bobbing within the fluid in the plastic container, but as it rolled in the liquid it seemed to be looking at him. He had barely been able to keep the vomit down long enough for him to reach the bathroom.

He should have rung the police straight away; it would have been the sensible thing to do. But that would have meant telling them that he was afraid and what he was afraid of. Which meant explaining what he had been party to. It didn't matter that he had been an unwilling observer.

That was why he had been sent the eye.

He had seen and done nothing to stop it.

That confession would have branded him for ever the man who did nothing.

Maybe it was finally the time for the truth to come out?

It was only a pity that he could not bear the shame of being around to own his part in it. Let them blame a dead man. Let them cast their stones. Let them damn the witness.

There was a reason he had come to this place and it was not that he thought of it as home. He had come here because, if he could muster the strength to go through with it, it would be O'Hare who found his body, not Mrs Moore. She did not need to see that.

FOURTEEN

F rankie Varg woke to the unmistakable noises of sex. It beat the dreams of burning cars that had haunted her all night. Thin walls and tired mattresses betrayed the lovers. She assumed it was an affair, one last urgent fuck before going back to real life. Good for them, she thought. She turned on the radio to give them a little privacy. The hotel gradually came to life; the sound of doors opening and closing, the rattle of pipes and splash of running water in neighbouring rooms created their own little theme tune. The double glazing wasn't thick enough to mask the sound of a delivery van arriving beneath her window. She could smell the fresh bread and cinnamon buns from her room.

It had been a long night. She'd finished too late to make the drive back to her own apartment and had no great urge to sleep in a familiar bed. That wasn't her. She craved practicality over familiarity, so by the time she had done everything she wanted to do the only logical choice was crash in the city and make an early start. It was purely practical. There was no one waiting for her back home, no cat to feed, and her plants were all plastic.

She kept a duffle bag in her car with a change of clothes and a few basic toiletries in it. She'd stayed here so many times several of the staff knew her by name.

She'd slept fitfully, if it wasn't the burning car it was a surreal warping of the post-mortem that plagued her dreams. The macabre incisions, the pale, pale skin, and the victim lying there, eyes glazed over, pencil-thin lips blue and begging for her to find her killer. It was an old phrase, cops being speakers for the dead, and somehow it had infiltrated her dream giving it a weird horror-movie quality. There had been no real need for her to attend the post-mortem beyond it being the right thing to do. Frankie was big on doing the right thing. Perception could make every difference in the world, especially when you spent half of your day treading on the toes of local law-enforcement agencies. She didn't want to give them an excuse to make her job more difficult than it had to be. She heard them talk, how she was a cold bitch who thought she was better than them, and that was the nice stuff.

It didn't matter how many times she attended an observation, it always had the same effect on her. They said you never forgot your first. It was the same with corpses. Her first post-mortem she'd been standing less than a metre from the body when the first incision had been made. But that wasn't the thing she remembered, it was the sound as the pathologist used the rib-cutters to sheer through the dead man's ribs and then spread the bones so that he could get at the no longer vital organs inside. That sound was like no other.

Her phone rang.

Frankie checked the screen, but there was no caller ID and she didn't recognize the number.

'Varg,' she said.

'Agent Varg?' an apologetic English voice asked, though for all the supposed English politeness didn't wait for an answer. 'This is Peter Ash.'

She knew the name. It was hard not to, given his partner had died during an active investigation just a few weeks ago. Everyone in Division knew that. She had worked one case with Mitch Greer. They'd connected. He was a good man. In that way the death of one of them hurt them all. It certainly rammed home the point that it could just as easily happen to them next.

'Good morning, Mr Ash. How are things in London?'

'Pete, please, and I'm sure it's wet and cold in London, but I'm not there. I'm in Paris.'

'The joys of EU membership, my Brexiting friend. Make the most of it while you can.' To be fair, the dust around the colossal clusterfuck that was the United Kingdom's withdrawal from the Union, the Single Market, and all of the concomitant bodies, including the Eurocrimes Division, was a long way from clearing. Right now, no one knew how things were going to fall one way or the other, but it was obvious that the easy cross-border co-operation was going to suffer. There was no way it couldn't. Hell, there was no way of knowing if Ash's part of the organization would be lost to the rest of Europe, or if they would continue to honour their commitment to the Continent's safety and cooperate in its blanket policing and protection.

'Luckily, we've already dug the tunnel,' Ash laughed. It was a kind laugh, an honest laugh.

'So, what can I do for you, Pete?'

'Actually, it's more what I can do for you. I think I have something that might belong to you. A tongue,' he said. 'I understand you're missing one.'

Frankie felt a chill chase up her spine.

'You did say a tongue?'

'I did.'

'My tongue is in Paris? How?'

'It was delivered by courier to a priest.'

'Why do I get the feeling your life is more interesting than mine, Pete? I don't suppose you have any idea why he might have been sent it?'

'The sixty-four-thousand-euro question. I wish I knew. And it's not like I can ask him, given he's been reported missing. No one has seen him since he received it.'

'Coincidence?'

'No such thing. And we're not talking some run-of-the-mill clergy, we're talking a bishop. Now, if it is Anglemark's tongue, what I'd want to know is why he'd be sent the tongue of a Swedish politician? There has to be a reason. I'm not buying random act of terror. Does your man have a connection to the Church?'

She thought about it for a moment but couldn't recall any mention of organized religion in his file. 'Not that I know of. But it's reasonable to assume anyone with political ambitions greases the palms of the Church one way or another. What is it they say, it's easier to elect a criminal than an atheist?'

'Why vote for anyone who believes in fairy tales? I like my stories grounded firmly in reality. Stuff I can understand. Like why would a cleric in Paris be sent the tongue of a Swedish politician? I want to know the story there.'

'And you're worried about your guy?'

'Wouldn't you be?'

'Statistically speaking, yes, and with good reason,' she said. 'But I would rather be working a missing persons case than a murder. I like the illusion of hope.'

'I'm all for catching a killer,' Ash said. 'My white-knight days are over. As far as I see it, this story plays out one of two ways, either the priest has met up with the tongue guy or he's gone into hiding from him.'

'Any leads?'

'A note, but hardly informative. The packaging, note, and tongue are on their way to the lab for processing. Maybe we'll learn something from them,' he said.

He walked her through it, right up until the point where he told her that he was about to visit the cafe where the priest had been instructed to meet the mysterious gift-giver.

'Remember to check the CCTV in the neighbouring streets, not just the cafe. Look for cars coming and going. Anything you mark as out of the ordinary.'

'I have done this kind of thing before.' He laughed again.

'Sorry. But this might actually be the break I've been looking for, it's hard not to give orders.'

'Don't sweat it. We're all on the same side. Laura my office administrator's just the same, she thinks she runs the show.'

'Are you sure she doesn't?' Frankie laughed. This was different. Easy. She wasn't used to talking to strangers beyond the brusque day to day of getting the job done. There was something oddly flirtatious about this connection she was sparking up with a comparative stranger. It was decidedly not her.

'You could be right,' he conceded. 'Anyway, thought you should know, so you can stop looking for it. Because I doubt very much that there's more than one tongue out there without a mouth to go with it.'

'The one thing this job has taught me, Pete, is that anything is possible in this crazy world of ours. Including the existence of some flesh-collector with a tongue fetish.'

'Nice,' he said, though the image was anything but.

She was already trying to link her politician and the priest, running through all manner of possible connections, but kept coming back to the most obvious, and frightening, one, that it was random. They had systems in place capable of finding even the most tenuous connections. She had to make use of them. 'Keep me posted about your missing bishop. You might get lucky with a happy ending.'

This time his laughter was a sharp bark, and she realized what she'd said. She didn't bother disabusing him of the image.

They had to work on the assumption that the priest was going to be found alive, even though every hour he went unfound the chances of that diminished. Frankie knew the numbers. The truth was almost always within them, even if you stubbornly refused to see it. There was a statistical likelihood he was already dead.

'I'll give you a call as soon as I have any news,' he promised.

Frankie said goodbye and hung up.

The murder of one individual was something with very defined parameters. It was something where plans could be put into place and followed through, where mistakes would be at a premium, and hope slim. But once a second victim was added to the equation, everything shifted exponentially, especially the room for mistakes. What if she was looking at a much larger case than she'd originally suspected? A tongue in Paris from a corpse in Stockholm meant throwing the investigation wide open. Everything they had reasonably thought they knew was wrong. Which made it her favourite kind of case.

FIFTEEN

Peter Ash left his hotel room a few minutes after ending the call to Frankie Varg.

He headed to the lobby to wait for Donatti.

They had agreed to visit the cafe together, though he would have preferred to have gone alone. It was the way he'd always worked with Mitch. Solitude suited his temperament. But he was the stranger in this even stranger city, lost in a language where the only thing he knew to listen out for was a sneer of Roast Beef. The Church man had the advantage of being fluent in the language and maybe it was a relic of when there were two Papacies but being sent by the Vatican still carried a fair amount of weight. The trick was to use Donatti's position to the best effect.

He took the stairs rather than the rickety old caged elevator, which looked like it was hanging on by a wing and a prayer – or more pointedly a worryingly thin cable. Pete wasn't great with heights, or confined spaces, and the fact the caged elevator offered a rather open view of the mechanisms and gears hauling the car up and down didn't instil confidence. The service stairs were nowhere near as grand as the main staircase. The floral carpet was worn down to the brown thread weave in the middle from the endless up and down of a century's worth of cleaners. There were black scuff marks on the wall where carts had banged up against the brickwork.

Pete pushed open the fire door at the bottom of the stairwell and emerged on the far side of the reception. He wasn't surprised to find the Italian already waiting for him.

Donatti sat on a large leather sofa reading *L'Équipe*.

He was dressed for business, in an immaculately tailored black suit with a crisp white shirt with buttoned-down collar. The top button was undone, a sole concession to informality. His Italian leather shoes were polished to a shine so perfect the staff manning the reception were reflected in them. Pete felt like a slob in his own wrinkled sports jacket and washed-out denim jeans, and there was no hope of his wine-coloured suede trainers reflecting anything but the crumbs he dropped from his last meal.

Donatti folded the newspaper and rose, offering a smile as Pete approached.

'Ready to take on the world, my friend?' Donatti asked, dropping the newspaper onto the mahogany table for the next time-killer to enjoy.

'Ready for a decent coffee,' he said. 'Anything in there?'

'The paper? Nothing.'

'Well, that's something. I've just had a chat with my colleague investigating the Jonas Anglemark murder in Stockholm.'

'The owner of our tongue?'

'We have to assume so.'

Donatti nodded. 'I am sure he will be delighted to reunite the flesh.'

'She,' Pete corrected. 'But yes, even if it opens up a whole slew of new questions, like how a Swedish politician's tongue ended up here.'

Donatti raised a hand in apology. 'The sins of living in my male-dominated world makes it far too easy to make assumptions.'

'It's all good, Padre.'

'Do we know anything about the victim?'

'Some,' Pete said.

He talked as they walked.

He told Donatti the little he knew. It was a judgement call, and under other circumstances he might have been more circum-spect, but he didn't for a minute think the Vatican had flown his old friend to Paris merely to help find a missing priest. The Church, like the invisible God they served, tended to move in mysterious ways. Maybe he really was just there to do someone a favour? Or maybe he was following a deeper investigation of his own? The only way he'd find out one way or the other was if they worked together.

The cafe was easy enough to find. They stood across from it for a moment, looking at the wonderfully Parisian windows with their gold lettering, and the plush awning that would come down later if the sun dared show its face. The place looked as if it had last been refurbished in the fifties and worn the same decor since then.

They crossed the street and went in and were immediately hit by the twin fragrances of coffee and smoke, with an undercurrent of fresh pastries.

The furniture was worn, the wallpaper sun-faded, but it was welcoming in a way that the faceless coffee chains could never be. The obvious problem, though, was that there was no way this little slice of Parisian culture was the kind of place that would have installed CCTV. He hadn't noticed any cameras in the street, either.

They were relying on the unreliable, the memories of the staff.

Already, half the tables were occupied, and seemed as though they had been for several hours. Pete heard the unmistakable sounds of cooking coming from the direction of the kitchen.

There was no one at the counter, so the two men took up residence at one of the vacant tables by the window.

A waitress with her hair pulled back in a ponytail to keep it out of her face bustled out of the kitchen a moment later, balancing a couple of laden plates to the next table.

Donatti caught her eye and offered one of those smiles that seemed to completely change his face. He spoke to her in fluent French, and without any discernible accent as far as Pete could tell. The exchange was too quick for Pete to follow.

'Parlez-vous Anglais?' he interrupted, feeling like a fool.

'Of course,' she smiled. 'What can I get for you?'

'I'd kill for a coffee so thick and black you can stand your spoon up in it,' Pete said.

'That we can do,' she promised. 'Anything to go with it?'

'What's good?'

'I ought to say everything,' she said, 'but I'm partial to the pastries. Our baker is a magician.'

'Then I shall put myself in your hands, black coffee and pastries sounds like a perfect way to start the day.'

She jotted a few words down on her pad, then slipped the pen behind her ear. Before she could turn her back, Pete asked, 'Were you working yesterday?'

She hesitated for a moment, unsure, then nodded.

'Sorry,' he said, producing his badge. 'It would be really helpful if we could ask you a few questions?' The sight of the badge had one of two effects, it either reassured the innocent, freeing them up to talk, or silenced the guilty.

'Of course. Anything to help. I was here all day. Family business,' she said, which explained everything.

'Ah, well, they'll work you into the ground, then tell you you're doing it all wrong,' Pete said.

She glanced in the direction of the kitchen and saw a large man standing in the doorway. 'My father doesn't like me to spend too long talking. Talking isn't working.'

'My old man was just the same,' Pete said.

Donatti took a piece of paper from his pocket. It was a photograph of the missing man. Not a snapshot. It had been taken during a photoshoot to go with the press release for his new appointment. Even the Church needed to manage its image in this day and age. Or especially the Church. 'Do you remember this man coming in yesterday? It would have been early afternoon.'

She took the photograph from Donatti and shrugged. 'He looks familiar. People come and go all the time. We see maybe one hundred, one hundred fifty faces a day. Sometimes more.'

'He would have met someone here, if that helps,' Pete said, hoping the gentle prod might help her remember something.

'Man or woman?'

Pete was suddenly struck by the realization that Donatti wasn't the only one jumping to conclusions. Tournard could just as easily have come here to meet a woman as a man. He gave the Vatican emissary a glance and saw that he was thinking the same. 'I want to say man, but the truth is we don't know, I'm afraid.'

'I really can't remember.' Then there was a flicker of recognition. 'He's a priest?'

'That's right,' Donatti said.

'That explains why I recognize him,' she said, and Pete felt that little flare of hope drain away. That was the problem with public figures, even if you never met them face to face they inevitably left some kind of false memory behind. 'Has something happened to him?'

'That's what we're trying to find out,' Pete said.

Donatti slipped the photograph back into his pocket.

'I'm sorry I couldn't be more help.'

She left them.

'We're going to have to report him missing,' Pete said.

Donatti nodded. 'And at risk. But it would be better if the

story was kept out of the press for a little longer. Could you hold off, just a little while?'

Ash made a face.

'You think he's dead, don't you?'

'The truth? Yes. But that doesn't mean he is. Just because he was told to meet someone here, doesn't mean that he actually came. Would you in his place?'

'I don't know,' Donatti admitted. 'Perhaps if I was feeling guilty.'

'Not me. I'd run. As far and as fast as I could. I wouldn't want that man catching up with me.'

SIXTEEN

It was almost ten.

A plate of warm croissants joined the coffees.

'My father said to tell you the man you're looking for was here yesterday,' their waitress said. 'He didn't see him, but overheard someone making a joke about God's tool on earth mixing the ordinary people.' Pete assumed it was a dirty joke, or at least in poor taste given the fact she used the word tool over instrument. 'They don't tend to mix, the Church and normal people. But that's God's Army for you.'

Ash couldn't help but smile as Donatti tried to will himself smaller in his seat. The other man hadn't needed to reveal his more unearthly employer, and maybe that was just as well. Not that he should be held to account for all the sins of the Church. Or maybe that was his job? Ash never really understood how it worked for people who believed in this stuff. He tried to keep an open mind, but it just didn't make sense to him that someone would believe in something so obviously made up – and that went for Joseph Smith's magic underpants and L. Ron's aliens burning in a volcano as much as it did Moses downloading the ten commandments to his tablets from the cloud . . . He offered her a smile, and a question.

'I don't suppose your father remembers who he overheard? That could be a big help.'

She shrugged. 'I can ask.'

She disappeared back into the kitchen only to return a few seconds later. 'Sorry,' she said. 'He wasn't a regular.'

'I don't suppose he saw who the priest was with?' Donatti asked. 'Even just male or female would help tremendously right now.'

'Sorry,' she said again.

'Would your father recognize the man if he came back?' Ash asked, reaching for his wallet.

'I doubt it,' she said. 'He doesn't venture out of his kingdom very often.'

'I understand completely,' Peter Ash said, teasing out one of his cards. He held it out to her. 'But just on the off chance the guy does come back, and the stars align and somehow your dad recognizes him, I'd be incredibly grateful if you could ask him to call me.'

'Sure, *Peter*,' she smiled as she read his name slowly off the card. 'It's the very least I can do for the man who trusted my taste in pastries.'

'And if he doesn't come back, well you've got my number,' he said, which earned him a laugh.

'Not sure that counts as progress,' Donatti said as the girl headed back to the kitchen.

'It would have been nice if we could have reduced our pool of suspects by fifty per cent, but beggars can't be choosers.'

There wasn't much to be gained by staying in the cafe, besides calories. They ate the buttery croissants in near silence. Ash watched the heavy black hands of the Deco clock tick around. He finished his coffee then made a call to Laura back in River House.

She answered on the second ring.

'Hey, Law.'

'Hey yourself, stranger. I take it you're not coming in today?' The question was light-hearted but had an edge to it. Probably because there was a better than even chance he was either in a gutter or curled up in bed. He couldn't blame her. She was a natural worrier.

'Don't worry,' he said. 'I'm on a case. Sort of.'

'Sort of?' He heard the rattle of keys as she ran a quick search in the system. 'You're not registered on any assignment.'

'Hence the "sort of,"' he said.

'Go on,' she said. He could hear the exasperation in her voice, but knew that she was smiling, too. Any case was progress. Christ, getting both legs into his jeans in the morning felt like progress. And there was no getting around the fact that even just a few months ago he would more than likely have hopped on the Eurostar without getting approval. So, the fact he'd actually let someone know that he was leaving the country was progress, too.

'I'm in Paris,' he said. He could almost hear the sigh that she released.

'Are you now?'

'Arrived last night.'

'Did you now? And why would you run off to Paris, pray tell?'

'I'm helping an old friend from the Vatican try to find a missing bishop.'

'Which sounds like the set-up of a bad joke. So, how on earth have they managed to lose a bishop?'

'A surprisingly difficult question, there, Law. But not through carelessness. It's connected to Frankie Varg's murdered politician in Stockholm.'

'I saw that one,' Laura said. 'Struck me as an odd case to get flagged by Division.'

Ash brought her up to speed, careful not to be too explicit with the details given that he had no idea who might be listening. 'What I need you to do is find a connection between the two men.'

'You make it sound easy.'

'A politician and a priest, a thousand miles apart? Piece of piss. I have faith, Law. If anyone can find a link, it's you. So, dig. Somewhere their worlds collide, even if it's something ridiculously random like the fact they attended the same six-year-old's birthday party. I want to know what that point of intersection is. The note that came with the finger mentioned Bonn. That must mean something. So, start there.'

'This isn't my first investigation,' Laura said.

There were all kinds of databases being compiled that amalgamated all manner of records. The world was focused on data these days. Data farms. Social-media profiles. All those clickbait quizzes. There was a wealth of information out there in the public domain that even a decade ago wouldn't have been anywhere near online, but it was still pretty fragmentary. Law enforcement had their own systems that focused on criminal behaviour, on crime statistics across the countries and criminal pathologies, building on the networks established by Interpol, but even that was lacking. Some countries just didn't prioritize the maintenance of electronic records, while others weren't big on sharing.

'Anything else come in I need to know about?'

'All quiet. Ish. I did hear someone moaning about possible changes in the building.'

'Ah, politics. Fantastic.'

'You're well out of it,' she said, and spent a couple of minutes trading grapevine gossip. The fact was no one wanted Ash or the unit in the building, but for some reason they all seemed to forget that Laura was one of 'them'.

Ash didn't give a shit. He either had a job or he didn't. It wasn't the end of the world, either way. People would still commit crimes, Brexit or no Brexit. Both Five and Six could get massive budget increases even as the number of beat cops in the capital was sliced brutally because no one could see the wood for the trees. It was all about dealing with the big-picture complications, the kind of things that were election-winning issues, not the minutiae of actually policing the streets. There was never enough money for that.

Anyway, the one thing he took from the conversation was that it was unlikely he was going to be saddled with a new partner any time soon.

And he was just fine with that.

SEVENTEEN

Frankie put a call into the pathology lab, letting them know a tongue had been found. The odds of two tongues floating around bodiless were slim, so the chances were better than good it was Anglemark's, but it still wasn't confirmed. The lab tech didn't sound particularly interested, or surprised that it had turned up a thousand miles away. It was almost as if they dealt with missing body parts every day.

'It would have been better if it had come to us first, given the profile of the victim.'

'To be honest, my biggest concern was biological over territorial. It's meat. Meat doesn't stay fresh for ever. I didn't want it rotting during transport.'

'We do have such things as refrigeration, Miss Varg. It's really quite civilized these days. Not to mention the fact that there are several courier services that specialize in the transportation of vital organs.'

'I'm not an idiot. It was a judgement call. I made it.'

'And I have to live with it. But that doesn't change the fact that you should have sent it to us. Not risked some *other* idiot screwing up our investigation.'

His tone made it absolutely obvious there were two idiots in the equation as far as he was concerned, and she was one of them.

'The tongue's in Paris.'

'Paris?'

'You know, capital of France as opposed to Texas. Big iron tower in the middle.'

'I know where it is. What I'm asking is how the hell it got there?'

'Curious, isn't it? And that's just one of the questions I'm trying to answer. My focus is solely on catching the killer. I don't care about jurisdiction or playing nicely with others. There's a killer out there who didn't just end a man's life, he cut his tongue out and shipped it to a bishop in Paris,' she said.

'Understood. By the way, we've got a name on your burn victim. Stefan Karius. Good old-fashioned police work. The car registration survived the fire. We worked back from there.'

Fire was a bastard. It would burn away the skin, removing all hope of getting fingerprints. Despite the charring and damage, that was all limited to the surface, so once they had an ID they could work back with DNA tests using the bone marrow against hairbrushes or toothbrushes or other stuff recovered from the home, check medical records for broken bones and other injuries that might show up on the skeleton. It all relied upon knowing who you were looking for, and in finding a name then it was relatively easy to make a positive ID.

'Poor bastard,' she said. That pretty much summed it up.

She hung up. She didn't have space in her head for more corpses. The discovery of the tongue had thrown her. It meant changing how she had been thinking about the politician's death. The missing priest held the key. Somehow. It didn't matter that the two men were a thousand miles apart, or that they moved in circles a world apart. There was a link. There had to be.

But for the time being she was going to have to concentrate on good old-fashioned police work, and that meant returning to the scene of the crime – first physically, then metaphorically. Her morning promised a walk along the riverbanks, familiarizing herself with every inch of the scene without every other agency trying to piss all over the territory like dogs. It promised to be more fun than a fruitless trawl through the CCTV footage. It wasn't as though the killer would smile up at the camera as he dumped Anglemark's corpse in the water.

EIGHTEEN

She showered and dressed and was ready to head out.

Breakfast consisted of a large latte, to go, and three filter-tipped cigarettes chain-smoked into her lungs for sustenance. It was always the way when she was on a case; a subsistence diet of nicotine and caffeine supplemented by anything she could grab on the run. It wasn't the usual health-obsessive Scandinavian lifestyle, but then she was hardly the usual blonde-haired blue-eyed Scandinavian. She didn't even bother lying to herself once a year with any made-up resolution about quitting. She liked smoking. She was a big girl. She got to choose what went into her body. It helped her think. When she dragged deeply on a cigarette that first hit of nicotine fired her synapses in ways that nothing else could.

She drew in a last lungful of smoke, then flicked the butt sailing away into the waters of Riddarfjärden, the Knight's Firth. It was a spectacular piece of real estate, but slightly off the beaten track. A few years ago, actually more than a few now, she realized, the city used to host a Water Festival here, with bands from all over the world performing on a stage pretty much exactly where she stood right now. She looked back towards the old church, remembering sitting up in the high banked seats there watching BB King with John Fogerty sat beside her. She couldn't even remember half of the acts on the bill that day. The Wannadies, Soundtrack of Our Lives, some Britpop band that had vanished without a trace. It was hard to believe it was nearly twenty years ago.

Most of the time the weird little square here was empty, though there was a small kiosk that opened in the summer to serve coffee. The island afforded a quiet little haven in the heart of the busiest city in Scandinavia. Every summer she took at least one day to come and sit by the water's edge, dangling her feet in Riddarfjärden and watching the world go by. There was something so peaceful about this spot, with views back onto Södermalm and the distinctive industrial presence of Münchenbryggeriet's towering chimneys on the distant shore one way, and the golden crowns of the City Hall the other.

All manner of boats came and went, churning up the surf.

It wasn't hard to see where the body had been found. The police tape was in tatters, but several bunches of flowers had been left by the water's edge. She watched from a distance as a couple of men knelt beside the river, heads bowed, and laid their own wreath with the other offerings. It would be much worse later, when Anglemark's name was released. Then the public outpouring of grief would be incredible.

Anglemark was the third major politician to be murdered in thirty years. Swedes had plenty of experience when it came to mourning the men and women who dared to try and change the world.

The yellow tape fluttered in the breeze where it had been torn away from its anchor points.

There was no real chance of finding any meaningful evidence here, she knew. And it would only get worse as the mourners made their pilgrimage to see where he had died, which of course wasn't here. Tidal patterns meant it was far more logical the corpse had been dumped from another one of the islands and this was just where it had washed up.

Techs back at the lab were already going through the tidal patterns and currents, cross-referencing the charts and recorded movements of the larger boats and ferries. They would come up with a pretty decent estimate as to where the body had been dumped before long, but right now it was still pure guesswork.

She was dragged from her thoughts by a voice.

'Real tragedy when something like this happens.'

Frankie turned around to see a middle-aged woman, her business suit finished off with a comfortable pair of trainers. She had a small dog by her side who seemed intent on marking the flowers as his territory.

'It is,' Frankie said.

'Do you know what happened? I mean beyond a body washing up here?'

'Not really,' she said, not exactly lying.

'We usually have a few a year. Normally they're suicides. Poor souls who decide to throw themselves off St Erik's Bridge. You have to feel for them. Anyone who thinks that is the answer must be in so much pain.' Frankie nodded. 'Of course, most of them don't make it this far along the shoreline. Though, that said, there was one last year, but that one wasn't a suicide if I recall. Some kid who'd had too much to drink and challenged his friends to a race to the other side. He split his skull open on the concrete footing and was dead before they got to the other side. So, you think this was a suicide?'

'It's not my place to say,' Frankie said, again not really lying, but definitely giving the truth a wide berth. 'Seems a nice place to walk the dog,' she said, changing the subject.

'He likes it here,' she said. 'This square is his little kingdom. He can be a real terror some days if he doesn't get to walk along the embankment sniffing every little pee-mail left by his friends.' She smiled at that, like she'd made the best joke. Frankie smiled down at the restless terrier. He seemed intent to sniff every inch of ground, more than once.

'A lot of people walk their dogs around here?' Frankie had lived in the city for the best part of fifteen years, since she moved down from Sala, a sleepy little village nearly a hundred miles north, but she wasn't a dog person. She didn't really pay attention to their walking habits.

'Plenty. As quiet as it is, remember, we're in the heart of the city. You're a couple of minutes' walk from the Old Town. You're on a direct path over the bridge to Södermalm. This is our favourite place in the whole world, isn't it, Buster?' she said to the dog. It looked up at her with big brown eyes, recognizing the sound of its name.

'Even at night?'

'Sure, they need to do their business before they go to sleep, just like us. Winter walks tend to be shorter, but in the summer you can see people strolling along here as late as midnight.'

The dog gave another tug and the woman ruffled its corn-coloured curls, then said her goodbyes.

Frankie watched as she was tugged after the terrier, which despite its size was obviously far stronger than it looked. She didn't know much more than she had when she'd started out, but it had been good to remind herself of the geography of the small square and lock the landscape in her memory again. There was every chance he might have been dumped out the back of the City Hall and left to drift the couple of hundred metres to where she stood. In all probability there were probably a dozen other places the killer might have dumped the body in the water for it to wash up here, and most if not all of them would be isolated.

The question was, did he know the corpse would wash up at the foot of the old church? Was there a message in it? This was the old monarch's burial church, home to the Order of the Knights Seraphim. It wasn't just some old church. It was one of the oldest buildings in the city, and the very first church built on the islands. Was this the killer's way of signalling a link to the missing bishop?

NINETEEN

Tolstoy was scratching at the inside of the heavy old oak door when Father Michael returned.

He had given Dooley as long as he possibly could, respectful of his wish for solitude, but as ever there were things he needed to do. The parish never slept. He smiled at that, imagining this tiny village being awake at midnight. He checked his watch. Elspeth Moore was no doubt inside already, cleaning the already clean church and arranging fresh flowers.

He could hear the dog's discomfort through the timbers.

Father Michael opened the doors on a frantic bundle of black fur and barking as the dog leapt out, agitated. He tried to calm the animal, but it jumped at him in a constant flurry of motion that belied its age. Tolstoy pressed his paws against his chest and licked at his face, then scuttered back a few steps only to run at him again and repeated that over and over. This wasn't his usual excitement. Every time he ran away a little further, venturing deeper into the church only to come haring back to the priest.

'What is it, buddy? What do you want to show me?'

The Labrador didn't hesitate.

Tolstoy darted back inside the church, claws skittering on the stone floor as he ran ahead.

The priest closed the oak doors behind him, noting the amount of damage that the dog had done with his claws.

The lights were still on inside, which was unlike Dooley.

'Father Dooley?' he called softly.

There was no immediate sign of him. Not at the altar or in any of the first rows of the pews, which was where he would usually be found if he was in thought.

Tolstoy raced backwards and forwards the length of the aisle, then started barking at one of the closed confessional curtains. There was that panic again in the old animal's bark.

Father Michael slipped behind the second curtain.

'Father Dooley,' he said, taking up his usual seat inside the confessional. 'I hope you haven't been waiting all this time for me?' It seemed unlikely, but with the old man anything was possible. 'Would you like me to hear your confession?' This last one he asked softly, observing the sanctity of the act and the confessional itself, and when there was no reply he wondered if perhaps the old man had fallen asleep on him, so he repeated it, slightly louder this time. But Dooley falling asleep wouldn't explain Tolstoy's strange behaviour. 'Are you all right in there, Father?'

Still no answer.

There was no sign of movement through the screen, but the old man was obviously in there, leaning up against the far wall. Father Michael peered through the screen as he said Dooley's name again. There was no sign of him stirring.

As much as he hated having to do it, he had no choice but to break the sacred trust and draw back the curtain to wake him.

Mumbling a quiet prayer of apology, he pulled back the curtain even as he realized he was standing in something wet. The carpet was sodden beneath his feet.

It took a moment for his brain to make the connections as the horror of the confessional started to make grotesque sense to his mind. He would never forget what lay behind that curtain for as long as he lived.

Father Dooley lay slumped in the chair, his head resting against the back wall. There was so much blood. That was all he could see for the longest time. One of Dooley's hands lay in his lap, while the other hung limply by his side. Blood dripped down his fingers to the floor, though most of it had already bled out of the old man's veins. A box-cutter lay six inches out of reach. Father Michael stood frozen, unable to reach those few inches to check for a pulse he knew couldn't be there.

Tolstoy stepped into the blood, nudging at the old man's hand with his nose, whining.

'Come away, boy,' he said and started fumbling inside his cassock for his mobile phone.

He was shaking as he dialled the emergency services operator.

'Ambulance, please. And police,' he said, giving the church's address before the phone slipped from his grip.

It hit him then, the full savage shock of his friend's suicide.

He fell to his knees in prayer, unaware of the blood soaking through his cassock.

A scream brought him back. Elspeth. She'd arrived to clean the church. It was almost as though a light had been switched on and he could suddenly see what he needed to do; Dooley was beyond his help, but he could comfort her. She needed him. His strength. His support. Father Michael stood up quickly, drawing the curtain to hide the worst of it. Not that it would take the image of the beloved old man out of her head.

'There's nothing we can do,' he said, and hated that he was telling the truth. 'There's an ambulance on the way.' Which was pointless unless they could somehow raise the dead. 'The police, too. Come on, let's go back to the cottage until they arrive.' He put a comforting arm around the elderly woman and walked back with her. The dead held no fear for him, but Dooley had committed a mortal sin. How could he have fallen so low?

The cleaner echoed his thoughts. 'Why would he do such a thing?'

He shook his head. He didn't have an answer for her. Not just why, but why *here*, in this place? In the confessional.

TWENTY

He needed to go back to the beginning.

What did they have? Really? Apart from an assumption that Monsignor Tournard had gone to meet a man? Nothing. Nada. Zip. Zilch. A big fat zero. There were no CCTV cameras in the vicinity likely to turn up an easy lead – or a difficult one, which he'd have happily taken right about now. London would have been different. The paranoia on his home turf meant pretty much every angle and street corner, every alleyway and green space was heavily surveilled. There were more cameras than rats, last he'd heard. He had no idea whether that was true or not, but if it was it wasn't because Rentokil were doing a bang-up job.

The obvious thing to do, like it or not, was enlist the media. Make an appeal for witnesses. The problem was he'd given Donatti his word it would stay under the radar, at least until the situation escalated.

And that was how he was thinking now, it was only ever about until, not if.

Until then he was limited to the resources they had at hand, which included the footage from the camera outside the Monsignor's office and apartment building. And all that gave him was confirmation of which direction he turned as he exited. It was hardly revelatory, but it showed that he was walking rather than waiting for a taxi, and that he turned towards the maze of streets that eventually lead to the cafe. Not exactly massive breaks in the case, but scutwork was important. And with discretion in mind, he couldn't farm it out to some junior. The more people involved, the more official it became, and the more official it became the sooner the details would leak into the press. It was a pretty simple equation.

Donatti was more than happy to pull every ecclesiastical string he could, but they both knew that it would fall to Ash to make things happen once the manhunt took them outside the realm of the Church.

He called in.

Laura had sourced some traffic-cam footage, and the feed from a couple of public buildings hooked into the city network. The term she used was 'Better than nothing, but only just.' Which translated to the unsurprising reality that the Catholic Church's cameras, assuming they had them and didn't rely on the fact that their boss saw and heard everything, weren't connected. What his own trawl had given him was the precise time Tournard had left the building and the direction, which meant he had something for her to work with.

Next, he called through to one of his opposite numbers in the French side of Division to arrange access to the city's surveillance network. They made all the usual noises about being stretched thin, about limited resources, lack of manpower and wanting to help, in the end saying as long as he was prepared to do it himself, they were happy enough to provide access. Once the bishop was declared officially missing or turned up dead, different priorities came into play. He knew arse-covering when he ran into it.

Ash followed in the Monsignor's footsteps. He walked slowly, head up and looking around like a tourist. He wasn't sightseeing though, he was scanning shop facades and apartment buildings for tell-tale signs of cameras. It wasn't so long ago the Batacalan theatre attack had shocked the world, and while the Parisians made a big show of life going on and were back out the next night in their bistros and strolling hand in hand down their boulevards, the truth was it had changed the city for ever. It had become as paranoid as every other major city in the world. And that meant cameras.

Or at least he hoped it did.

Of course, logically, there was very little he expected to learn from the exercise. Tournard had reached his destination after all, but Ash was playing a hunch. There was a fair chance the Monsignor had been watched, and more likely than not followed to the cafe. The mysterious stranger wasn't just going to risk turning up to an empty table and hanging around long enough for people to get a good look at him, was he? Not when it was easy enough to follow someone in a place like this without being seen. Easier still when you knew their destination. And following him took care of another problem, making sure Tournard hadn't brought the law into this.

It made sense.

It's what he would have done.

In the absence of any other leads it was worth chasing down at least. Ash walked to the first junction and waited for Laura to call back. A young Parisian girl with an artist's portfolio balanced under her left arm struggled with lighting a cigarette as she leaned against the wall. A much older woman, one of the city's *grandes dames*, wrestled with shopping bags stuffed to overflowing with fruit fresh from a market stall and the other staples of life, nicotine and coffee. A dark-haired kid with his hair shaved into a weird rat's tail kicked a yellow football along the street, bouncing it off the doors of each house he passed. He had a peculiar déjà vu moment standing there, and realized he'd been here before, a long time ago. His father had brought him here for his tenth birthday. He'd liked to do this little ritual where they visited children's homes and dropped off gifts on their birthdays. They were never expensive, but that didn't matter. It was a measure of the man's good heart. Ash hadn't taken any birthday gifts in a long while. Not since his dad had died. He would change that this birthday, make a new ritual to honour the old man.

The phone vibrated in his hand.

'Talk to me,' he said.

'The priest turned right where you are,' she said. 'I scrolled through the next five minutes' worth of coverage, not sure exactly who I was looking for out of the foot traffic. But eight people turned in the same direction. Eight's not a huge suspect pool, so I've done screen grabs of them which I'm sending over now. Profile shots were the best I could do, though. Sorry. It's a brisk walk to the next camera. I'm scrubbing the footage at the moment to see which of the eight stayed with him.'

'Good work, Law. Let me know when you have anything.' He killed the call.

Ash took his time again, lingering at a couple of shop windows, including an old-fashioned ironmonger's and a haberdashery with a window full of pin cushions and pinned-up fabrics. He could smell the cinnamon from the cafe already.

His phone rang again before he reached it.

'What have you got?'

'Straight on. The original eight became three, but he's been joined by a couple of newcomers, too. So we're following five possibles now.'

'Narrowing it down,' he said appreciatively. 'How far to the next camera?'

'A couple of hundred metres, but we've got two major crossings and at least three minor side streets between where you are. If he's good, the chances are he'll break away from pursuit and come around to the cafe from another direction now he knows the old man hasn't brought in reinforcements. If he does, then we're out of luck. There are no more cameras on the other approaches between where you are and the cafe.'

'Makes sense. But let's hope you're wrong, eh?'

The boy lost control of the ball and ran out into the path of an oncoming car. The driver hit the horn as hard as he hit the brakes, as the kid stooped to scoop up the ball and then dashed across to the other side. Ash shook his head, but the driver seemed amused. Maybe it was a regular thing? Or maybe the kid would never grow up to be Cantona?

Back home, Ash might have taken a moment to talk to the kid, point out the physics of soft flesh versus hard metal and all that, but the kid was maybe eleven, meaning his English was going to be worse than Ash's French, and the whole thing would get very muddled very fast. So, he let it go.

Laura said, 'Looks like your man took one of the side streets before the next camera. We don't see him again.'

'OK,' Ash said. 'Not ideal. Please tell me you've got better news? Like a guy with a string of garlic around his neck and a big sign saying *Le méchant* above his head.'

'No signs saying the bad guy, and no shockingly crude stereotypes. But only two of the five following Tournard made it this far. So, three made the turnoff. I'll process the best screen grabs I can get and get them over to you in a minute.'

'You're a star. Do you think we could clone you?'

'You couldn't handle two of me,' she said. 'You can always show your appreciation by sending me out on a jolly next time you get a juicy case. Somewhere warm preferably. Think of all the airmiles you'd get.'

'You know I would, if I could, but Division would never sign off on me putting you out in the field. And just imagine they did, and decided to send you to Germany? Can you imagine that lot taking kindly to you telling them how to do their jobs?'

'It isn't the 1970s, Pete,' Laura laughed.

'You say that, I say Brexit, m'dear. Take a look at them prejudices. And that as they say is game, set, and match.'

'You're terrible.'

The rest of the walk was fruitless.

He marked a couple of offices that might have some form of system, but their cameras were angled inwards, not interested in the street at all. And for them to be of any use it meant the guy he was looking for would have had to drop into the small convenience store for a packet of cigarettes or a paper or something. Meaning move on, forget about it.

Ash was still scouting out the area when the images came through from Laura. She tagged them with a short text saying she was running them through Division's facial-recognition software but didn't expect to get a match.

Once he opened the file he understood why.

He wasn't sure if their own mothers would recognize any of the three men from the pictures.

TWENTY-ONE

A sh showed Donatti the shots.
'Recognize anyone?'
The Vatican's man shook his head.

They had met up again in a much more modern coffee shop this time. The prices were double, the coffees more worried about the art in the foam than the quality of the beans. Of course it looked more Parisian, decorated for the tourists who wouldn't give the extra euros a second thought. Frothy coffee was probably the only growth industry on the Continent. He couldn't even remember seeing a coffee shop back home before *Friends* made them into these cool alternatives to pubs.

'So, you think one of these three men followed the Monsignor from his office?'

'It's a possibility,' Ash said, 'but by no means a certainty. All we know for a fact is that they walked the same streets at the same time before we lost sight of them. But it could be one of them.'

'Or none of them.'

Ash nodded.

Donatti studied each profile in turn but betrayed no hint of recognition. Even enhanced they were still relatively indistinct. The youngest of the three was maybe late twenties or early thirties. The oldest was in his sixties. The third man could have fitted anywhere in between. And according to Laura, none of them walked with any sense of urgency. Not like people on the way to or from work, so probably tourists. Meaning a reduced likelihood of being recognized if they canvassed the area.

'We should show them to Blanc, the Monsignor's secretary. Perhaps he has noticed one of them hanging around recently?'

Ash shrugged. There were worse ideas. Thinking aloud, he said, 'If Tournard's new to the job, there's a good chance this has to do with some previous appointment, something in Germany given the Remember Bonn message that came with the tongue, it's more likely his previous secretary would know, surely?'

'Possible,' Donatti said. 'I shall reach out. Have copies of the photographs sent to him. Double-checking with Blanc doesn't hurt, either.'

Ash nodded. 'I'll leave that to you.'

'What are you going to do?'

'Need to check with the lab to get the result on the tongue.'

'I still don't understand what you think that's going to tell you. Other than confirm that it is your dead politician's.'

'Never dismiss science, my friend. You might have a god who sees all and knows all,' Ash's smile undercut the words, 'but I've got one who deals purely in hard provable data. Maybe between the old and the new we'll get lucky.'

'The devil is in the details?'

'Most of the time.'

'So, beyond that – what? We wait?'

'It's difficult without bringing in the local police,' Ash said. 'But if Tournard *was* followed we know whoever he met didn't have a car. Which means he still has to be local.'

'I am not sure I agree. There are too many variables for your scientific certainty there. One, we could be dealing with two men, an accomplice to drive the car. Two, the kidnapper could have arrived several hours early, parking the car for a convenient getaway, and spent the rest of the early morning familiarizing himself with the area. Three, they could have taken an Uber. Four, taxis exist. Five, they could have walked happily away from the scene together, like old friends, and kept on walking.'

Ash couldn't disagree with any of the scenarios. They were all viable possibilities, and he'd considered them all to one degree or another. There could well be someone else; a man or a woman who drove a car to the cafe to collect the two men when they left. It made sense if there was more than one person behind whatever was going on if you factored in the fact the politician in Sweden died maybe twelve hours before Tournard took delivery of his tongue. They were dealing in fine margins.

The only thing he could think was that Tournard must have gone with the man willingly. It was the only thing that made sense. He said as much.

'Any sort of scuffle or commotion in the cafe, we hear about it. It's not a big place, and that old man spent most of his morning standing in the doorway glowering at us while his daughter interpreted. He would have seen trouble kicking off. And willingly doesn't mean he wasn't afraid. People don't pay enough attention to social cues being put out by strangers to be able to tell if they are agitated or acting under duress. And if he was genuinely afraid, he'd try to conceal it, wouldn't he? So, I completely buy him leaving of his own free will.'

'Free will means different things to different people,' Donatti agreed.

They went their separate ways.

The call to the lab was frustrating.

They emailed through some results, but the language issue meant he was looking largely for any familiar Latin terms he recognized from cases he'd worked back home. He forwarded them on to Frankie with a short note hoping her pathologist was fluent in Google translate.

Then he stood in the middle of one of the many bridges over the Seine, the spectre of Notre-Dame to one side, the accusing point of the tower in the other, and realized he had nowhere to be and nothing to do. By rights he should have been on the next train back to London. There was nothing he could do here until they went public. And if Donatti had his way that wasn't going to happen until a body turned up.

That word again: *until*.

The problem was he really didn't want to go home to the ghosts of London.

Twenty-four hours.

He could afford that. He'd give his old friend that much, as a courtesy, then he was escalating the investigation.

TWENTY-TWO

Frankie Varg listened while Peter Ash talked. A lot. He talked too much for her liking. Men who talked too much were afraid of silence. People who were afraid of silence were running from their own thoughts. It wasn't difficult. He talked because he was hiding from the guilt he felt over his partner's death. You didn't need advanced degrees in psychology to work this stuff out. There was nothing particularly original about the man.

She listened as he filled her in on the shortcomings of his Parisian investigation. Walking the bishop's route was thorough, and she could appreciate the process of elimination behind isolating the three indistinct faces. He might talk too much, but he was at least competent. That was a plus, even if she fundamentally disagreed with him making promises to keep the links to her murder out of the news. Memories were short and got fuzzier by the hour. Someone had seen the bishop in the moments leading up to his disappearance. But if they didn't know he was gone, how could they come forward to help?

And every hour he was gone was an hour closer to the inevitable.

Silence helped no one. But, considering Jonas Anglemark's name was yet to hit the news-stands, understandable. She'd fielded a couple of calls from TT, the news service, asking for comment, about the fact the politician hadn't been seen in some time.

'What are your plans now'

'Logically, head back to London tomorrow, coordinate things from there. Or if a body turns up, hand it all over to Division for the French to run with. It's not like I'm far away.'

'We can always use an extra body over here,' she said, the offer out of her mouth before any of the many reasons why it was a bad idea reached her brain.

'I'd love to,' he said, and her stomach lurched, 'but I can't see Division giving approval when I'm the only active agent in the UK.'

'Ah, yes, permission. But they were happy for you to go to Paris?'

'I think they're easing me back into things gently. I'm sure Laura's shielding me from the politics. She knows how it all gives me a brain ache.'

'Laura? Is that your new partner?'

Ash laughed. 'Much worse. She's the boss. She runs the London office.'

'Ah, yes. Of course.'

She'd been to London several times. She'd hear Skånska slang and the Noll-åtta dialect on Oxford Street and in Covent Garden more often than she'd hear English. It always amused her how her fellow countrymen called Stockholmers after the city's phone code. It wasn't exactly a cutting-edge insult. She'd done the usual tourist things and almost melted her credit card in the process. It was always different experiencing a city through the eyes of a local, though. His London was no doubt very different to hers, and not merely because he spent his time rooting around in the filth and hunting the kind of people who lived in it.

'Any luck with finding a connection between my man and yours? Or with Germany?'

'You know how it is,' Ash said. 'We need more data to narrow the search parameters.' Which was an easy thing to say and a considerably harder thing to do. Reliable information could not simply be conjured out of thin air because you needed it.

And even if the bishop turned up dead, that wasn't going to add to their knowledge pool. At least not immediately.

Her watchword had to be procedure, because the moment the news broke, the press would be swarming all over her and the chance of taking a breath before she drowned beneath all the attention was minimal. Procedure. Doing things the right way. Don't hope for a lucky break. Follow protocols. And that meant following Ash's example, and quite literally trying to walk a mile in Jonas Anglemark's shoes.

'I'll loop you in if Law turns anything up. We're in this together, after all.'

She wished she could say the same thing about the other inter-agencies she was forced to interact with; with each wanting to cling on to their precious knowledge in fear of someone else getting the glory for cracking a case.

And that, of course, perpetuated the cycle of mistrust and made her reluctant to share her own discoveries. This one was different though; on the back of Palme and Lindh, the whole nation was going to be demanding justice for Anglemark's murder, and very public justice at that. There would be no time to worry about treading on toes or putting noses out of joint. She wasn't doing this for the man, she as doing it for the whole of Sweden, and that made it different from any case she'd been involved in. How did you carry the weight of a nation on your shoulders? Where did you even begin to start?

It was time to try those dead man's shoes on for size.

TWENTY-THREE

I n the end he followed the siren song back to London, intending to clear his head, catch up on sleep and do some thinking away from the case that wasn't quite a case.

Donatti had his back. He told his old friend he'd return in twenty-four hours, but it wouldn't end up being that long.

'There's been another one.'

He heard the words, but couldn't place the voice, and without that recognition that one could have been anything. 'Sorry?'

'There's been another one,' the woman said patiently. This time he recognized the voice; it was Frankie Varg.

'Body or body part?'

'Both.'

'I'm listening.'

Things had just become interesting. Not that he was about to say that out loud, but another body, and more body parts, meant more opportunities for the killer to screw up. He glanced across at the clock. He could be in either Paris or Stockholm before lunch.

'Where?'

'Your way. A village in Surrey, retired priest, Catholic, decided to end his own life in the confessional of his old church.'

'Priest suicide? Unusual, but there could be a lot of reasons for an old man of the cloth to kill himself,' he said, not needing to elaborate.

'He received a package that morning. There was a card with it, just like the other two.'

'Bonn again?'

'Remember Bonn,' she agreed. 'An eyeball this time.'

'Tournard's?' It was the logical assumption; even though the bishop's body hadn't been found, he was out of the first forty-eight hours, which meant the chances of him turning up alive were greatly reduced.

'It's possible,' she said. 'Whatever happened in Bonn he couldn't live with it.'

'No other corpses turned up sans eyeballs?'

'None so far. Not in Sweden, and not in Paris according to Etienne Reynard.' Reynard ran the Paris Division. He was the epitome of the permanently harried French cop who looked like he had just stepped out of a François Truffaut movie. They'd worked together a few times. The man had chain-smoked his way through sixty Gauloises a day for the duration of the investigations. He drove a battered old 2CV that changed gears on what looked like the indicator stick. The man was a proper throwback. He even did that thing where he'd pause on the threshold of walking out of an interrogation and look back to say, 'Oh, this is probably nothing, but . . .' and that but was never nothing. Ash liked the guy, even at the risk of proximal lung cancer. 'I've got feelers out to other offices, especially Germany. Not turned up anything yet.'

'I'll get Laura to trawl through local and international reports. If it's there to be found, she'll find it.'

'You think she'll be OK if we coordinate everything through her? I'd rather not risk some nosy reporter over here stumbling on what we're dealing with before we go public. And if we're going to be working this together it makes sense.'

'She'll love it. Give it a week and she'll be asking to move up your way, assuming you don't have polar bears?'

'We don't.'

'Great, let me sell it to her.'

'Of course. I completely understand. I wouldn't want an outsider putting extra work on one of my team, either.'

'We're on the same wavelength. OK, I'll head into the office. I'll take a look at our dead priest while I'm there, but give me the cheat sheet: what do you know about the guy? Any obvious link to Anglemark or Tournard?'

'The Church?'

'Was your politician Catholic?'

'I don't believe so. We are not very Catholic here. The Church of Sweden is Lutheran. Unofficial estimates put the number of Catholics here at between one and one and a half per cent of the population. Improbable, but not impossible. It would be foolish of us to become fixated with the religious aspect of this, I think. Remember Bonn. That points us to a place, if not a time. That is the true point of connection, not the fact they believe in the same version of God. Are you a Catholic, Peter? May I ask?'

The question caught him off-guard.

'Why?'

'Because our personal beliefs influence the way we consider the evidence, even if only subconsciously.'

He shook his head, even though she couldn't see him. 'It won't affect me.'

'So, you are?'

'I was,' Ash said. 'Altar boy. I feasted on the body of Christ and got drunk the first time on his blood. But that was all a very long time ago. I have a seriously low bullshit threshold these days. Christ, if anything I'd *love* to find a connection back to the Church. There's so much wrong with organized religion.'

'So your beliefs – or lack of – might make it easier to blame the Church rather than trying to shift the blame away from it,' she said, touching a nerve.

'Let's just say that I don't like being told what to do.'

'Ah, a rebel. But good to hear.'

'Is it?'

'Yes,' she assured him. 'If you find it easy to condemn the Church the chances are you'll challenge the evidence rather than just accept it at face value, whatever they say, however close you might be to one of them. We can't afford to let them close ranks if this points back to some past horrors they've buried.'

'I agree,' he said. 'The evidence speaks for itself. We don't put words in its mouth.'

'I like that,' Frankie said.

'Then I guess it's you and me,' he said.

'Always and for ever,' she said and then laughed into the ensuing silence. 'It's a song,' Frankie promised him, 'not a proposal.'

TWENTY-FOUR

Laura arrived back at the office ten minutes after he did. River House was humming with activity. If ever there was a place that didn't sleep, this was it. Every hour of the day. The demands of keeping the country safe didn't let up. They earned the nickname Spooks for good reason.

She slipped her jacket over the back of her chair and dropped her bag beside it.

'Coffee?' he asked.

She held up a takeaway cup that he hadn't noticed her carrying. 'One of the few perks of civilized living,' she said. 'So . . .?'

'So what?'

'So Frankie?'

'What about her?'

'Let's just say there's a definite change in inflection when you mention her.'

'All in your head,' he laughed.

'Is it now?'

'Yup.'

'You looking for a new partner?' She didn't need to say to replace Mitch.

He shook his head. 'Nope, nothing long term. A marriage of convenience. We're looped into the same case, that's it. We break this, make the arrests, and go our separate ways.'

'If you say so,' Laura said. She sat in her chair and raised her coffee to her lips, obviously enjoying teasing him a little too much. 'I assume she's the reason I've been graced with your presence, too? Which, hold on, I'm having a psychic moment, yes, I can feel it coming through from the other side . . . yes . . . it means more work for me.'

'The psychic hotline is on fire,' he said.

'That, or Division called through an hour ago, asking if I'd be willing to act as coordinator for the pair of you.'

'Ha. Sorry about that. I wanted you to hear it from me.'

'Hence the impromptu visit. You should have called.'

'Favours demand face-to-face begging.'

'You mean so I can't say no?'

'Would you ever? Think of it as something fun to sink your teeth into. And maybe there's a jolly to Sweden in it for you.'

'Hmmmm,' she said, then her face cracked into a grin.

It took a moment for Ash to realize that he'd been played.

He took it on the chin.

'So, what are you actually doing back here?'

'Catching up on the information that came in overnight.'

'Frankie hasn't filled you in already?' The playfulness lasted one more second, then disappeared; and it was all business.

'She called me this morning,' he said. 'Gave me the heads up that we've got a new body, and another random body part, meaning we've gone from two killings to a serial pattern. I wanted to check what we'd got in the system before I head out.'

'You're going to the scene?'

He nodded. 'It's a lot closer to home,' close being Langley Vale, a small village of maybe two hundred people on the Downs just outside Epsom. It didn't get much closer to home for him. An hour and a half's drive at most, even with traffic. 'I've already talked to the first officers on the scene, and they're happy it's a straightforward suicide. They confirmed the message on the note and the eyeball and were more than happy to slope their shoulders and let us take over.'

'Definitely suicide?'

He nodded. 'But the arrival of an eyeball in the post and the implicit threat of the accompanying card was enough to make him choose death over whatever else was on the table. Meaning he jumped rather than waiting to be pushed. So he remembered Bonn and he couldn't live with those memories.'

'Poor man.'

'Possibly,' Ash agreed. 'Now, somehow, we've got to find what links a retired priest seeing out his days in his comfortable little parish here, a missing bishop in Paris and a dead politician in Sweden. Because something does connect all three of them.'

'I'm going to add Father Dooley to the search parameters, see if it narrows things down. If you want to make yourself useful while you wait, you can pick me up another cup of the good stuff.' She held up the takeaway.

TWENTY-FIVE

There was little to be learned in the church itself, and Father Michael O'Hare, the new priest, was obviously uncomfortable in the place where his predecessor had committed a mortal sin, even with the body removed. No amount of scrubbing would get the blood out of the carpet and the inside of the confessional was for ever tainted.

'The bishop is coming tomorrow,' O'Hare said. 'He'll know what to do.' It was obvious that he didn't. 'I've lost people, of course. And buried a boy who hanged himself in his bedroom just last year. There is incredible sadness to it every time, but there is a distance, too. They are your parishioners. Your flock. You tend to them as best you can. But he was my *friend*. I can't begin to imagine his pain, that he could be so troubled as to think the only answer was death. How does it happen, officer? From your side. How do people break like this?' He didn't wait for an answer from Ash. 'I thought he was happy. He was enjoying his retirement. Not that he *wanted* to retire. But we had an arrangement. He could come and go as he pleased and this would always be his church. I was only ever looking after it for him.'

'We can never know what is going on inside someone else's skin, Father. Pain isn't something we wear on the outside like bruises. If only it was. That would save a lot of people from suffering in silence. All we can do is listen if they want us to hear.'

The priest nodded. 'That is the part I am having the most difficulty with. Father . . .' He struggled to say the dead man's name. There was a sense of complete loss about him as if he was unable to think for himself any longer. 'Father Dooley. He didn't think that he could talk to me?'

Both the loss and the manner of its discovery had damaged something in the other man, and from bitter experience Ash knew it would never fix, not fully. It would linger in his mind and come back to hurt him again and again. The only sense of healing was that given time it would haunt him less frequently, and the pain of it would dim because of the distance. The soul built calluses over raw wounds until they became bearable. But no amount of time would change the fact that every time he came into this place he would see Patrick Dooley lying there in the confessional, wrists slashed, his dog walking through his friend's lifeblood. He couldn't imagine the priest would ever become so dulled to the memory that he would feel at home in this place again.

'I understand that there was a note,' he said, leading the man back outside into the glorious daylight. The bright blue sky might have been painted in by a child, so incredibly blue was it. There were no traffic sounds; despite the fact that there were maybe two hundred houses in the village it was suitably removed from the busier roads that ran from Epsom proper up the Downs to Tattenham Corner.

'Yes, yes,' the man said, glad of something else to think about. The change in his demeanour was obvious the moment they stepped over the threshold. In the most basic of ways it was as though he had left his troubles behind. 'The police took it with them.'

'Can you remember what it said?' Ash already knew but was looking for a way to keep the man talking. If there was something inside he needed to say, he'd need to find the words and nine times out of ten they were hidden within others and the only way to get to them was just to keep talking. That was the similarity of their jobs, both traded on the human need for confession.

'Just that he was sorry, that he couldn't carry the burden any longer. He explained that he had chosen the church as he didn't want Elspeth, his housekeeper, to find his body.' O'Hare breathed deeply, nostrils flaring as he sniffed back emotions halfway between anger and sadness. 'He thought I would be better able to deal with it.' He shook his head. 'I'm not sure that he was right.'

'Could you take me to his home?'

'Of course,' he priest said. 'I have to admit that I don't really know what I am doing. We don't have many dealings with law enforcement here, despite the odd crime prevention seminar in the Church Hall and neighbourhood watch meetings. I don't mean to sound callous, but is this liable to take a long time? For them to release his body for burial, I mean. Father Dooley was much loved by the people here. They will want the chance to mourn him.'

'Honestly, I don't know. But I should be out of your hair pretty soon, then you'll be called to the Coroner's court. A few days, maybe?'

'You aren't here to investigate his death, though, are you? This is about that *thing* they found in his desk.'

'You have to admit, it is unusual.'

'Horrible. It's horrible. I can't imagine why he would have something like that. Was he in trouble? I don't . . . I mean . . . Where would he get an eye from?' The priest's hands were shaking. 'I mean . . . was he . . .? Did he . . .?'

'I think that someone sent it to him,' Ash said, putting the other man out of his misery.

'Who would do such a thing?' O'Hare's hand went instinctively to his mouth. His face blanched. 'Why?'

'That, I'm afraid, I don't know. Perhaps there's something in the house that might shed some light upon it? I understand that he was the parish priest here for a number of years.'

'Oh yes, many years. He dedicated his life to this church. Even after I took over from him, most of the parishioners would still seek out his wisdom. He was a good man.'

'I'm sure he was. You can't dedicate your life to helping others and not be. Do you know anything about where he was before he came to Langley Vale?'

'Not really. Our conversations revolved around the everyday life of the parish.'

It came as no surprise that they would talk about the commonalities of the lives they lived and how they ran parallel to each other, even if they only overlapped for a relatively short time. Going back before that, trading stories of life already lived, that needed friendship. This was a man who believed in the sanctity of the confessional, the act as opposed to the place, and that extended beyond death.

'I have to ask this, and please don't take it the wrong way, but can you think of anything out of the ordinary that he might have been involved with?'

'What are you suggesting, Dooley was mixed up in some kind of criminal activity? He was an old man, not some criminal mastermind.'

Ash held up a placating hand. 'I know, I know. I'm not saying that at all. But I'm trying to work out who sent him that eye, and why, because I think it was intended as a threat, or a warning.'

The man said nothing for a moment, pausing at the end of a short garden path no more than fifty metres from the church. 'Here we are,' he said, meaning the cottage. 'All I ask is that you won't upset Mrs Moore any more than she has been. As you can imagine, first she has had to cope with the death of her friend, and then in gathering his things she found the eyeball in the Father's desk.'

'It was a good thing she did,' he said. And it really was. Without it this would just be a tragic case of an old man who couldn't wait for his allotted time. Because Elspeth Moore had gone rooting through his personal effects looking for the papers she would need for the registrar they had a link to two other murders half a continent away. Today was actually a good day. Just not for Dooley.

TWENTY-SIX

The first thing Peter Ash noticed was that the roll-top desk was closed. One corner of the small study was stacked with boxes filled with a lifetime of sermons no longer needed and untouched since Dooley had switched the vicarage for this small house across the road. Langley Vale was basically four streets in a natural dip on the far side of the famous racecourse with a farm behind it.

The roll top was locked.

He looked at her without needing to ask the question.

Mrs Moore took a deep death and let it out as a heavy sigh before she retrieved the key from its hiding place in the Toby jug on the mantelpiece.

'Would the Father usually lock his desk?' Ash asked her. He fitted the small brass key into the lock and turned it. There was a hollow click.

'What would be the point of having a key if you don't use it?'

Ash shrugged. 'I don't think I've ever had a drawer that locked, even at work.' He rolled the wooden lid back to reveal a jumble of papers. A cursory glanced revealed no obvious order to them.

'He'd never let me tidy in there,' she said.

'Every man needs his secrets, I suppose,' Ash said, without really thinking about it. 'My father used to say that and keep anything he considered precious in the shed, which was a no-go area for me. People are strange. You found the box yesterday?'

She nodded. 'I knew he kept his birth certificate and other important papers in there, things Father Michael would need to take to the registrar . . . but I was looking for his address book when I found it. There were people I needed to tell . . . for him . . . you understand? People who cared about him. I didn't want them learning about what had happened from the newspapers.'

He nodded. 'Any idea who his next of kin was?'

'There's a cousin, but she's never been here. I don't remember him ever visiting her.'

'And the police took it away with them?'

She nodded. 'The book, and the box with that *thing* in it.'

'Did they take anything else?'

'What else would they take?'

'I know it feels like a horrible invasion of your friend's privacy, Mrs Moore, but I promise you I'm not trying to make things worse, either for you or for Father Dooley.'

'I don't see how things could get worse for him,' she said, with a surprising edge of bitterness behind her words.

'Well, yes. But . . .' He stopped rifling through the papers to look at the woman, properly look at her, and offered a sad smile. 'When you look at me, what do you see?' He didn't let her answer. 'A man. A cop. Maybe a tired-looking man. A troubled man. Someone looking for answers. But I'll tell you what you're really looking at, Elspeth, you're looking at a man who has given his life to be an advocate of the dead. Everything I do, I do to try and bring some sense of closure and comfort to those left behind. I do it for the victims. Some cops don't, some do it for justice, to catch the bad guys. But that's not how I think about it. Something horrible happened here, and it goes beyond a man taking his own life. I just want to find the truth.'

'And if that doesn't help?'

'Then I've let everyone down. So, can you talk me through it. You found the box?'

'Yes. It was a small Tupperware container, you know the sort of thing you keep leftovers in?' He nodded. 'I opened it and saw . . . I saw . . . the eye looking back at me. I dropped the box.' The memory was genuinely distressing. 'When I picked it up I saw the card that lay on top of the envelope.'

'Can you remember what was written on the card?'

She nodded. 'It was a strange message. Only two words. *Memini Bonn*. And then there was a time and an address down in town, like an invitation.'

TWENTY-SEVEN

Laura had already arranged for the box and its contents to be delivered to their lab for processing.

The local cops had Dooley's address book but were happy for evidence transfer as they had traced the cousin and didn't see any need for them to hold on to it any longer.

Ash rang through. The conversation was short and sweet.

'The coroner's ruled Dooley's death a suicide. We've got a suicide note and there's no evidence of anyone else's involvement. It's about as open and shut as we get. And put bluntly, we just don't investigate why someone feels like they have nothing left worth living for. But there is the eye—'

'Which is the heart of my investigation,' Ash assured the other man, resisting the weird compulsion to say tongue or eyeball in place of heart.

'And I'm happy for you to take over. I can courier it over?'

'It's fine, I'm in the area. I'll drop in and collect it.'

'You do that.'

The book was with the desk sergeant when he arrived fifteen minutes later. The station had gone through several facelifts over the last thirty years, sloughing off the square functionalism of the seventies for gradually more and more progressive and modern facades until it resembled a Holiday Inn. Despite Epsom itself being considerably bigger than the village on the hill above it, the station wasn't anywhere near as busy as it might have been. But then, the place reeked of entitlement not homelessness and criminal desperation.

He signed the evidence out and called Laura when he was done.

'Got it,' he said. He resisted looking inside it until he was well away from the desk sergeant, and even then he was surreptitious about it, flicking through the pages without taking the address book all the way out of the envelope. The first names he checked for were the most obvious, Jacques Tournard and Jonas Anglemark. Neither were in there.

'Many names?' she asked.

'Considerably more than in mine,' Ash told her. 'But then I've been a practising misanthrope for quite a while now.'

'You like to pretend, anyway.'

'Looks like he's been collecting names since the dawn of time. I bet there's people in here who have been dead for a decade.'

'It's kind of sweet,' Laura said. 'I haven't written down a telephone number in years. If my mobile died I'd be screwed.'

'You're such modern girl,' Ash said.

'Woman,' Laura corrected.

'It's like playing six degrees of Kevin Bacon. We add them to the mix and start to see the overlaps between clusters of them that shouldn't be there given the geographical and social disparity of the victims. There has to be an overlap. Find that intersection, we find our murderous Kevin Bacon.'

'Or another dead Bacon,' he finished for her.

TWENTY-EIGHT

'We've got something.'

Laura was at her desk, one hand gripping the wooden edge, the other holding on to the mouse. The cursor hovered over a box on the screen.

'What am I looking at?'

'It's tenuous, but it's a connection. Tournard was involved in setting up an orphanage in Poland shortly after the war.' Ash nodded. 'There were a lot of children who needed looking after, we'd made a lot of orphans. And far too many slipped through the cracks.'

'I can't even begin to imagine,' but that wasn't strictly true. He'd done a lot of imagining over the years. How could he not when his father was himself an orphan, and as far as Pete's family tree went every root and branch dead-ended in one of those places? His dad didn't talk about it much. Pete didn't press him about it, either. He figured there were some things best left forgotten. Now, of course, they weren't just forgotten, they were lost. It was strange not knowing anything about where you came from, but that sense of rootlessness was very much a part of what made him who he was. 'But doing something, that makes Tournard a good man.'

'You'd like to think so,' she said, but the way she said it made him wonder if she disagreed. 'But sometimes hope is worse than not being able to help at all.'

'I think I'd always rather hope,' he said. 'So, what's the connection with the other two?'

'Dooley spent six months volunteering there before he was given his first parish.'

'OK, that's a solid link. That feels like we're getting somewhere. What about the Swede, Anglemark? Where does he fit in?'

'Like I said, it's tenuous. Don't get your hopes up. But before he first ran for office he was a reasonably successful entrepreneur. He had several business interests in the construction industry, one of which was involved in a project to renovate and extend the building.'

'Please tell me they were there at the same time.'

Laura shook her head. 'Not even within a year of each other. I told you, sometimes hope is worse. It could just be a coincidence.'

'It's hard to believe we can find a definite connection linking all three and it's not the one we're looking for. This was definitely Poland, not Germany?'

'Definitely Poland.'

'OK.' He was thinking on his feet. 'Maybe the connection's not the orphanage but the charity that ran it? Maybe that's where the links go back to Bonn? Some dark secret that was going on there, and the three of them knew about it?'

'That's a lot of maybes.'

'It is.' Another thought occurred to him, though he wasn't sure how relevant it might be. 'Do me a favour, Law. Check if this is the only orphanage that the charity ran. Maybe there were others?'

'In different countries? I like the way your mind works. I'll see what I can turn up,' Laura promised, turning back to her screen. 'Once you cross my lips with caffeine.'

'Consider it sorted.'

'I'll wait while you make the pilgrimage to the home of the coffee gods.'

'Anything else happening?'

'Nothing devastating. Looks like your new friend just updated the system a couple of minutes ago, so you never know.'

'I'll check it out once I've taken care of your brew,' Ash said.

'Nice to know you've got your priorities right,' she grinned.

The truth was, without her there would be no point. It was already hard enough to carry on without Mitch Greer. They'd been in this thing together from the start, the Three Musketeers. She was the heart of the team, though she preferred to call herself the brains. It amounted to the same thing. She thought in terms of data and how to use it; how to connect and to eliminate the strands. He couldn't think like that, as much as he tried to. His mind worked on the principle of osmosis. He just soaked and soaked and soaked stuff up until it all bubbled out of him. Of course, sometimes it just felt like he was drowning.

But even then, even as the tides threatened to sweep him

away, she was always there, his rock. Though she wouldn't have appreciated being called a big lump of stone at the best of times, even if he tried to explain the analogy of life being a rushing river full of whitecaps and her being the only thing for him to cling on to.

'I do love you, you know,' he said, not looking at her.

'Of course you do,' she said. 'I'm loveable. Now go and fetch that coffee, there's a good boy.'

TWENTY-NINE

'We might have found something,' Ash said.

'Might?' Frankie asked.

'It's a stretch at best, but it's something concrete, and it links all three men.'

She listened as he filled her in. Realistically, it was more than she could have hoped for. 'I could kiss you,' she said. The other end of the long-distance connection stayed quiet. 'Obviously I don't *have* to.' This time her words were greeted by laughter.

'Sorry,' Ash said. 'I just keep thinking about what it doesn't tell us, rather than what it helps us with.'

'I get that,' she said. 'And it might ask as many questions as it answers, but it's a genuine intersection. These lives crossed. We know that for sure now. This old man in London, our gay politician in Stockholm, and our missing cleric in Paris. Their lives touched, even if only geographically, and never at the same time. It's a real connection. That's—'

'Got nothing to with Bonn,' he finished for her. 'I've got Laura digging into the charity. Let's see if she can unearth any links to Bonn. A conference, maybe, something about at-risk kids across Europe post-war. Anything like that. Because it's there. It has to be.'

'All roads lead to Bonn,' she said. And then she wanted to kick herself. 'Hold on, hold on, hold on . . . The body. Was there anything missing?'

'The priest's post-mortem is scheduled for this afternoon, but no one has mentioned any missing body parts. It was a suicide. He didn't answer the summons. He killed himself rather than go.'

'Meaning the killer has no new body part to send on to their next victim.'

'Assuming that it doesn't just end here?'

She thought about it. 'It doesn't.' She was sure of it. Serial killers didn't just stop killing. And that's what they were dealing with, a cross-border killing spree. The pattern was escalating. And fast. They already had two bodies, but there had to be a third to account for the eye, and that meant a fourth victim they didn't know about, and if the pattern held and one of Dooley's organs or extremities was meant to go to the next, that meant a fifth possible intersection of lives. There was still so much they didn't understand about what was happening, but today was going to be the day it all changed, because Jonas Anglemark's death was about to hit the wire. 'We need to confirm whose eye it is.'

'Hold on,' Ash said, and then cupped his hand over the headset so all she could hear was muffled voices, as a woman talked to him.

Laura.

'You still there?' he asked almost a full minute later. 'Laura's got some more on the charity, and why our original searches dead-ended. It opened several orphanages in Eastern Europe in the late 1980s.'

'So well after the initial post-war effort.'

'Children always need helping. And it isn't like we just suddenly stopped killing each other. We make orphans all the time. We're doing it right now somewhere in the world.'

'True,' she agreed, thinking of the horrors of Aleppo.

'And the reason we didn't turn up these other orphanages immediately?'

'The charity rebranded. Changed its name. That's why I kept hitting a brick wall.'

'How often does that happen?'

'I don't know,' she said. 'Not often, I'd guess. But if they were a global concern, maybe they were looking for something that translated across national boundaries? It doesn't have to be a sinister reason,' she said, despite the fact they were looking for exactly that, some sinister reason that might explain the trail of bodies. 'They're called The EuropaChild Foundation, registered office is in Rome. It might be worth one of us paying them a visit.'

'It's on the list,' he said. 'Dooley left behind an address book with almost eight hundred names in it. Laura's going through them one at a time looking for any that link back to the charity. Any one of them could be a potential target.'

'Or killer,' she said.

'That's my regular little ray of Swedish sunshine,' Ash said. 'I'm going to see if Donatti can get a look at the Monsignor's address book, assuming Blanc maintained one for him.'

'And you think they'll help?'

'Right up until the moment Tournard's body turns up, then they'll batten down the hatches.'

'Then we better hope the eyeball isn't confirmed as his,' she said.

'It's not. Wrong colour,' Ash replied.

'Are you sure?'

'The eye was brown. I'm looking at a photograph of the Monsignor right now. His eyes are blue-grey. Definitely not the same colour.'

'Well, that's bad news for someone else then, as that means we've got another corpse out there missing an eyeball.'

'And another unknown victim in the wind. Just to be sure we're on the same page, we're thinking grudge, right? This has to be personal.'

'Driven by hatred,' she agreed. 'Sending part of the previous victim to the next, it's meant to instil fear. It's meant to do to the recipient exactly what it did to Patrick Dooley. It's meant to make them give up. But what if it is more than just fear? What if the body part itself is relevant? Dooley received an eye, Tournard a tongue . . . You see, you speak, that kind of thing?'

'I like the way you think,' Ash said. 'I mean, if every victim received a finger, we'd assume that was a message, wouldn't we? That the killer was pointing the finger, or something like that. So, it makes sense the body parts are chosen for a reason. And they're parts of the body that aren't easily identifiable. You can't just run a tongue through the tongue database to get a match like you could a finger. So, if it's deliberate, the question is why a tongue? Why an eyeball? Both are considerably more difficult to excise than a finger. And your theory about the message, sight and sound, I like it. It works. Can I say something stupid?'

'Try me.'

'What if we're literally missing something here?'

'How do you mean?'

'The Monsignor received a tongue and a note to meet someone, a note that also mentioned Bonn. The priest was sent an eyeball and a similar note, also mentioning Bonn. The thing is though, and I can't believe I haven't asked you this before now, but was your politician sent something? A similar note. A random body part? Or is he victim zero, where it all begins? Because that makes a difference, doesn't it?'

She thought about it. She'd checked his office and his apartment in Vasastan, and nothing had turned up there. But he kept a room in chambers, too, and had a summer house out in the archipelago. Uniform had checked his room in chambers, and SAPO had cordoned off the summer house, so by rights if there was something to be found it would have turned up by now. But that wasn't the same as there being nothing to find. 'We haven't found anything.'

And this had bothered her from the beginning. Anglemark must have been lured to the rendezvous, same as the other victims. Everything about this all seemed so carefully orchestrated. The planning left little margin for error. And that meant there must have been some sort of message to lure him out, whether it was delivered to his office, or to one of the other residences. Any sort of threat sent to chambers would have immediately raised alarms with SAPO, and any suspect package – especially one containing human flesh – would have run afoul of the Riksdag's security.

No threat was going unnoticed.

It was impossible.

'SAPO are deconstructing every aspect of Anglemark's life. They're going through his phone logs and retracing every step he made over the last month, looking for any anomalies. Assuming he was lured to a carefully chosen meeting place, it can't stay secret. There are always traffic cams, CCTV, eye-witnesses. They will reconstruct the last hours of his life.'

'Changing MOs doesn't make sense, so even if there wasn't some grisly souvenir, I'm betting there was a card.'

'You're right,' Frankie said, 'changing MOs doesn't make sense. So if every other victim was lured to their death with a note telling them to remember Bonn you can bet Anglemark received one, too.'

'Then where is it?'

'I can't think about that now. I have a press conference in ten minutes. I am supposed to sit in front of the cameras and tell my country what has happened without telling them anything.'

'I don't envy you.'

THIRTY

The room was as sterile as the briefing they delivered. An array of cameras and microphones caught every angle and every missing nuance as the man beside her, Henrik Frys, leaned forward. He was well aware of the cameras and that every word and change of expression would be analysed and repeated on the endless news cycles of the world as soon as they were out of his mouth. Everyone in the room already knew what he was about to say, word had leaked out last night, tipping their hand and forcing the press conference.

Frys lowered his head before beginning to address the gathered reporters. Frankie felt for him. The next few words out of his mouth would write a new chapter in the history of their country. They would be in text books and on documentaries in twenty and thirty and forty years' time and talked about long after they were themselves dead.

He looked up.

Frys said, 'It is with great sadness that I must confirm that the body of a man fished out of Riddarfjärden two days ago was in fact Sweden's Minister for Children, the Elderly, and Gender Equality within the Social Health Department, Jonas Anglemark—'

And before he could go on, the first question was called out from the gathered reporters. 'Did he take his own life?'

Frys's glare lived up to his name. He waited to answer, and when he finally did it was to ignore the question. 'I would appreciate it if you could save your questions to the end, thank you. Our thoughts and the thoughts of everyone in our nation are with his partner, Mikael, at this incredibly difficult time. There are not the words to express our grief. It feels unreal. Jonas was working side by side with us just a few days ago, passionately advocating for the victims of the Syrian conflict who even now wait to discover the outcome of their asylum appeals and whether they will be allowed to stay permanently in their new homes. Jonas was an incredible man. He was passionate. Fierce. Loyal. You hear things like this all the time, but he was the best of us. He believed intensely that as the open and caring society we claim to be it falls to us to protect the weak, to take in the needy and nurture them. Without that guiding goodness, we are nothing.

'And yet, personally I feel a great sense of anger at his loss, and what it means for our society. For the wounds it inflicts upon the hearts and minds of our cities, because he was right, we have a duty to those who cannot help themselves to do everything we can to help them. I feel a sense of bewilderment, wanting to understand how it could happen, again. How he could be gone, like that, from our lives. I feel a sense of shame that people will walk our streets tonight and not feel safe. Everyone has the right to feel safe in their own city. But most of all I feel an intense sadness that I have lost a man I called my friend.'

There were tears in his eyes, and they were reflected in the eyes of many of the assembled journalists who hung now on his every word, hurting.

'So, I ask you to join me in a moment's quiet reflection, to think about the friend we have lost and what he means to us, and then I will hand you over to the officer leading the investigation into Jonas's death, Francesca Varg.'

Frys lowered his head again.

This time there were no questions.

The silence that fell over the room was freighted with grief.

Frankie closed her eyes and didn't open them again until she heard Henrik Frys say her name.

'Detective Varg?'

She nodded. She didn't have the same stirring words to move them, but what she had was, she hoped, more important in terms of how the next days and weeks played out.

'It is believed that Jonas Anglemark died in the early hours of Sunday morning, more than a week after his disappearance. We are currently appealing for witnesses, for anyone who might have seen something around Riddarholmen, Gamla Stan, and the Parliament on the night in question, or anyone who believes they have information that could shed some light upon his whereabouts during the days he was missing to come forward to help us with our investigations.'

'You're treating it as murder?' the same journalist called.

Frankie nodded. 'We have reason to believe that he was the victim of a criminal assault, yes.'

The questions kept coming.

'Do you have any leads?'

'We are currently pursuing a number of avenues which we hope will give us a better understanding of the events leading up to his death.'

'Are you looking at any particular groups or individuals?'

'At this moment in time we are not limiting the scope of our investigation to any one suspect pool.'

'Could it be an assault on the LGBTQ community, with Anglemark singled out because of his profile as a gay man?'

'At this moment in time we would rather not speculate,' Frankie said.

'Could it be linked to his advocacy for the Muslim immigrants?' a woman at the back called over the heads of the assembled journalists.

'Again,' Frankie answered, 'at this moment in time we would rather not speculate. It benefits no one if we look to assign blame to the very people Jonas spent his entire life trying to help.'

'Right-wing extremists then?'

Frankie ignored the question. It was painfully obvious where the press conference was heading. 'For all that we've lost, it is important we don't lose sight of who we are. Of who we want to be. We owe it to Jonas Anglemark to carry on with all the good work that he has done advocating for the vulnerable people in society, not looking to blame them for what has happened. So, please, if anyone watching has information they think might help the investigation I would urge them to contact us. We all want the same thing. Justice for Jonas Anglemark. And I can assure you we will find the person responsible for this crime. You have my word.'

She pushed back her chair and rose, indicating her part in the charade was over.

THIRTY-ONE

Peter Ash had been right.

Frankie couldn't get it out of her mind for the entirety of the press conference. They were missing something. Anglemark *must* have received some physical form of communication to draw him out. Even if it wasn't a body part. The killer had an established pattern, a way of doing things that felt safe and familiar to him. He wouldn't have started out improvising. It didn't make sense. A man who took a tongue and an eyeball didn't improvise. They added an imperative to the invitation; Frankie was working under the hypothesis that their inclusion was nothing more subtle than a threat. Fail to make the rendez-vous, this is what happens to you.

She was a great believer in instinct. It was what set good cops apart from great cops. That ability to see threads that bound the lies of the heart together. Sometimes you didn't need to see them to know that they were there, like in this case. Something had happened in Bonn that tied all these people together. The threads were there, and like secrets, they couldn't stay hidden for ever, not once she started pulling at them. They would eventually unravel. That was just the nature of threads. And it wasn't just her, this time. Ash and his resource manager – that was the term Division used: the last time she'd encountered it had been out on active duty, and then it was used as a euphemism for bodyguard – pulling at those invisible threads.

Something had to give.

She looked at her phone.

Three missed calls.

There was a voicemail waiting. She knew what it was going to say before she listened to it. Yet another link in the chain higher up demanding to know what progress was being made. The call had come through while she was on air. She'd felt the phone vibrate against her thigh. She didn't have anything more to say to them than she'd said in the press conference, but of course they wouldn't be content with that, so she needed to work out *exactly* what she was prepared to say before she hit reply.

So, work it through. Think smart. If he hadn't received the summons through the mail in his office, and there was no sign of it in his apartment, how had the killer reached him? It didn't make sense that some random telephone threat would draw him out, but it was possible, though the risk factor was high. Electronic media made so much more sense.

And that meant Kalle Lindholm. Kalle lived and breathed the shadowy half-world of digital surveillance. He was as close to a verified genius as she'd ever met and had all the social grace of a brick to the side of the face, but that was just all the more reason to love him.

'Ah, if it isn't the wolf herself,' the voice said before she had even had the chance to speak. 'Are you going to blow my house down?'

'Only if you ask nicely,' she said.

'I see you drew the short straw.'

'So you know why I'm calling you, then.'

'I figured you'd want to use me and then cast me aside, like usual.'

'That's really not fair, Kalle.'

'Isn't it? You remember what you promised me last time I stuck my neck out for you?'

'I do,' she said.

'So why should I trust you'll pay up this time?'

'Because I'm sorry?' she said.

'Of course you are, Frankie. You're so sorry it's taken you eleven months to call back. You must be really cut up about it.'

'It's not personal,' she said.

'Of course it is. By definition it's personal. What else can it be? I put myself out there, you left me hanging.'

'You don't really want the prize, anyway, Kalle. I know you, the fun is in the chase. Once you win, you lose interest. I'd hate for you to lose interest in me.'

'That could well be true,' he agreed with her, 'but it's beside the point. You owe me.'

'Double or quits,' she said.

'Double? OK, I'm liking the sound of that. You got a sister you want to bring along?'

'That would be telling.'

'And this is for the Anglemark case.'

'Yes.'

'Let me get this right, highest-profile crime in a decade and you come to a black-hat hacker rather than go through official channels?'

'You're too clever for your own good,' she said. 'Which is why I like you.'

'What do you want?'

'Something someone higher up the food chain has decided I don't need to know.'

'Oh yes?'

'I need access to Anglemark's emails.'

'You want me to hack a murdered politician's email account? I'm going to jail for this, you know that, right?'

'Not if you are good. Chances are I won't need to read the mails. I'm after specific mentions of Bonn, or The EuropaChild Foundation. Specifically, anything that came in in the last ten to twelve days.'

'And you don't want to go through channels?'

'Not if I can avoid it.'

'You do realize I expect sex for this, right? Lots of it. Very nasty sex. The kind of thing you don't want to imagine your parents doing.'

She laughed at that. 'I know what you're expecting. If you're lucky you'll get a Big Mac.'

'That sounds positively perverted.'

'Well, it's bad for your health,' she agreed.

Kalle laughed. It was a deep, guttural, and distinctly unattractive laugh.

'So, can you do it?'

'For a Big Mac I'll do anything.'

'I knew you were the only man for me.'

'Damn, woman, if only you weren't talking about an actual burger,' the hacker said. 'I could fall in love with a woman like you.'

'Which is why you're only getting the Big Mac. I don't do

love. Now, listen up, I'm going to tell you something I shouldn't, but you need to know. There's been at least one other death and a disappearance connected to Anglemark's murder.'

'Hence the Bonn connection and the charity? You think you've got a serial killer?' That shouldn't have excited him as much as it did.

'It's possible.'

'What other possibility is there?'

'Multiple killers working in tandem. We have three victims from three different countries.'

'And the other shoe drops. Now I understand why it's on your desk, not the Secret Service. That explains everything.'

She wasn't about to tell him that she'd been bought onboard before they knew that there was more than one victim, but that suddenly set her mind racing on a very different train of thought. If someone important was blocking her investigation they already knew the case crossed international borders before they came calling. But that immediately made it a government-level conspiracy, and that way led madness.

'And this charity? The EuropaChild Foundation?'

'Just a name at this stage. I'm not really sure how it connects, if it even connects, but Bonn is crucial, that much we do know. Two of the three victims received threats telling them to remember Bonn.'

'Leave it with me, wolf. I've got your back. Any mails referencing Bonn or traffic involving the charity. You sure there's nothing else you need once I'm in there?'

'That's all I need from the emails.'

'I like the way you said that, because it's absolutely obvious what you're really saying is hell yeah there's something else I need. Come on then, spill.'

'Do this, and you never know, I might just weaken,' she said.

'Oh, you tease.'

'Anglemark has two addresses in the city, an apartment in Vasastan and a rented room in chambers, but there's a family home in the archipelago and a stuga up beyond Kebnekaise . . .' Frankie let the statement dangle for a moment to see if he would bite.

The silence was deafening.

She let it roll on, knowing the power of silence.

Finally, he broke it, but only to say, 'I'll call you back,' before killing the call abruptly.

She stood there like an idiot, phone still pressed to her ear even though the hacker was long gone.

She walked down a narrow set of concrete steps and out onto a busy street. Sometimes being surrounded by so many people was the best way to keep your secrets. She crossed the road, walking under the colourful neon awning of one of three cinemas and on to one of the new espresso bars that had sprung up in this part of town. She raised two fingers, meaning a double shot, and tapped her contactless card against the card reader.

She was leaning up against the bar savouring the bitter strong aroma when her phone rang.

His voice sounded different. The acoustics around him were strange. Hollow.

'Better make this quick,' he said.

'What's wrong?'

'I'm locked in a stall in the men's room.' She didn't laugh at his crude tradecraft. 'I didn't want anyone overhearing me. This is strictly hush-hush, right? For your ears only. I'm serious. No matter what happens, you didn't hear this from me. Do I have your word?'

'You don't even need to ask.'

'Yes, I do. I'm serious, Frankie. This Anglemark guy. He ain't what he seems. I mean he was the gay crusader, right? He was everyone's image of the perfect LGBTQ knight, the wholesome gay politician with the model partner at his side. The kind of man it was easy to accept, who was a passionate advocate of children's rights, especially vulnerable immigrant kids who'd come in with the most recent wave of asylum seekers. It was all a carefully manufactured image.'

'What are you saying?'

'I'm not saying anything. You need to discover this shit for yourself, Frankie. The guy was a sick fuck. All I'm going to do is point you in the right direction, the rest is up to you.'

Frankie made writing gestures at the barista who took a pen from beside the cash register and passed it to her. She scribbled the address down on a folded napkin.

'I'll call you if I find anything in the emails,' he promised.

'I owe you,' she said, staring at the address she had written down.

'You do, more than you can possibly imagine. But I know you're good for it.'

The phone went dead. Frankie drained the small espresso in a single swallow. She felt a wave of guilt surge through her, hot with the coffee. They both knew she wasn't good for it. She'd used him like she always used him, letting him try and flirt his way out of that paper bag he hyperventilated into because it made it easier for her to get what she wanted out of him. But he'd let her. That made him complicit, didn't it?

So why did she feel as dirty as she did?

There was no way a Big Mac was going to pay off her debt if his tip came through. Maybe she'd have to stump up for extra fries.

THIRTY-TWO

F rankie grabbed a wild-game burger from the street vendor outside the espresso bar, eating as she walked. The fat juices ran down her chin. She used the napkin to clean herself up.

She didn't know what she expected to find at the address, but it promised to be incendiary.

And that was enough to give her hope.

She logged the address remotely, using an app on her phone that one of the tech boys had been developing. It was a long way from perfect but meant she didn't have to keep rushing back to the office to catch up on mindless paperwork. She made no reference of what the address was, how it pertained to her investigation, or where she'd obtained it, just in case someone came looking. She knew she was acting like some paranoid Big-Brother-fearing conspiracy theorist, but so be it. When the prize behind Door Number Three was a grand conspiracy running from top to bottom through the government a little circumspection was smart. But procedure dictated a certain amount of breadcrumbs or their lack would be suspicious. It was a delicate balancing act.

Like most police officers in Sweden she carried a Sig Saur P226, loaded with Speer Gold Dot hollowpoints. Rules required they carry one shot in the chamber to reduce the chance of accidental discharge in pressure situations. Very few officers ever discharged their weapons, with only twenty or so warning shots registered in any given twelve-month period. It wasn't like on television. They weren't gunning down suspects in street shootouts.

The address was within walking distance, as so many were within the main islands of the city. Stockholm was built across fourteen islands with road and rail bridges spanning the waterways around them. Most commuters used the extensive subway system, as the main city centre was held hostage by a couple of main choking points that were the only way on and off the island. It was simply faster to use the trains than it was to try and drive anywhere, and given the medieval nature of parts of the town and the incredibly narrow cobbled streets parking was a bitch. Back in the seventies and eighties lots of the older Germanic buildings had been demolished in the name of progress, replaced with harsh brutal Functionalist blocks, but the roads themselves hadn't been widened, and real estate was so precious no one wanted to waste it building car parks.

It took Frankie a little more than twenty minutes to leave the prosperous financial district behind in favour of one of Stockholm's less salubrious back alleys.

The yellow-painted walls were broken up by iron-banded grilles over windows which were probably older than America. A year ago there had been trouble in this part of town with rough sleepers setting up a cardboard city. Footage of the police going in heavy handed to evict them, confiscating their mattresses and sleeping bags, had been all over social media. There had been another video, this time black balaclava-wearing football fans going on a rampage through the same cardboard city. They'd filmed themselves beating the immigrants huddled up on their pathetic mattresses and released the video to stir up anti-immigration fears, claiming the streets were unsafe. This was the kind of stuff that Jonas Anglemark had stood up against, decrying the casual fascism of these people.

But that was her city now. It was on edge, just like the rest of Europe, with rapidly rising racist sentiments in the face of seemingly unending immigration, with the worst of them not understanding the basic difference between an immigrant and an asylum seeker.

The whole idea that these people had gone through hell to get to the promised land and a new life only to be forced to live like rats made her feel sick.

She recognized the street; there had been a major raid here that led to the discovery of a slum landlord who was claiming aid to support several unaccompanied children, only to cram a dozen undocumented refugees into each room, charging them half of the money they managed to beg each day for the privilege of being there. Those who weren't begging were being forced into prostitution, and more than half of the kids in that building already had drug problems. Every city had places like this; the kind that politicians pretended didn't exist.

Which made it interesting that Anglemark had spent any sort of time here. What kind of connection could he have to a place like this?

There was a thick iron-banded oak door like something from a medieval castle between her and the answer to that question.

At some point in the last few years the building had been divided into apartments. If the facade was anything to go by it was in a state of disrepair.

A couple of crusty teenagers were perched on a low wall sharing a joint in plain sight. They were dressed like something out of the grunge era with layers of plaid and torn denim.

Drugs were a hot-button topic in Sweden. It was only a decade since the public attitude to someone smoking a joint was up there with cheating on your taxes, and in Sweden cheating on your taxes was the crime of the century.

Times changed, especially with the raft of asylum seekers who were used to a very different drug culture back home.

It wasn't Frankie's job to bust the kids, so she let them get on with it.

She checked the buzzers beside the door. The address Kalle had given was for a second-floor apartment. She checked the names beside each one, but none of them meant anything to her. Even so, she used her phone to take a photograph so she could cross-reference them later.

The name of the occupant in the apartment she was looking for was Dahlberg. She pressed it and waited. There was no response. She thought about trying every button, but didn't need to as the door opened in front of her and a twenty-something Middle Eastern man with thick black stubble and black stones for eyes pushed by her. She stepped through behind him.

Motion sensors brought the light back to life as the door closed. There was a porthole-shaped window on the landing at the top of the first flight of granite steps. There was no light beyond the first landing. She stood under the hanging wire, looking up at the coupling where the bulb should have been. Whoever owned the building wasn't investing in the general upkeep. Thick layers of dust lay on the wooden banister. Pots of dried paint lined up beneath the window, hinting that maybe once upon a time someone actually cared. A cleaner hadn't set foot in this place since at least New Year, she realized, seeing several streamers and party favours that had been trodden underfoot.

She climbed to the second floor.

There was no doorbell outside the Dahlberg apartment. She listened at the door. There were on obvious sounds coming from behind it. She heard a baby crying in the opposite apartment and someone shouting somewhere upstairs. Both things were very out of place for an apartment block in the city. Swedes weren't social animals. They hid behind their doors and didn't make a sound for fear of standing out. It was like the way they all dressed in uniforms of blacks and greys and avoided bright colours. No one wanted to be seen.

Frankie was beginning to wonder if Kalle had sent her on a wild-goose chase, or if she'd somehow made a mistake with the address.

She knocked again, this time much harder, and the door swung open slowly without resistance, which immediately set her instincts jangling. She reached for the Sig Saur, calling out, 'Hello?' as she went inside. 'Armed police. I'm coming in,' she said, loud enough for her voice to carry to every room in the small apartment.

The last thing she wanted was to trigger some fight or flight response by surprising anyone inside.

'Police,' she called again, still standing on the threshold.

The door opposite opened.

A young girl of perhaps four or five years old peered out through the crack long enough to see Frankie flash her badge before closing it again.

She'd been a cop for a long time and been in situations where she just had to trust her gut plenty of times. Something was off here.

She stepped inside and pushed the door closed behind her with her heel.

She didn't want any nosy little girls following her inside.

The ceiling was thin. The argument upstairs was louder in here than it had been out in the hallway. 'Police,' she called for a third time. 'Don't make any sudden movements. Stand in the middle of the room with your hands behind your head.'

There was no answer.

The moment she opened the door into the lounge she knew why.

The body of the man lay sprawled out on the couch.

His drug paraphernalia cluttered the coffee table. Rubber tubing was still tied off around his arm. The needle was on the carpet. She slipped the gun back into its underarm holster and took a pair of latex gloves from her pocket.

Even through the latex his skin was icy to the touch.

There was no trace of a pulse.

The smell of vomit hung in the air, stale. It mixed with the stench of faeces where he'd evacuated his bowels in death. His chin was crusted yellow.

Frankie stood up to distance herself from it.

She needed to call it in.

The fact she'd flashed the girl her badge would hopefully be enough to stop them forming a posse to deal with the intruder. Not that this felt like the kind of place where neighbours went the extra mile for each other.

She made a call to the local station, putting it in their hands, and promised to stay on the scene until they arrived. They warned that it could take fifteen minutes before anyone got to her. 'It's not like the body is going anywhere,' the dispatcher noted. It was that familiar callousness around drug deaths.

But fifteen minutes would hopefully give her all the time she needed to work out who the dead man was and how he tied in to Jonas Anglemark.

If there was something that linked him to the apartment.

She took a look around.

The room was furnished better than she had expected. It wasn't expensive stuff, but it was decent IKEA starter-home furniture. She had been in similar apartments where every piece of furniture was on its last legs. Most of the stuff in here looked almost new. There were a few signs of age and wear, hence the almost, but it was better than some of her own stuff. The pictures were tasteful, the walls a soft shade of blue, the rugs plush beneath her feet, and the hardwood floor oiled and polished. This wasn't the home of a junkie despite evidence to the contrary lying on the sofa.

The first thing she noticed was a lack of photographs. There were no personal flourishes beyond a few dog-eared paperbacks on the bookcase. The spines marked them all as bestsellers, all in their Swedish translations rather than the original languages. She checked the fridge. There were no plastic containers with body parts inside. There were two bottles of imported beer and a carton of milk that had passed its expiry date. There was nothing else in the way of sustenance inside, so maybe this wasn't the kind of apartment where someone lived, but rather somewhere they crashed from time to time when they were in the city.

The bathroom was no more personal. There were a few expensive toiletries with designer labels, but they were all near empty. The shower mat was bone dry.

She tried the first bedroom. The bed was unmade, the sheets sweated into the outline of the last sleeper. There were obvious semen stains on the fabric – large irregular discoloured circles. There were a lot of them, like a weird living Kandinsky collage. Sweat stains made a poor man's Turin shroud out of the pillow case. There was plenty of evidence of sex and sweat and very little else. She found a couple of changes of clothes in the wardrobe. Like the furniture it wasn't designer stuff, but it was good-quality functional material. Again though, there was nothing personal in here.

She went through to the smaller second bedroom. It was being used as a study, and instead of a bed there was a beautiful leather-inlaid desk and a desk chair that probably cost a month's salary.

She settled into the chair and tried to imagine Anglemark using this place as his refuge, a bolt hole away from the public eye. But why would he need one?

Frankie tried the drawers.

There was a desk diary in the first drawer she opened. Most of the pages were blank, but a few had the initial B beside the date. She riffled through the pages, stopping on the day Anglemark had died. A card had been slipped between the pages. She knew what it said before she picked it up: *Memini Bonn*. And an address and time halfway across town. It was proof positive that Anglemark was tied to Tournard and Dooley. That same imprecation, remember Bonn, presumably in Latin because that was the language of the Catholic Church.

But how did Kalle know about this place? What went on here that it was even on the hacker's radar?

And how did the dead man fit in?

Or more accurately, dead men. Both Anglemark and the corpse on the couch had reason to be here on their last days.

Frankie was beginning to think she knew the answer.

She slipped the card into an envelope she found in the second drawer and put it in her pocket, returning the diary to the drawer.

After a quick glance at her watch she guessed she had maybe five or six minutes before the beat cops arrived. If there was anything else to be found it needed to be found quickly.

Using her phone Frankie took as many shots of the apartment as she could, not sure what she was looking for in them but not wanting to risk missing the obvious.

But it was the corpse that warranted most her attention. She realized what it was that bugged her about the dead man's pose. There was no way that he could have been comfortable reclining like that, even if he was stoned. And in death it just looked unnatural. There was a half-drunk bottle of whiskey, cap off, and the classic tableau of aluminium foil, cotton-wool balls, tarnished spoon for cooking the drug, and the lighter with which to cook it, and of course the hypodermic on the floor.

Frankie took half a dozen more shots of the table and the stuff on it, and then some of the dead man.

It was only as she knelt to get a decent shot of the vein damage in his arm that she realized he was much younger than she had originally thought.

Death could age a corpse, making it appear more wasted than it had been in life.

She checked his pockets and found a wallet that identified him as one Björn Dahlberg and listed a date of birth in this millennium. She couldn't believe he was barely eighteen, but the ID looked legit. She would have guessed him at closer to thirty. Mid-thirties even.

Things were beginning to fall into place. Dahlberg's name on the buzzer added a layer of anonymity for Anglemark. There was no way the teenager could afford a place this central, no matter how shitty it was, it was still prime real estate. Kalle's comment about Anglemark being a bastard made sense. Here was a man

who had it all. Who was a paragon of virtue in the gay community. Someone who presented that perfect face for the new
Sweden, an open caring society, a place where race, creed, colour,
and sexuality didn't matter because everyone was equal. Everyone
bled red, the rest didn't matter. He was good. Better than good.
He put himself out there as the best of them.

The insult levelled so often at politicians couldn't have been
truer in his case. He was a two-faced liar, and this was his secret
place, his second face. When he wasn't campaigning for those
vulnerable kids and fighting for the rights of those asylum
children, he was fucking around behind his partner's back with
some young drug-addled twink he kept as a toy.

She shook her head, not wanting to believe the reason behind
his murder could be as banal as that.

It was disappointing.

She'd expected more from him.

Something gnawed at the back of her brain.

It was too neat. Like it had been served up to her. Anglemark
had done his best to keep this place a secret and to be fair had
done a damned good job of hiding it as far as legal searches
and official records went, but a hacktivist like Kalle Lindholm
had not just known of its existence, but what went on within its
four walls, and its address, too.

Which begged the question: did that mean he knew about
Björn Dahlberg?

And did the killer?

The card urging Anglemark to remember Bonn was here,
not in chambers or his own apartment, or any of the places he
kept out of town. It was here. Meaning either the killer had sent
it to this address, and thus knew the Dahlberg connection, or
Anglemark had brought it here himself and hidden it because
he considered this the one safe place in his world.

She was still trying to make sense of all of it when she heard
a knock at the door. She had company. Fifteen minutes. Right
on time.

THIRTY-THREE

Another cafe, another dead end.

This time it was a small, and desperately old-fashioned place; the kind that still had a brass bell on the door that chimed every time it opened and closed. A small bird-like woman approached as he entered, all smiles as she ushered him to a two-top and took his order.

Dooley had already been dead by the time he was supposed to meet his nemesis. The coroner's time of death pronouncement had a little wiggle room, but he was several hours cold by the time stamped on the card.

He put his warrant card on the table, not making a big thing out of it. It didn't do to spook anyone. 'My name's Peter, I'm with the Eurocrimes Division.' She nodded like that meant something to her, which of course it didn't. The badge did all the meaningful talking for him. 'I'd like to ask you a few questions about yesterday if that's OK?'

'Of course, happy to help if I can, officer.'

'I'm interested in anyone who came in alone, specifically around two to three in the afternoon, maybe looked like they were expecting to meet someone that never showed?'

'A lot of people come here for a drink and a chat, you know how it is. Lots of people come in by themselves these days, too. It's not like it used to be when it was embarrassing to eat alone.'

'I understand,' Ash said.

'It means that folks don't stick out like a sore thumb any more. People use this place differently. We have some guys who come in with their laptops and sit for three or four hours on one cup of coffee. We have others who are leaving before the dregs in their cup have gone cold.'

He nodded. 'I'm sure you see all sorts. But think about yesterday afternoon, maybe someone came in and went out again without ordering?'

'You heard the bell? I'm like Pavlov's Waitress. That rings,

I've got you in a seat faster than you can say milk and two sugars, dear. Besides, yesterday was quiet. It always is, midweek. We have our regulars, of course. I could probably make you a list of every person who came in through those doors. Most of our custom is on patterns. Like ten thirty, the mother and baby group lets out and we get half a dozen mums who need their sugar infusion to survive the oncoming storm of toddler days. Then it's the office crowd who are on a grab and go schedule with their takeaway lattes and sourdough sandwiches. The third wave comes when the schools finish and we get the sixth-formers coming in to hang out for an hour or so before going home. Used to be they sat around inside the Ashley Centre, killing time or shoplifting, but now it's all frothy coffees and poetry.' She smiled, obviously very fond of the young Byrons and Shelleys who frequented her humble abode. 'We get the gentle artistic souls, mainly from the art college, the others all want to hang out at the Starbucks down the road.'

'There are worse kids to have as regulars,' Ash said, and meant it. 'I don't suppose you have cameras watching the street?'

She shook her head. 'The cost isn't worth it. We're not a Nero or Costa. We don't have a problem with vandalism or theft.'

'You're very lucky.'

She didn't disagree.

He thanked her, and decided to canvass the area, making a list of cameras in the area and the kind of coverage they offered. It wasn't as bad as Paris, but it still wasn't great as most of them were traffic cams linked to the lights, and their focus was squarely on the road.

It was all about patterns of behaviour; people were creatures of habit. They took comfort in the familiar and repeated what had worked before. It stood to reason that he watched his victims. That reduced the element of surprise and the room for things to go wrong. So, if he'd followed Tournard to their meeting, it was reasonable to expect repeated behaviour. But where would he start watching the old man? Nearly eighty thousand people lived in the borough, even if Langley Vale itself was maybe two hundred at best. Epsom wasn't so small that there was only one way in or out, but there was only one sensible way from the Downs to the town centre. But even so he couldn't just sit at a bus stop and wait to be sure the old priest was on time. People were random. They didn't follow predictable patterns: like Brownian random motion playing out on a massive scale, they bounced off each other and got side-tracked by signs, hungers and thirsts, and distractions. Unless they had a destination in mind, then they followed the shortest possible route from A to B. But even then there were just too many opportunities for things to go wrong. A double-decker bus reinforced that as it drove slowly by obscuring the other side of the street for a good forty-five seconds. A lot could change in even that short time. So why risk missing your man by lying in wait any sort of distance from their destination?

There were far too many places on the busy street for someone to hide in plain sight.

He was thinking about this all wrong.

He needed to break out of this mindset. He gave up, deciding to head back into River House.

He was halfway back to the car when his phone rang; it was Laura.

'What's the good news?'

'You only want the good? Or are you up for the bad, too?'

'Give me the good news first.'

'OK, I've managed to pull together a list of the orphanages that the EuropaChild Foundation has helped set up. Most of them are across Eastern Europe and were set up after the Berlin Wall came down.'

'I'm sure their money was welcomed with open arms,' Ash said, cynically.

'You remember what it was like. The governments in most of those countries didn't have the resources or were using them to shore up their regimes in the wake of civil unrest. They were happy to let foreign aid take on the financial burden, but most of the orphanages themselves were eventually taken over by either the government or local groups. A few have been closed down, of course, as the need for them has diminished.'

'That's good to hear at least.'

'I've whittled the list down to the ones still open and run by the charity, rather than reabsorbed into state control.'

'Any of them in Germany?'

'Like I said, good news, bad news. That's the bad news. Or some of it at least.'

'You're breaking my heart here, Law.'

'I've had Division run a historical search on crimes involving victims being sent body parts. We've had two fresh hits.'

That immediately changed things. He stopped dead in his tracks. 'I want to know everything.'

'The first match turned up in Seville, Spain, though it didn't get flagged immediately because the recipient's cause of death was determined to be a heart attack. His daughter found a finger in a plastic container in the fridge when they were clearing the house out. The guy lived on his own since his wife died five years earlier. The initial police reports describe him as a loner. It is believed he died several weeks before his body was found.'

'Close-knit family. How long ago?'

'Just over a month.'

The implications washed over him. A month. He looked over his shoulder, suddenly conscious of just how public he was, before he said, 'We've had a killer out there for over a month and we've only just realized?'

'Natural causes. No one was looking for a murderer.'

'Even so. I don't suppose the local plod turned up a note? A nice little "remember Bonn" warning to link things definitively to our case?'

'If only. Looks like daughter dearest either boxed up or burnt anything that might have been of use, cleaning the place out. Not one for sentimentality, I guess.'

'And the other victim?'

'Rome, Italy.'

'Rome? That's on Donatti's doorstep. Surely it was on his radar?'

'Maybe, maybe not. You know what it's like over there with the Vatican police, the Polizia di Stato, and Carabinieri, it's not like all of these forces are all lovey dovey. Chances are because it's got zero to do with the Church he doesn't even know about it.'

'I don't know . . . he's got a habit of hearing things,' Ash said, already going through a list of possibilities why the Church man might hold out on him. 'So, what do we know about the vic?'

'This one was sent to a judge. His wife opened it and, assuming it was some sort of Mob threat, reported it to the Carabinieri straight away. The judge is in protective custody.'

'Has he missed his meeting?'

'Not yet. It's scheduled for this afternoon, three o'clock.'

Ash checked his watch, even though he knew that it was physically impossible for him to make the journey, lose an hour in the time zone change, and make the meeting.

'The Carabinieri have a body double taking his place to see if they can lure the suspect out.'

'He won't be there.'

'What makes you say that?'

'Patterns of behaviour. He didn't turn up to the meet when Dooley didn't show, but he did turn up for Tournard's because the Monsignor was there. He's watching them. He knows the judge is a no-show. He'll know it's a sting.'

'So, does he come back for the judge a second time?'

Ash found himself shrugging, as if she could see his response. 'Yes. Absolutely. There's no forgiveness here. No absolution. You don't get lucky and get to live just because you missed the showdown. If anything you sign your death certificate by not taking that meeting, that's the threat isn't it. Don't show, you get chopped up into little pieces and mailed across Europe.'

'And show up and you only lose one extremity. Deal or no deal?'

'He's got a grudge list. One by one he's facing them down to settle old scores. Whatever happened in Bonn they're being made to remember their role in it. And he isn't going to stop until he has made each and every one of them face up to what they did.'

'Unless we stop him.'

'That's the plan.'

'There's no room to manoeuvre,' Ash said. She assumed he meant for them, but he didn't, he was thinking like the killer. The man was working to a tight schedule. He was in Stockholm less than a week ago, in Paris only a few days ago, and London yesterday. Now he's supposed to be in Italy this afternoon?

'I want you to get onto the Civil Aviation Authority, run a check for any travellers who have flown from Stockholm to Paris to London and on to Italy in the last week, or any two from four.

There can't be too many of them. Then get those passport numbers to border control at the other countries and see if they entered by any other means, like the Tunnel. We've got a map here. Let's follow it.'

'On it,' Laura promised.

'Dooley has fucked things up for him. He is missing a body part. And now the judge is off limits he's oh for two. He's going to need to adjust, and it's in that window of adjustment he fucks up. His schedule's off. He's got no room for manoeuvre. He's rigidly locked into this pattern of threat and vengeance, he's not going to just jump to the next name on the grudge list. He wants these people to remember Bonn, and the body parts are part of the message. They have to be. And he needs them or the message doesn't work.'

'Makes sense,' Laura said. 'But surely he can just kill somebody else for the necessary body part?'

'He's not a murderer,' Ash said. 'Not like that. He's not killing randomly. He's working to some sort of justice. He isn't about to hurt someone he doesn't believe deserves to be hurt.'

'So, he sees himself as the good guy here?'

'Doesn't everyone think they're the heroes of their own lives?'

'Good point,' Laura said.

'Do we have an ID on the finger?'

'I'm waiting for the print to be processed and sent through. Rome have promised it within the hour.'

'An hour? Jesus, it's not like we're in a race against time or anything. Let me guess, the lab closes for a siesta?'

'Wish I knew. I'm trying to hurry them along, but frankly getting anything back feels like a miracle on the loaves and fishes level right now.'

'Well, I've got faith in you, Law. You're my own personal Jesus,' Ash said. 'But next time maybe you could shoot for a useful miracle, like the wine one.'

THIRTY-FOUR

The two men who arrived at the Dahlberg apartment were sharply dressed, in dark suits that no doubt came from the same bespoke tailor's shop. They weren't beat cops. She knew they were SAPO before they flashed their identification. SAPO. The Swedish Security Service.

She produced her own Eurocrimes Division identification, but neither of them seemed the least bit interested in it.

'We'll take it from here, Miss Varg,' the shorter of the two, who still stood close to six three, said, as they pushed their way into the living room.

'Take over?'

'The security of government officials falls within our jurisdiction.'

'I don't see any government officials,' she said, looking pointedly at Dahlberg's corpse. 'And given how miserably you failed Jonas Anglemark isn't this a bit like shutting the stable door after the horse has well and truly bolted off to horsie heaven?' Probably not the smartest thing to say, but their assumed superiority just pissed her off.

'Which would be all well and good, but this has nothing to do with Anglemark,' the taller of the two suits said.

'How can you possibly be sure?'

'Because we are good at what we do.'

His partner asked, 'Do you think he was killed here?'

'No,' she said, 'but . . .'

The man raised his hand to silence her. 'Do you have *any* reason to believe that this man was responsible for Anglemark's death?'

She shook her head.

'And there you have it. This has *nothing* to do with your investigation, Miss Varg.' He scratched at the underside of his nose, and in the process let his jacket fall open just enough to reveal the butt of his own service weapon in a shoulder holster.

This was a pointless hill to die on. When it came to picking your battles with SAPO and the suits of the Riksdag it was always better to let the small things go. She had what she needed from here. The rest was just a tangle of red tape that would take up far too much of her time to extricate herself from if she chose to fight the politics of it. Better to let the boys have their win so they could walk away thinking their dick-swinging had done the job. There were better hills to die on. Always.

'OK, boys, you win. Your case. But do me a favour, one of you give me your number so I know who I've handed the crime scene over to, then I'll leave you to it.'

'Ah, Miss Varg, you seem to be under the misapprehension that this is a crime scene? That would explain a lot. Let me set you straight. There is no crime scene. What we have here is a junkie who has, not so tragically, overdosed. He might have just as easily stepped in front of a subway train at T-Centralen. It is a waste of life, yes, but it is not a crime.'

She looked the pair up and down and just shook her head. 'I'm still going to need something I can put in the report. Not all of us have the joys of just writing "it's above your pay grade" in the file and moving on.'

'It's your lucky day,' the shorter of the two said. 'You don't need to write a report because you were never here.' She started to object, but he cut her off. 'Understand, if you *were* here I would have to start asking some very serious questions, not least what led you to this place, and put you in the middle of our investigation. Bear in mind if there was anything in any way suspicious or, dare I say, illegal about the way the information was gathered there would be ramifications. And even if it was all entirely above board, your source would almost certainly suffer. No one wants that.'

She maintained eye contact with the man. Still not a hill worth dying on, she told herself. But she was damned if she was just meekly going to roll over. 'Perhaps you'd give me a call if you come across anything that might be of use in *my* investigation.'

She reached into her back pocket for her wallet and offered her own card.

He didn't take it.

'I know where to reach you,' he said. 'Rest assured, should anything of importance come to light, I will be in touch. We are, after all, on the same side.'

She still didn't break eye contact.

'Now, if you wouldn't mind?'

She bit her tongue.

Better hills.

Frankie left the apartment. She took the stairs down to the ground level without a backward glance. This wasn't about hiding some scandal. They hadn't been surprised or, to be brutally honest, bothered that there was a dead kid on the sofa. Their primary concern had been territorial. They were more worried about containing and controlling the scene. They knew the secrets of that apartment, and they obviously went beyond Anglemark fucking a twink because he was bored with his perfect little life at home.

So, assuming Anglemark kept everything at arm's length, ownership of the flat, everything else, it was conceivable the kid was the mysterious Dahlberg, or it was a hot couch. The kind of roll-on roll-off casual sex hook up arrangement where there was no Dahlberg, or everyone who walked through the door was Dahlberg. It wasn't her problem if the guy was unfaithful. She didn't care if he went from gloryhole to gloryhole pleasing himself and every other gay man in the city. All she cared about was who killed him, and why. And if his personal proclivities had something to do with it, great, otherwise, they were irrelevant.

She'd got what she needed out of the place, definitive proof of the pattern. *Memini Bonn.*

A police car rolled up outside the apartment building just as she turned left at the mouth of the alleyway, heading back towards the subway. She heard the car doors slam as the uniformed officers clambered out.

The secret service had beaten the beat cops to the punch, despite the fact she'd called in to dispatch to report the incident, giving the uniforms what should have been an unassailable head start. What that told her was that SAPO were monitoring either her calls or had an alert in the system set to trigger as soon as the address came up. One choice was considerably better than the other. She discounted the possibility of uniform tipping the secret service off purely and simply because they'd still responded to the call, and SAPO would have shut that down.

The fourth alternative was a variant on the same, that Kalle had sold her out, which made no sense, why help and hinder at the same time, unless he just wanted to be seen to help but not actually help?

The only other possibility was that SAPO were monitoring his calls and for a black-hat hacker who survived through a mix of skill and paranoia that didn't exactly seem likely.

The only answer that made any sense to her cop brain was that they were watching her or the house, and of the two she knew which one her money was on.

THIRTY-FIVE

Rome. The eternal. But sadly not frozen in time.

The telephone was a fine invention, but Ash was more for the face-to-face encounter. So much was lost without the nuance of body language and those micro-emotions that gave away the truth behind the words, those tells were always there if you knew what to look for. He wanted to sit down with the judge, Paulo Maffrici.

It was late by the time he landed, and the taxi driver tried to pull a fast one with his change. The guy was all chatty, and as Ash handed over the fifty the guy palmed it and held up a five saying it wasn't enough. Ash flipped open his wallet, making sure the word police on the top of his identification was there for the man to see, and asked him, 'Are you sure about that? You might want to check again.' The guy nodded and promised it was an honest mistake, which of course it was anything but. He drove Ash to the hotel Laura had booked him into, which was down on the Tiber in Trastavere, the old workers' quarter. He always liked this part of the city because it had very little in the way of pretence about it, unlike the more ancient areas around it. Good food, cheap; good wine, again cheap. He didn't have Donatti to play host, but that was fine.

He took a walk to find food. The thing about Italy was that despite the fact most sensible people back home would be nursing their nightcaps by now the locals were just sitting down for their evening meal. He found a little place along Piazza di Sant'Egidio. The prosciutto and mozzarella, on a bed of rocket and toasted flatbread, came on a wooden chopping board along with a selection of olive oils and balsamic. It tasted even better than it looked. He washed it down with a couple of glasses of red wine picked from a precious wall balanced floor to ceiling with bottles.

Setting his knife and fork aside, he called Laura on her mobile, knowing she'd pick up despite the hour. There was nothing nine-to-five about their relationship.

'I've arranged for you to see the judge at eleven,' Laura said. 'But, I should warn you, he isn't a willing interviewee. I had to call in a few favours to get you a sit-down with him. He seems . . . difficult.'

'That's a nice way of putting it,' he said.

'He's not big on talking. I guess it shouldn't come as a surprise seeing as he's been heavily involved in prosecuting organized crime in the city, and according to our local boys has received no fewer than three hundred death threats in the last decade.'

'So what makes this one different? Why suddenly go into protective custody if you're a fully paid-up member of a Threat of the Month club?'

'It was the wife that reported it, not the judge.'

'That, or the message this time makes it a credible threat, because he remembers Bonn,' Ash said.

'He's adamant that you're making a wasted journey. Claims it is just some crackpot, and that he's got nothing to tell you that isn't in his statement.'

'That's fine. Sometimes it's not the words. And, you know me, I don't trust anyone to tell me the truth unless I'm looking them in the eye.'

'Please tell me you're not about to call a high-ranking judge a liar?'

'There are plenty of liars in high places. Power is no indication of purity, you know that.'

'Just don't go getting the guys there riled up, Pete. It's all well and good to go in like a bull in a china shop every now and then but you never know when we might need their help.'

'You know me. I'm a fucking delight.' She barked a harsh laugh in his ear. 'I'm going to be discreet, promise,' he said, more seriously. 'I want to look into his eyes when I say the words EuropaChild Foundation. I want to see if there's a flicker of recognition, or if it genuinely means nothing to him. It's a split-second thing, while his reptile brain tries to decide how best to lie. Then I'm going to ask him what happened in Bonn.'

'You know he'll deny all knowledge of Bonn. He has to if he's going to maintain it's all a big hoax.'

'I know,' he agreed. 'I want him to lie. I want him to know I know he's lying. I'm not afraid of a judge. I don't give a shit about the political niceties of a corrupt justice system like Italy's. He can't fuck up my career any more spectacularly than I've already fucked it up myself. So, I can push harder than the Carabinieri.'

'Don't interrogate a bloody judge, Pete.'

He smiled at that. 'I promise.'

And with that he killed the call and went to take in a little night air. This part of Rome was a different beast to the main tourist traps. Youths parked their Vespas along the side of the road, and gathered in groups around old boom boxes blaring out tunes so loudly the speakers distorted. Girls danced in the street with boys; girls danced in the street with other girls; boys danced in the street with boys. They linked hands and jived along with the tunes in a very obvious mating ritual. Some of the boys, too cool for their own good, perched on the stones of a broken wall, hands cupped around the thin dog ends of hand-rolled cigarettes, blowing smoke whilst the pretended they were living *la dolce vita*.

He walked alongside the Tiber then back to his hotel, and bed.

He slept the sleep of the damned: fitful, broken, and tangled up in febrile dreams.

He woke to a pre-breakfast call from Donatti. He answered it hazily, throat raw and words weak as he rolled over, saying, 'Ash?'

'Ah, Peter, my friend, what is this I hear? You are here in my glorious home and you did not call me? Did we not have an agreement that I would show you my city as only a local can?' He sounded far too awake for his own good.

'I thought you were in Paris?' Ash said.

'Yesterday's news. I had accomplished all I could there, which I admit was distressingly little, and am now resigned to the fact that it is only a matter of time before we hear the worst.'

'It was always the most likely possibility,' he agreed. 'And even more so now that it looks as though Tournard's disappearance is part of something bigger than just the murder of Jonas Anglemark.'

'Just? Isn't that a terrifying word in this context, my friend? I assume that is why you are here, to talk to Judge Maffrici?'

'You really do hear everything, don't you?'

'My boss sees everything, hears everything, and knows every-thing,' the Church man said. Ash could hear the grin in his voice.

'That's got to come in handy.'

'You can't seriously believe Maffrici is involved?' Donatti said, changing the subject.

'There have been developments. I know I promised to share intel, but I really can't discuss this stuff now, Ernesto.' He hardly ever used his old friend's given name. He hoped that would go a long way to explaining just how serious things were now, and not just for the missing Tournard. 'But I will give you this much: he may be able to shed some light on an aspect of your search.' It was more than he should have said. Donatti wasn't an idiot. He could join dots and see patterns with a clarity that evaded most cops Ash had met. The guy had a way of making assump-tions that hit way too close to the mark. 'Needless to say, that is between you, me, and your boss. No one hears a word, you understand? No running back to the Holy See to tattle. It's imperative no one knows what I'm looking for. All it needs is someone to overhear a careless word and they'll close ranks.'

'I understand, my friend, and value your trust. I cannot believe it. Maffrici involved . . .' he tailed off.

'It's not certain that he is,' Ash half-lied. He might not have concrete proof the judge was up to his neck in it yet, but he was involved. The finger and its accompanying note were all the proof he needed of that. 'I'm more interested in knowing how you found out that I was coming.'

'We both have our secrets,' Donatti said. 'You show me yours, and I'll show you mine. Isn't that how it works?'

'That's a very British expression, but no can do.'

'Pity. I hope we will get to spend some time together before you leave? There is so much I would love to show you. It always helps to know your friends, I think, when you know where they come from.'

'I'll see what I can do,' Ash said. 'No promises. But maybe we can have a beer before I head back to the airport.'

'We should do that,' Donatti agreed, taking it as a done deal.

Ash ended the call and dropped the silent phone onto the bed.

He felt the fine hairs along the nape his neck prickle.

It came down to patterns of behaviour. We all have our tells, our giveaways. It wouldn't have been difficult for Donatti to call in a favour from someone in Rome's police, one law man to another, so they'd tip him off about Ash's arrival. And in a city like Rome it is hard to imagine someone rising to the rank of judge without developing some sort of ties to the Church, if not directly with the Vatican itself. It was a small city in that regard. Power begat power. Influence fed off influence. A man like Donatti, in a city like this, was one of the hidden powerbrokers. They used to call them kingmakers. It wasn't difficult to imagine the network of influence the man had amassed during his rise until finally he was so connected the Vatican turned to him as their fixer.

He was a man who got things done.

But that wasn't what was interesting – or at least it shouldn't have been, not by itself. He'd always known Donatti had his own agenda here, and they were only working in tandem whilst their purposes aligned. So, no, what was interesting was why the Church's fixer was so interested in Ash's travel arrangements. It wasn't just that he'd extended an invitation to Rome, either. So, it had to be Maffrici, didn't it? Occam's razor. The simplest explanation is always the most likely.

Which meant a connection between the Vatican itself and the disappearance of Monsignor Tournard, Jonas Anglemark, Patrick Dooley, and Paulo Maffrici. That was the simplest explanation for Donatti's repeated requests for circumspection, and requests for time in delaying Tournard's case being escalated to Missing Persons. And the simplest answer meant Donatti had his own motivations, especially when it came to calling so early in the morning.

The simplest explanation demanded he turn over a stone he would never have thought to turn over if Donatti hadn't called. They'd run all sorts of background checks into the victims and the EuropaChild Foundation, but what they hadn't done was run the same checks for links between the Vatican and the orphanages. Or, more directly, between Ernesto Donatti, the foundation, or any of the orphanages it ran.

Sometimes he hated the simplest explanation, because it cut right to the heart of the matter, and that wound could do serious damage to the matter of the heart.

THIRTY-SIX

T he serviceman at the security gate had been expecting
him, even though he showed a certain amount of disdain
at his presence.

He scrutinized both Ash's passport and his Eurocrimes Division
identification and was happy to let Ash enter but wouldn't allow
the taxi to drive up to the main door of the safe house.

Ash didn't make a fuss, but rather asked the driver to return
in an hour to collect him and promised a healthy tip. He pointed
to a spot on the side of the road a little walk from the house's
wrought-iron gate and tapped his watch. One hour. Of course,
there was every chance the judge would dismiss him almost as
soon as he arrived, and Ash would be left kicking the kerb for
most of that hour.

The house itself stood back from the road, behind a high
yellow wall that was topped with climbing plants. It was not how
he imagined a safe house; a gravel driveway swept through the
lush garden. There were swings to the left, and a terraced area
to the right where more people sat, this time reading the daily
news and sipping at early morning cappuccinos. He was early.
More than quarter of an hour ahead of schedule, mainly because
he wanted to rattle the judge and catch him before he'd had time
to calm himself in preparation for their interview.

He walked up the driveway, gravel crunching under his
shoes. The sun was already high enough in the sky to make
the heat noticeable. Give it another hour or so and it would be
close to unbearable.

The people reading in the shadow of the terrace paid him
no heed. No, that wasn't right, he realized. One of them, at least,
watched him closely as he walked towards the main door.

A second uniformed officer waited for him at the foot of
a short flight of stone steps up to the door.

Ash nodded to the man as he puffed out his chest. It was a
curiously male ritual, he thought, and a rather pointless one as

a kick to the bollocks was a universal leveller, no matter how broad your ribcage or glorious your plume of peacock feathers. He was all for practicality.

The second man checked his papers again, then patted him down, looking for a weapon. 'I'm British,' he said. 'We don't carry guns, we stop our criminals with a stern voice.'

The sentry did his best to keep a straight face but couldn't stop the smirk.

He rang the doorbell.

'I could have done that,' Ash said.

A woman opened the door. She smiled. It seemed genuine enough, the tiny lines around her eyes wrinkling as well as those at the corners of her mouth.

She ushered him inside. 'Please,' she said. 'This way. The judge is expecting you.'

Her heels clicked neatly on the marble floor tiles as she walked ahead of him. There was a confidence to her walk that spoke of belonging. She was in charge here, not any of the muscle heads he'd seen outside. He heard voices echoing through an open door as they swept through the hallways. The house was surprisingly spacious, with plenty of ostentatious wealth on display in the form of vases and marble heads.

She paused on the threshold and motioned for him to go inside.

There were two men, one he knew well.

He did his best to mask his surprise at the sight of Ernesto Donatti leaning forward in the plush armchair, talking to Maffrici like they were the best of old friends.

Seeing Ash, the Church's fixer broke into a wide smile and held out a warm hand, which, Ash noted, was busy holding the thick end of a hand-rolled Cuban cigar. Curls of smoke rafted up across the other man's face.

The judge was a big man, both in height, towering over Ash as he rose to his feet in greeting, and in girth as his legs struggled with his weight. He looked a good twenty years older than the photograph Laura had sent him. Stress had a way of exacting its toll. Sleep deprivation, likewise.

'Peter, my friend,' Donatti said, overly loud, overly cheerful all things considered, 'I would like you to meet Paulo, my other dear friend.'

'Such a small world, wouldn't you agree, Mr Ash?' Maffrici said, holding out a meaty ham-hock of a hand for Ash to shake. His grip was firm but stopped short of being uncomfortable. He wasn't looking to exert power or prove his manliness in it. Ash had met plenty of people who tried the power-shake to prove they were the alpha male in any given first meeting, usually what he did then was take a grip of their shoulder like the hand clasp couldn't possibly be enough to prove how very happy he was to meet them, and counter their downward pull with a move of his own that if he wanted to could put them on their knees. He really didn't have a lot of time for macho bullshit.

Ash liked to think he was a decent judge of character, and his first impression of Maffrici was that here was a man who would have been comfortable no matter which side of the law he had chosen to make his life.

'Please, join us.'

Ash took the third seat on the far side of the small table, while the judge offered him the choice of smokes from a humidor that probably cost half of his annual wage. He declined. Likewise, he put his hand across the top of the crystal tumbler on the table in front of him as the man moved to fill it from the whisky decanter.

'Thank you so much for seeing me. I'm sure you're a very busy man.'

'Ordinarily, yes, but at the moment I am at something of a loose end. I can't so much as walk to the news-stand down the street without a small coterie of armed men escorting me. It's too much effort, to be honest. So for now I am content to try and enjoy this enforced holiday.'

'Holiday,' Ash said with a smile.

'It sounds better than house arrest,' Maffrici said.

'Now, now, Paulo. It's for your own protection, and you know that,' Donatti said.

'I appreciate your concern. You are a dear friend, Ernesto, but even you must admit this is –' Maffrici waved his hands to encompass the whole room as he searched for the word he wanted – 'overkill.'

'Better overkill than just the second half of the word,' Donatti said, no trace of humour in his response.

'Well, yes. Now, Peter, may I call you Peter?'

Ash nodded. 'It's my name.'

'Ernesto has told me a great deal about you.'

'Then you have me at a disadvantage,' he said.

'I seriously doubt that. The picture Ernesto has painted of you is of a methodical man, one who does his research. I do not think you would have come as far as Rome without learning something of me first.' Ash shrugged, not denying it, not confirming it. 'I merely wanted to know a little about you. I knew that Ernesto was liaising with your Division, so it seemed only prudent to ask him.'

'Quite a coincidence.'

'Fortunate, perhaps, but not a coincidence. I know so many people who share your line of work. It stands to reason that your paths will have crossed at one point or another. That is not coincidence, merely probability.'

'Well, neither of you good people need me here,' Donatti said, getting to his feet. 'I think it best I leave you to discuss whatever it is you must discuss, and Peter, I look forward to our meeting again this evening. Until then, my friend.'

'There's no need for you to go,' Maffrici said. 'Honestly, you know all there is to know already, Ernesto. There's no need for secrets between us.'

'Ah, but there really is every need,' Donatti said, giving a slight bow of the head towards Ash. 'Peter no doubt has other questions he would have answers to, and in his place I would not want an audience when I was asking them, so I will do you both the courtesy of giving you a little privacy. As you say, he has come a long way, leaving you alone is the very least I can do.'

'Thank you for understanding,' Ash told the other man. It really would be better to do this without interruptions and having to worry about the Church man putting two and two together and realizing how close he was getting to home. And not having to ask him to leave saved them both the embarrassment.

The judge reached to a push button beside the lamp on a table beside his armchair and the summons was quickly followed by the click of heels on the hallway's marble tiles.

The door opened.

Maffrici told the woman, 'Father Donatti is leaving, please see him out.' The judge shook the emissary's hand before he left them alone.

'If alcohol is a problem, perhaps I can offer you coffee instead? It is after all, our national drink. We take our coffee very seriously.'

'I'm fine,' Ash assured him.

'So, to business then. What do you think you can ask me that the local police have not already done? Had I opened the package myself I would not even have bothered to inform the police about it.'

'Really?'

'As I am sure you are well aware, I receive a lot of threats. Too many. But if you go against the Mafiosi in this country you paint a target very squarely on your back. I am used to their crude attempts at intimidation. There are a lot of people in Rome who would see me hurt. That is just the way it is. Indeed, enough of my fellow judiciary have found themselves victims that I would be a fool not to think I am on someone's hit list, wouldn't I?'

'Occupational hazard,' Ash agreed. 'Even so . . .' He took his notebook out of his pocket, even though he knew the questions he'd written in there off by heart. He'd taken the time to craft them in such a way, he hoped, that they wouldn't immediately cause an international incident.

He double-checked what he'd written then closed the book.

'OK, I have to ask, even when you're used to receiving threats, didn't you think a finger through the mail was a little . . . extreme?'

'It was not a horse's head in my bed,' he said, with a wry smile. 'Yes, it was a threat. If you are trying to intimidate someone that threat needs to feel real. A finger makes it feel real.'

'But you wouldn't mention it to the police? I find that hard to believe.'

'My wife is not as used to these scare tactics as I am. I try to shield her from this kind of nonsense, but sometimes I fail. You must remember, I've been sent bullets with my name engraved on them. I have been sent photographs of my grandchildren playing. I have been sent a lock of my wife's hair—'

'How the hell does that happen?'

'They must have collected it when she was in the salon. We ran DNA tests to confirm it was hers. As you can imagine, that one was inventive enough to cause some concern.'

Ash nodded.

'And you called the police that time?'

'I did, and believe me it proved to be futile. All it succeeded in doing was wasting a considerable amount of their time and resources.'

'So, let me see if I've got this straight in my head, a finger is less threatening than a lock of your wife's hair?'

'Yes. It was not her finger, after all. There have been a lot of threats in between, but this was the only one that came inside my home. It became personal. Does that make sense?'

'To a degree,' Ash said, thinking about it. He wasn't sure how he would have reacted in the man's place, but he was right, there was something immediately more intimate about receiving a lock of your wife's hair through the mail than some dead stranger's finger. It was the message that made the finger a more pressing threat, which had been his line of thinking all along.

'Now, your turn to answer a question for me, I think. What makes you suspect this is a credible threat?'

Ash didn't see any point in lying or telling half-truths. 'You're not the only person to have received a body part in the mail.'

'So Ernesto said. A priest in Paris? Surely that has to be a coincidence. We are nine hundred miles apart. I don't move in the same circles as a monsignor. I deal with the worst this country has to offer every day, and very few of them are ever repentant. And any who are, it is generally because they have been caught, not because they have found God. I'm sorry, I just can't imagine we have any enemies in common.'

'See, that's what I would have thought as well,' Ash said, baiting the hook.

'You believe we do?'

'Here's what Donatti couldn't tell you, Monsignor Tournard is not the only victim.'

He watched the judge's reaction and saw the markers of genuine surprise in his expression. The big man shifted uncomfortably in his chair and leaned forward a fraction. There was a marked change in his demeanour. Suddenly he was interested.

'There are more?'

'At least three.'

'Three? Who? How is this possible? Four victims, all recipients of dead flesh through the mail? Surely this should be front-page news?'

'I'm afraid I'm not at liberty to give you any names, and I have only told you this much because I'm sure that I can rely on your discretion.' The hook was fully baited now. He waited for Maffrici to bite. He knew the judge would update Donatti the moment he left, especially if they were in this together – whatever this might be. It was a price he was prepared to pay.

'Of course. I completely understand, but if I knew who these others were, perhaps their names would be familiar, trigger some sort of memory?'

Interesting choice of words, Ash noted. Memory. Remember Bonn.

'Believe me, the moment I get clearance to share their names, I will be back in touch.'

Maffrici sank back into his armchair, the momentary fascination already fading as it became just another crime in a life of crimes.

Ash needed to keep him on the hook.

'Well, I can tell you that we are following a number of enquiries, looking for possible connections between the victims. There are some things I would like to share, perhaps they will mean something to you?'

The judge didn't respond immediately. He held the cigar between his lips, seeming to count to some silent tally in his head before letting the smoke leak slowly out. He closed his eyes for another long moment, savouring the flavour of the smoke, before telling Ash to, 'Fire away.'

Ash opened his notebook again, making a show of looking at the grid of names he'd written down, but again he knew them all off by heart. This was where the games began. He'd deliberately written several lies in there because he didn't want to simply come straight out with the EuropaChild and the orphanages they controlled. It was a dance. He wanted to see if Maffrici reacted differently to those names than how he did to others.

'OK, first, do the words Forza Romana mean anything?'

'The new fascists?' he laughed. 'Really, Mr Ash? Of course they mean something. What I believe you are asking is have I had any dealings with them? Perhaps pronounced judgement on any of their number? The answer is I must remain removed from political leaning in my job, so it does not matter to me if I pass sentence on supporters of Forza Italia or Romana, they are all the same to me.'

'That can't be easy.'

'It isn't, but I can only do my best.'

Ash nodded. 'Tell me, have you ever visited Tel Aviv?'

'No. I have never been to Israel.'

'Moscow?'

'I'm sorry, what is it exactly you are trying to do here? Because it seems to me you merely making wild guesses with nothing to substantiate them?'

'I have supporting evidence, trust me.'

'Really? Because I'm not sure you do.'

'I know it may appear scattershot, but that is the nature of my Division, Judge. All of our investigations cross national boundaries. It can make it seem as though there is nothing to link our suspects, but like any other force we are circumspect in our investigation. In this case, for instance, all of our victims thus far have some kind of connection to the Catholic Church.'

'The problem is it is far too easy to make a connection to the Church. Everyone living and working in Rome is connected somehow.'

'Indeed, and in your own case it is obvious that you would have more ties than I could possibly count. But, finding Donatti here, while a surprise, merely confirms what I mean about connections. The ties that bind you are at least tight enough to bring one of the Holy See's fixers to your door. That would not happen for just anyone.'

'So, you are basing your case around Church involvement?'

'Let's just say I'm keeping an open mind.'

'Of course you are, Peter. Of course you are. But, and forgive the crude vernacular, you're just pissing in the wind. You don't know anything. Your questions prove that.'

'See, that kind of response goes a long way to convincing me I know a lot, I mean, you're trying to get a rise out of me. But you know what else it does? It tells me you *do* know something. And that just gets my blood pumping, mate. So, now for one of the big questions, what about the note?'

'The note?'

'You know the one, came on a little card right along with the finger. Short message with a meeting place. The police sent a body double to the rendezvous yesterday.'

'Yes, yes, of course, the note. What about it?'

'Was the meeting place familiar? Somewhere you would regularly go? Where you might be recognized?'

'I've been there a few times. Not often. I hardly see how that could be important.'

'Well, now, I think it might be, because all the victims were invited to places they were familiar with.' Which he didn't know for sure but saying it like it was a fact was a good way of working the judge. It was all about keeping him talking, and making him think that he knew more than he did without really telling him anything. 'What it means, beyond a shadow of a doubt, is that whoever sent you that note knows enough about your habits to know you are familiar with the place. And that means you have been under observation, Judge. The killer has been watching you.' He let that sink in. 'And not only was he watching you, at some point he followed you there. He may even have sat at the table beside you. You could have raised a glass to each other or rolled your eyes at the score in the Juventus match. Doesn't that worry you? Because I think it should. I think it tells you this guy can get to you, no matter how many bodyguards you surround yourself with. He knows you well enough to identify the third aspect of the Holy Trinity: means, motive, and opportunity.'

'People are watching me all the time, Peter. You have seen that for yourself. What other measures could I realistically take? An armoured car to and from the court? Wearing a Kevlar vest as I sit in judgement? I cannot show these people that I am afraid. They would get too much mileage out of that. My position would become untenable. I cannot show the slightest weakness.'

'I get that, Judge. I really do. I can understand all about saving face, about jutting your chin out and telling the world to take its best shot. That's incredibly human. Stupid, but human. I just need to make sure you get it, this isn't some idle threat. This isn't just a lock of your wife's hair. This is credible. You are in danger here.'

'I'm touched by your concern but, as I told you, I have nothing to tell you because I don't know anything.'

'The note talked about Bonn.' Maffrici shrugged. 'You've never been there?'

'Been there?'

'Or anywhere else in Germany?'

There was a pause for a moment; a beat; a split second where Paulo Maffrici seemed almost human. He shook his head. He held out a hand as though to say look, I have nothing, not even words. 'Berlin,' he said eventually. 'I attended a conference there once. But it was years ago. And Munich, but I was even younger then. It isn't a country I've had cause to visit.'

'Not Bonn?'

'No, not Bonn.'

'Hmm. Have you come across the EuropaChild Foundation? A children's charity?'

He breathed in deeply through his nose, then shook his head. 'No. It doesn't sound familiar. Should I have?'

'Possibly, but as you can see, it's just one of several lines of enquiry that I'm following.'

'I really am sorry I haven't been more help,' Maffrici said, rising from his chair. The move signified that their meeting had come to its natural end, whether Ash had more questions or not.

The rather expensive carriage clock on the mantel above the fire told him he still had twenty minutes to wait before his taxi was due to return, but that was fine, because he knew categorically the judge was lying to him. That momentary relief about Bonn had been a sure sign he was lying.

He knew precisely what that note's sender had been imploring him to remember, and he was relieved that Ash didn't. That was the only way to read that relief.

The woman with the heels showed him out. She didn't engage in any small talk or offer so much as a glimmer of a smile this time.

The bodyguard on the terrace watched him walk down the gravel driveway away from the house. Another armed guard stood beside him, making a show of resting his hand on his Beretta. Ash stooped halfway down the track and turned to look back at the house.

The judge was standing at the window, watching him.

He was already on the telephone.

THIRTY-SEVEN

The taxi was waiting for him.

He waited until he was back in his room to make the call.

'I'm going to stick around a few extra days,' he told Laura once he'd brought her up to speed. 'He knows something. He knew the foundation's name, it was obvious by the way he reacted. I didn't tell him what they were involved with, and he didn't ask. Someone who didn't already know would ask, because it helps you position it in your mind. It's how we make connections. But that's small fry. He knows about Bonn.'

'What's the plan?'

'Initially, just watching. The hotel is sorting out a hire car. I'll collect it after lunch.'

'Then why go back to the hotel? Just enjoy the sights.'

'This is the kind of place where everybody knows everybody else. It's weird. They all stop and embrace each other in the street and loudly proclaim their joy at the encounter, kissing each other cheek to cheek to cheek. If I'd had the driver drop me anywhere but the hotel word would have made it back to Maffrici. I'm absolutely sure of it. That guy's like the fucking Godfather.'

'You don't think you're being a little paranoid?'

'Just because you're paranoid doesn't mean people aren't out to get you,' he barked out a bitter laugh. 'You got anything?'

'And there was me thinking it was going to be all about you. Nice of you to ask,' she said.

'OK, what have you got?'

'An owner for the finger.'

Ash stood up and walked to the window. It offered a view of the gardens, and across the street another hotel that was almost a mirror of it. 'Well, don't keep me in suspense.'

'That would be one Monsignor Jacques Tournard.'

'Bollocks.'

'I assume you're going to tell your friend Donatti?'

'I'm not sure that he's any friend of mine.'

'How so?'

'Oh, let me count the ways. First, he calls me up at the crack of dawn, ostensibly to invite me for a drink, despite the fact I didn't tell him I was in the city. Then he turns up at the judge's house. He was there when I arrived. The pair were thick as thieves.'

'Well, a judge and a Vatican emissary, you'd have to assume that Rome is the kind of place where their paths would cross on a fairly regular basis.'

'Only Rome and Vatican City are different countries, not just different districts. The Holy See has its own police, its own justice system. Maffrici is a Roman judge. Never the twain shall meet.'

'Seems a little extreme, but maybe you're right. I don't claim to understand the subtleties of international politics. But the way I see it, Donatti goes wherever the Church's influence reaches, and speaking as a born-again atheist I'd say there's nowhere the Church's influence is more pernicious than in Rome. Roman Catholic, the clue's in the name.'

'Are you suggesting that I give him the benefit of the doubt?'

'I'm just saying that he could be useful, right? It's his city. He's the Church's fixer, that's how you described him. He's going to know everyone who could be useful. That doesn't mean there's anything underhand going on. Besides, I thought you liked the man.'

'Fair enough, and yes I did, or do. I'm not sure. There's something that's just gnawing away at me. I feel like I'm being played.'

'Well, you know him better than I do. I only know what you've told me about him, but I figure at the very least if he is as connected as you say, then he's going to be expecting a call from you, if only to sort out that drink.'

'True, and now we know it's Tournard's finger, there's no way we can keep things between ourselves. This has to escalate.'

'So, do it that way, fall back on procedure.'

'OK. I'll do that. Do me a favour, keep Frankie in the loop.'

'Of course. I've got a list of people with connections to the foundation, so I need to talk to her anyway.'

'Any other interesting names on there?'

'No one to speak of. No one of the status of Tournard, Anglemark, or Maffrici, to be honest. They're not exactly out there in the public eye. It's proving to be a real bastard to find out much about them.'

'Fantastic, keep at it.'

'I'll try to pretend that you weren't being just a little patronizing then,' she said, though she sounded more amused than annoyed. 'I'll give Frankie a call first, then let you know if she's turned up anything interesting at her end. Now, try not to get yourself killed.'

She hung up before he could respond and he knew she didn't mean like Mitch, and he knew it was just something to say, something that a month ago wouldn't have meant anything more than it needed to, but now even such a stupidly obvious sentiment came freighted with other meaning. He tried not to read anything into it, because for a couple of days he'd actually managed to feel relatively normal.

Donatti answered on the second ring.

'Peter, my friend! I was beginning to give up hope. I have a wonderful vintage brandy here with your name on it.'

'And I fully intend to take you up on it.'

'How did it go with Judge Maffrici?'

'As you'd expect. Like he said when you were there, he didn't have a lot to tell me, but you already know this.'

'Me? How could I possibly?'

'Because he called you before I was even halfway down the drive, my old friend.'

Donatti fell silent for a moment.

It didn't sound like he was about to admit it, but then he wasn't denying it either, which was as good as a confirmation.

Ash knew the next words out of his mouth would be to change the subject.

He wasn't disappointed.

'So, tell me, any news on Monsignor Tournard?'

'Sadly, that is the main reason for my call,' Ash said, then paused for a moment. Ideally this was another face-to-face conversation, because the reaction would be telling. He realized in that moment that the way he thought about Ernesto Donatti was changing.

'You've found his body?'

'No, but the finger Maffrici was sent, it was Tournard's.'

Donatti cursed in Italian, fast and angry. 'You're certain?'

'It's him. But this means I'm going to have to circulate his disappearance to other agencies now, and there may well be questions about why we have kept it secret up until now.'

'From the press?'

'Interagency. We need their cooperation. That's how Eurocrimes works. They are going to want to know why we didn't alert them the moment we realized this was part of a bigger crime. We are conducting an investigation into a serial killer here, like it or not, and we've been hiding it from our own people. There are going to be repercussions.'

'Of course, of course. I'm sorry. I know you stuck your neck out for me. I will shoulder the blame.'

'It doesn't work that way,' Ash told him. 'And to be honest, I don't care. This has always been about the crime, not the protocols. There's a link between all the victims—'

'You've found the connection?'

Ash caught himself, and deliberately held back. 'We've turned up a few possibilities,' he said, careful to repeat the same bogus links he'd already shared with Maffrici, guessing that the judge had already fed the deliberate lies back to the Vatican's man.

THIRTY-EIGHT

I t finally felt like things were coming together. The biggest problem facing Frankie was that the killer was still a shadow. Normally she'd be looking at a profile by now, seeing the forensics slowly tighten the noose, and know that the only thing needed to banish a shadow was the metaphorical single flickering flame. But she felt curiously disconnected from this guy, and it wasn't just that he seemed to be two steps ahead of her all of the time. Somehow he kept up a punishing schedule of revenge, moving from country to country with such regularity it was next to impossible to track him. This was one of the flaws of the open border policy across Europe. It was possible to leave Sweden, driving over the Öresund's bridge, take the ferry from Rodby in Denmark to Puttgarden in Germany and disappear into continental Europe without once having to show identification. Those frictionless borders made the notion of tracking passenger manifests for patterns of travel next to useless. The only time the killer's passport would have been checked, for sure, was when he made the journey from Paris to London, and even then if he'd flown into Dublin first he could have avoided that.

Even if they had a name, following him would be next to impossible if he knew what he was doing. And the 'Memory Man', as she'd started to think of him, knew what he was doing. His vendetta was meticulously planned and ruthlessly executed.

With the finger identified as the missing monsignor's, and the next target being in protective custody in Italy, there was at least a grim hope that he'd be forced to improvise now, and when things were out of his control it was the best hope they had of him screwing up.

One thing she found interesting was Ash's change towards Donatti. He didn't say as much, or at least not in so many words, but her British counterpart was obviously starting to think of his erstwhile friend as at least complicit, and at worst guilty. But of what? The actual killings? That was unlikely, to say the least. But a Vatican cover-up? That wasn't out of the realm of possibility.

Without concrete evidence that Tournard was dead, the mail-order digit was proof he hadn't made it into hiding, which meant they couldn't keep his disappearance off the books. He was at risk. They needed all the resources they could muster for the search. And that meant the media. The problem with that was that once the genie was out of the bottle there was no putting it back in. Reporters weren't stupid. Most of the crime-beat reporters cultivated good links within the departments. Someone some-where would mention the link between the monsignor and the politician and they'd be flooded with calls all claiming to know who was behind the abduction and murder. Every crank and nut-job would come crawling out of the woodwork with their crazy conspiracy theories, and all that would do was allow the real killer to go underground.

Now that they had identified EuropaChild and started digging into the orphanages it had funded, Laura had found another point of interest: both the British priest, Dooley, and the dead Spaniard, Carlos Ramirez, had worked for a while at the same facility. Though as before there was no overlap in their time there, meaning it was more than likely that the pair had never met. It was still an anchor point their lives shared, and in the normal course of things so many people from so many different countries and walks of life shouldn't have shared so many anchor points, with or without overlap. It couldn't be coincidental.

The connections to the other victims remained tenuous at best, and no matter how many stones they turned over, there didn't seem to be a single anchor point between the judge and anyone else on the Memory Man's grudge list.

Maffrici was an outlier.

So, why had he made the list?

Carlos Ramirez's death certificate listed cause of death as natural ventricular failure. He had died at home, but his doctor had been treating him for a heart condition for several years, which meant that no one raised so much as an eyebrow at his passing. It was expected.

But she couldn't shake the feeling that someone like Ramirez coming into contact with a sociopath demanding he remember some horrible thing they had done, didn't need a gun put to his temple to die. He had the means of his own end built into his failing body.

It made a sick sort of sense to her.

She looked at the card she'd taken from Anglemark's diary again. It was in a plastic evidence bag. She intended to take it to the lab for testing. She knew the only prints they'd pull from it would belong to the politician himself. But that wasn't the lead she was looking at. She knew where the Memory Man had lured Anglemark.

She'd be able to trace his route. She'd be able to build a coherent picture of his last hours. That was how you solved a crime like this – solid policework.

It didn't matter how meticulous you were in the planning, there was always going to be a breadcrumb waiting to lead the good guys to you. It didn't matter if it was a single frame from a CCTV camera, witness testimony, or scene of crime forensics, there was always something left behind. All it took was one little chink in the otherwise flawless armour and they'd have something to work away at. Pull enough at the smallest thread and eventually you were left with a great big hole.

Anglemark had been missing for over a week before his body was found. He hadn't been in the water more than a few hours. It was all about the missing time. And she finally felt like she was beginning to get somewhere with that.

She read Anglemark's post-mortem report again.

He had died of suffocation and there was very little water in his lungs, meaning he had been dead before he had gone into the water. In terms of fluid in his lungs, rather than sea water there was a considerable quantity of blood, which confirmed his tongue had been removed perimortem. Deep ligature marks on his wrists indicated that he had been restrained, and dental records proved that two of his teeth had been damaged in the course of the mutilation. Hardly surprising if the man was conscious at the time. She could imagine his horror as he realized what his assailant was doing, and his frantic efforts to stop him.

Frankie flipped through pages in search of the toxicology report. There were traces of Rohypnol in his system; enough to have made him pliable and less resistant.

Did the Memory Man lace their drinks at the meeting, and rely upon their almost drunken confusion to steer them back towards wherever he intended to keep them? Because he kept them, didn't he? That was another parallel between Tournard and Anglemark. They had both been unaccounted for, and for a number of days. The killer had to have a place ready in each of the cities, too. He couldn't just rely upon finding somewhere quiet on the fly. That was something they should be looking at: land registry for purchases, records for abandoned places, empty industrial units, and such. Places where he could hold his victims without fear of someone accidentally stumbling across them. Find one of them, in any of the cities, and you unlocked a whole host of forensic evidence, because that was the thing about a safe place, somewhere that the killer felt he could let his guard down, that he could prepare the kill and carry it out, there was no way he couldn't leave behind proof that he'd been there. And that proof would be what locked him up.

She called Laura.

'The problem is even if the killer rented a place there's no guarantee that he used his own name, or even the same name every time. Pete's sure your guy is anal when it comes to the planning. Each abduction nailed down to the last detail.'

'I agree,' Frankie said. 'It is the only way he hasn't been caught. There are too many places where things could go wrong for him not to have worked the details out like some sort of OCD compulsion. Can I ask you something?'

'Of course.'

'You know Peter. Is he coping?'

'You mean with Mitch's death? Right now, this is the best it's been in a while. He's always been driven. It's his personality. I can't slow him down. And to be honest, I wouldn't want to. He is who he is.'

'Please don't take this the wrong way, but from the outside looking in, I'd say that he's more than driven. It's like he believes he's the only one who can bring our Memory Man in. He needs to remember he's not alone. Division is a dysfunctional family, but it's a family all the same. We are in this together.'

'Talk to Pete. Remind him that he can lean on you. Just don't expect him to actually do any leaning. At least not for a while.

The last person he let in ended up . . . well, you know what happened to Mitch. Everyone does.'

'He's lucky to have you in his corner,' she said.

The other woman laughed at that, a laugh that was so obviously filled with love even from a thousand miles away. 'You should definitely tell him that.'

THIRTY-NINE

The hotel concierge apologized for the budget hire car. It was the kind of thing money-conscious tourists and less well-off locals drove. It fitted in. It was small enough to handle Rome's labyrinthine streets, and there were so many identical ones on the road there was no way he was going to be marked or remembered. That made it easier to tail someone.

There was, at least, a relatively new satellite navigation system. He punched in the address he was looking for and followed the voice he didn't understand telling him to *prendi la prossima a destra* and *andare dritto alla rotonda* because he couldn't work out how to change the language settings.

Ash drove past the house without glancing at the guard. Even a well-trained bodyguard wouldn't remember the face of a random driver unless that driver was stupid enough to stop looking at the road and make direct eye contact.

There were more cars now, but it was still far from busy. The three cars ahead of him were all Fiats of varying colours.

He drove about eight hundred metres past the safe house, following the flow of the traffic.

The road bent naturally to the left.

He followed it until he was safely out of sight of the safe house, then pulled over. He waited a few minutes, the window rolled down, and leaned with his forearm half out of the door. It was hard to enjoy the heat. He turned the radio on. He didn't recognize the song. It didn't matter, he was simply changing one of the obviously identifiable aspects of the car. First pass he'd driven in silence. For the return, he rolled the window down and cranked the music up.

He pulled up outside one of the neighbours and let the music keep playing for a full thirty seconds before he killed the engine.

He was playing a hunch.

It was obvious that the judge wasn't enjoying his confinement and wasn't the kind of person to sit idly on his hands. Ash had the odds at sixty–forty, but with nothing better to do than stake out Maffrici, those were odds he was happy to take. Maffrici was a loose end. And he'd made a point of telling Ash how many times he'd been threatened, and how even the Mob didn't scare him. So, maybe those odds were closer to fifty–fifty? Either the judge would head out or he wouldn't. But if he *did*, then things got interesting, because there was no way he was just taking a trip to his favourite trattoria. If he broke protective custody it was because he was doing something.

Ash's gamble was that that something was either confronting the killer, keeping the meeting he'd failed to make once before, or trying to warn someone he knew was in danger.

And the more he thought about it, the more likely it felt that Donatti would be the one to help him.

Not that Ash would have admitted he was baking in a tin can on a hunch with zero evidence to support it.

The gate guard walked a few steps every now and again, stretching his legs. Ash watched as someone brought him a bottle of water from the house.

Twenty minutes later he stepped inside the gate and disappeared from a sight.

Either a shift change or a call of nature.

A moment later the gate opened and a black town car slid out of the driveway and headed towards the city.

Predictable.

Which in itself was a bad thing, because if Ash could work out the judge's personality well enough to guess he'd go walkabout after just one meeting there was no way the killer hadn't reached the same conclusion.

Ash started the engine and pulled out of the neighbour's drive to follow him.

He kept three or four cars between him and Maffrici's more out of habit than out of fear that he would be seen. He doubted the judge would even realize he had a tail. He certainly wasn't taking any evasive measures.

Ash followed Maffrici until he picked up the autostrada and headed east.

Less than ten miles later Maffrici indicated and took the turn off into the Colle del Tasso rest area.

He hadn't been driving for long enough to need a stop, even with a huge prostate. So this was his final destination.

It was a good place. Easy access from in and out of town, enough surveillance cameras if things went south and you needed a closer look at the people coming and going later.

He put a call through to Laura, giving her his GPS coordinates and telling her to move heaven and earth to tap into the live feed.

FORTY

Unsurprisingly, the address printed on Anglemark's summons was only a short distance from his secret apartment.

The red, white, and green awning announced that it was an Italian restaurant whilst the writing in the window promised genuine stone-baked pizzas. It offered takeaway and delivery as well as the sit-down restaurant. First impressions, it looked too nice for the average Swede's taste. The Swedish relationship with pizza was weird. It was all about the biggest, thinnest base and the cheapest ingredients. It was basically hangover food. Or had been until a couple of years when all of these fancy pizzerias had started to spring up in Vasastan and down on Söder. Suddenly it was all about artichoke hearts, asparagus, rocket, Parma ham, and parmesan shavings. But this wasn't the part of town where people would make a pizzeria a destination, no matter how hip and trendy it was.

There were traffic cameras on the junction at the far end of the street. There was also a sign warning people that there were traffic cameras in operation. That was uniquely Swedish. It didn't matter that the cameras were there for public safety, they were viewed as infringing on the people's right to privacy, and the will of the people was stronger than the law. She doubted very much that the Memory Man would have been careless enough to wind up on one of the feeds, especially with the signs warning him that Big Brother was watching.

Anglemark could have walked here from the apartment. It was far enough that he might have taken a taxi in bad weather; that didn't help much, but she made a note to check with the various taxi firms, to discount them as much as anything else.

The place was open.

Not that she'd have been able to tell without the bored-looking girl behind the counter. There wasn't a customer in the place, but it was still early. Swedes ate in shifts, mainly going out for lunch between 11:30 and 13:00, and then not coming out again until after 19:00.

There was no menu in the window.

The decor inside was considerably more expensive that she would have expected, given the location. The girl looked up as she opened the door and smiled. Frankie figured she was about eighteen or nineteen, probably picking up shifts to help fund college, and more interested in being anywhere but here.

'Hi there,' Frankie said, as the girl slid a pad across the counter in front of her.

'It's two for one before six,' the girl said. 'Eat here or to go? I'm sure we can squeeze you in.' This time her smile was genuine.

'I'm not here to eat.' Frankie fished out her identification out of her pocket.

'Eurocrimes? That sounds exotic. Please tell me this is about something glamorous. Something that's going to make the news.'

'It already has,' Frankie said. 'I'm investigating the murder of Jonas Anglemark.'

'The politician they pulled out of the water?'

'That's the one.'

'I read he had his tongue cut out? That's awful. I mean can you imagine?'

Frankie raised a hand to silence her before she could ask any more dumb questions, because contrary to what every teacher had no doubt told the girl for most of her life there are in fact dumb questions. It wasn't good that the detail about his tongue was in the public domain. That would make it harder to weed out the cranks. It also meant they had a leak somewhere between the coroner's department and her office. Though of course there was so much interest in the case it could have been from any of a dozen links in the chain.

'I'm looking into his whereabouts during the days running up to his death.'

'And you think he came in here?'

'I think he met his killer here.'

'Here? You're joking.'

'I don't tend to do that,' Frankie said. 'Do you have some sort of security camera?'

'We do—'

'Great.'

'But it won't help. It hasn't worked for months. Valentino,

that's the guy who owns this place, decided that it wasn't worth getting it fixed when it died.'

Frankie's heart sank.

She saw that the connecting wires were dangling loose.

Anyone who paid attention when they came in would have seen that and known that it wasn't working, which made it the perfect place for a kidnap. 'That's a real shame,' she said. 'I don't suppose you were working here last week?' She gave her the date.

'I only work until seven. Any idea what time?'

'Say around two o'clock, so after the lunch rush, like today.'

The girl made a quick search on the electronic diary: there were no reservations until seven on both evenings. 'That's not surprising though. We never have more than half a dozen people in after the lunch rush so no one bothers reserving ahead of time. Most places round here close up for three or four hours between services, but Tino likes us to stay open. Every hour we're closed is an hour we're not making money.'

'I had a boss like that,' she sympathized. She reached into her pocket for a photograph of Anglemark then laid it on the counter between them.

'Is this him? Good-looking guy.'

'Do you remember him coming in?'

'To be honest, he looks kind of familiar, but he's been on the news a lot, hasn't he? He's not a rock star or anything, but plenty of people would see him and think, oh I know him from somewhere . . .'

'OK. But think. Do you remember him coming in here? Meeting someone?'

The girl tilted her head to one side and looked at the picture again as if the shift in perspective might somehow shake an errant memory loose. 'He might have done, maybe. Honestly, I can't be sure. And even if he was, I can't be sure if it was even the right day. We got a lot of people in here, especially during lunch. You only remember the ones who stand out.' Which made sense. 'Let me see if Tino remembers. He would have been looking after the restaurant side of things.' She came out from behind the counter and crossed the terracotta floor to the kitchen doors, opening them to allow a waft of garlic and tomato to escape.

'Hey, Tino. You got a minute? There's someone here wants a word with you.'

The response was almost inaudible against the clatter of pans, but the girl nodded and told Frankie, 'He'll be out in a minute. He's working on the marinara base. I need to go and take over.'

Frankie took her word for it.

The girl slipped out through the door, to be replaced a moment later by a brute of a man in kitchen whites that were splattered red. He looked like some slovenly butcher, only instead of blood it was tomato sauce. He was sweating profusely. Tino used the sleeve of his whites to mop up the worst of it from his forehead.

'Do I know you?' he asked.

'Francesca Varg,' she said, showing her identification again. Tino did not seem to be as impressed as his waitress. He scrutinized it and handed it back with a shrug.

'What can I do for you?'

Frankie showed him the photograph which was still lying on the counter. 'Do you recognize this man?'

'Should I?'

'He was due to meet someone here last Wednesday.'

'*Diavolo.*' Devil.

'Sorry?'

'Diavolo. That's what he ordered. Classic Neopolitana pizza. Tomato base, buffalo mozzarella, spicy Naples salsiccia, peppers, goat's cheese, and basil.'

'You remember him?'

'The guy who was murdered. Yeah, I remember him, but he looked different. He wasn't wearing a suit. He was in jeans, and grey shirt. T-shirt underneath.'

'You have a good memory.'

The man shrugged. 'Not every day you read about a customer being murdered,' which was true. 'Besides, we talked a bit. He ordered in Italian, told me he'd spent some time in Milan.'

'And the man with him?'

'He didn't speak, the politician ordered for him. Gamberetti, hand-scaled shrimps, garlic, lemon, and parsley. It's good. But all of our pizzas are good.'

'Did you get a good look at him?'

'Gamberetti man? He didn't even look up when I brought the food out. He had his back to the kitchen door. I can tell you what the back of his head looked like.'

'Anything you can tell me might help.'

'He had hair. That's all I've got. What's so special about Gamberetti man?'

'He is almost certainly the murderer,' Frankie said.

The man's face went slack, his eyes glassy, as he wrestled with the notion he'd served food to a man capable of murder.

Tino mopped his forehead with his sleeve again.

'They sat here,' he said, showing her the chair the killer had occupied. He didn't touch the back, as though he expected her to suddenly start dusting for prints. The problem was in more than a week there had probably been a hundred other people in that seat. Any residual evidence would be long gone.

'Why don't we sit for a minute?' Frankie suggested.

Tino nodded with gratitude. She sat in the killer's chair. He sat across from her. 'Sorry,' he said, picking up a paper napkin carefully folded on the table to wipe his face again. It came away sodden. He had the complexion of an alcoholic on the verge of a heart attack.

Frankie placed her notebook on the table and looked at what little she'd managed to write so far.

'OK. Anything you can give me. How old would you say he was, ball park?'

'Younger than the politician. He was in good shape. I remember thinking he looked like he could handle himself.'

'And you said he had hair?'

'Razor cut, but not shaved.'

'Anything you can remember about his face? Anything at all. It would be really helpful.'

Tino shrugged. 'Sorry.'

'What about his clothes?'

'Grey fleece, I think. Something sporty. Like climbers wear. That's about it. Sorry,' he said again.

'Believe me, that's great, thank you.'

'I hope you find the bastard.'

'I will.'

FORTY-ONE

A sh had no intention of following the judge immediately. First, because it increased the likelihood the other man would make him; second, because he wanted to see if anyone else was following him. And that included Donatti.

This was someone he didn't want his security detail knowing he was meeting, or someone who didn't want to be seen visiting the house. Then again, it was Italy; maybe Maffrici was meeting his mistress.

He waited until the judge was inside the building before climbing out of the Fiat.

He followed him.

A group of noisy children rushed ahead of him, determined to be first inside the restaurant, the shop, or the toilet. A couple of frazzled teachers tried to wrangle them. He didn't envy them. They made no effort to keep the noise levels down. Not that they could have made themselves heard against the constant babble.

Maffrici had his back to him.

The judge scanned the dining area in search of whoever he expected to meet.

Ash noticed a hand go up to attract his attention.

The judge weaved his way between other tables and diners to reach him.

Ash moved through into the sitting area and took a seat at a table close enough to watch their body language without being close enough to overhear anything.

He slipped his phone out of his pocket and using the camera app fired off a sly shot of the stranger, not worrying about how it was framed. He enlarged the picture, but the distance and the shitty zoom feature meant there was very little clarity to the detail of the face, and it wasn't a face he immediately recognized, either.

He rattled off a quick message to Laura and attached the image. She'd find him if he was in the database if he was there to be found.

The man was older than Maffrici. He was thinner, too, and frail. There was nothing about him that suggested strength, certainly not the kind of strength needed to subdue or overpower anyone. So not the killer. Which, if his gut hunch was right, made the old man another potential victim.

The conversation did not last long, and whilst there were no raised voices it didn't appear to be a particularly friendly tête-à-tête. Maffrici was obviously in control. The other man looked less than reassured – if that was the purpose of their sit-down. He took a single swallow of his caffé, downing it in one. The caffeine was unlikely to calm him.

The judge got to his feet suddenly, scraping his chair back across the linoleum floor. A few heads turned in their direction, drawn to the unexpected noise, but Ash kept his head down, pretending to concentrate on his phone. It prevented the risk of accidental eye contact. Never had this generation's fixation with all things digital and cellular been so useful.

Maffrici left.

Not just left; he stormed out.

The other man remained at the table holding his small coffee cup. Even from this distance he looked obviously distressed.

It was a gift horse, of sorts. A perfect photo op if nothing else. Ash took another shot, being less subtle about it. He didn't cross the room to join the old man. Now wasn't the right time.

He waited ten minutes.

The man finally abandoned his coffee cup and rose slowly to his feet. He was unsteady as he crossed the dining area to the main doors. He didn't look around, which Ash found interesting. Assuming the judge had just told him there was a hit out on him he would have thought the old man's first instinct would be to look around to see where it was coming from.

Unless he knew?

Ash followed behind the old man, keeping a comfortable distance. Once he reached the car park the man was three rows of vehicles ahead. He crossed in the direction of his hired Fiat, gambling that it would take the old man a few moments to pull himself together once he got behind the wheel. From there it was a fifty–fifty shot on whether he took the Rome exit or followed the loop around and headed back the way he had come.

Ash saw him fumble with the keys at the driver's door of a racing green Renault. In the time it took the man to reverse out Ash was in place and ready to follow.

He joined the flow of traffic, trying to see far enough ahead to see which way the old man went. By the time he hit the autostrada the green Renault was nowhere to be seen.

He cursed himself.

Her call came in as he scanned the snake of cars up ahead, trying to use the curve to better see who was out there.

'I'm in, what am I looking for?'

'Too late,' he said.

'Aren't you a little ray of sunshine.'

'I lost him. Racing-green Renault.'

'Registration?'

'I'm sure it has one,' he said.

'Hold on. I'll see what I can find. I take it you're no more than a minute or so behind the guy?'

'Assuming I'm going the right way.'

'OK, I'll spool back through the feed from the exit camera, find you, then track back another minute or so for our Renault.'

She made it sound easy.

The line fell silent. He heard the distant flutter of her fingers racing across the keyboard. Ash concentrated on the road ahead. Red brake lights in the distance showed that the traffic was slowing.

'Got him,' she said. 'About eight hundred metres ahead of you.'

'What's the delay?'

'Looks like a car has broken down. They're getting it pulled over. You shouldn't be held up too long, but I'll track the Renault in case he gets away from you. I've got a registration, should have a name in a couple of minutes. Just running it through the STA network. Once I've got it I'll run it against EuropaChild.'

The traffic ahead of him had come to a complete standstill. He still couldn't see the Renault.

FORTY-TWO

Frankie left the restaurant knowing she'd made a small dent in the sheer overwhelming amount of stuff she didn't know, and it didn't exactly turn her thinking on its head, but it made her think and that was always a plus.

Anglemark had made the meeting.

It was definitely with a man, confirming that working hypothesis.

The meeting itself had been nothing to write home about, two people sharing a meal. Nothing to raise suspicion or make it memorable for any witnesses.

The diner had shielded his face, and in the process his identity, but she had a barebones description even if it wasn't enough to build a photofit around.

Valentino hadn't seen them leave, but they'd covered the bill, and left enough of a tip not to stick out in the memory either way. And there was obviously no commotion or disturbance when they left, otherwise it would have been noticed; so Anglemark accompanied the killer of his own free will.

She stood under the awning looking up and down the street. Where could they have gone from here?

It was one thing to walk outside willingly, but if Anglemark had even an inkling of what was to come surely he wouldn't have walked these streets with that same willingness? Did the Memory Man have something to keep him compliant? Something the politician was prepared to do *anything* to ensure remained a secret? *Memini Bonn.* What could have happened there that was so horrific it would make a man walk willingly to his death?

Her mind went to the dark places of the world she worked in, and all manner of crimes linked to vulnerable children. A paedophilia ring, child pornography, child-trafficking? None of the alternatives felt good, but to be fair, she'd been thinking along these lines from the moment Ash proved the link to the Catholic

Church. She wasn't proud of it, but preconceptions existed for a reason, didn't they?

And being found guilty of any of those crimes was not just a career-ender for Anglemark, it was a life-ender, wasn't it? Here was a man who had ostensibly devoted his life to the protection of vulnerable children. To be found guilty of any of them, even merely in the court of public opinion, would be enough to end the man. So, yes, there were some reasons a dead man walking would willingly take that long walk home.

She kept thinking about the camera. It was obvious it didn't work, because of the mess of wires hanging out of its guts, but to know that you had to go inside. There were three things to take away from that. The first, the killer must have known that or he wouldn't have chosen the pizzeria, and thus had visited the place before. The second, he may very well have checked out other restaurants in the neighbourhood before finding one that suited his purpose. The third takeaway, and the most important, thinking like the killer, you wouldn't want to give your victim time to gather their nerve or steel themselves to fight back, so you didn't want to march them through the streets; you wanted to get them off the streets as quickly as possible, so you chose the restaurant based on the proximity to *your* bolthole, not the victim's.

She looked up and down the street, knowing she was close.

She was looking for somewhere that felt empty, and a long time empty, not just the owner's at work empty. No lights in the windows, no obvious decoration, pictures on the walls, stuff like that.

The houses on the opposite side of the road were old, but not so old that they had the hollowed out into the bedrock basements of the really old places in Gamla Stan. There were places there that literally had been cells for fifteenth- and sixteenth-century criminals that were now wine cellars and coffee vaults. Like so many of the buildings, what once was a Hanseatic merchant's townhouse had been divided into apartments, probably a century or more ago. The real estate was just too valuable for the old houses to remain that way.

On her side were a row of shops, but even those had three and four storeys of apartments above their hoardings. What she didn't see was anything obviously derelict. She walked the length of the street, to the corner where the block was under renovation. Scaffolding had been set up outside, and plastic sheeting covered most of the facade. A sign advertised the contractors doing the work, and said they specialized in replacing old pipes. That was common enough; lots of these older places had the same rusted and rotten pipes in them from the forties and fifties that needed to be stripped out and replaced with modern materials. That was the thing about Stockholm, ever since the voracious culling of buildings with any real history to make way for those Functionalist monstrosities, people had become fixated with preserving what remained, so even when old buildings were essentially dead inside it was about patching them up not replacing them.

A couple of the buildings had HSB and SKB logos on the side, meaning they were owned by the massive letting companies, both of which had decades-long waiting lists for tenants, so she immediately discounted them. Too much paperwork, even if they were being rented out second hand. Condo boards kept records and voted on allowing sublets. Everything was listed in the minutes and filed with the tax authorities. So none of those would work. It needed to be privately owned.

Somewhere that had a decent turnover of people on short-term leases. A place where the owner didn't look too closely at the paperwork, preferring cold hard cash to the letter of the law. And the owner of that kind of place wasn't going to live there.

A door-to-door search would take hours, and Swedes didn't answer their doors to strangers. She could stand hammering on a door for a good ten minutes and the occupant would cheerfully ignore her. It was a part of the Swedish psyche that she'd never understood. Her own apartment building was a classic example; it had a door code to allow access, but after 9 p.m. the code was disabled and the only way you were getting into the building was with a key, even if you were an invited guest. Swedes, Stockholmers especially, didn't like visitors. She'd lived in her place for the best part of a decade and she'd yet to say hello to the neighbours who shared her landing and wouldn't recognize them in the street. One of them, she was sure, watched through the spyhole until she was gone before they risked opening the door because they didn't want to face a few seconds of awkward

social interaction. But that was just city life. Or at least
Scandinavian city life.

It did mean that provided the screams were kept to a minimum,
pretty much any old building with thick stone walls would work
for the killer's purposes.

She had to narrow it down though.

She crossed the street and walked the length of it again in the
opposite direction. As she suspected, nearly all of the houses had
cellars, several of which had been converted into laundry rooms,
though some offered additional accommodation, squeezing out
every drop of profit from the building. Most had only internal
access, but a few offered street entry down a short flight of steps.
Those had more in the way of isolation, curiously, as the steps
added a layer of distance from the pavement that the other
buildings didn't have.

The door to the nearest of the apartments below street level
opened and a moment later a young woman emerged, struggling
with a small child in a buggy. There was a neat concrete ramp
built into the short flight of stairs, allowing wheelchair – and in
this case pushchair – access.

The best intelligence was always local.

'Need a hand?' Frankie called down.

'No need,' the woman said, as she turned her back and negotiated the ramp backwards. The baby giggled away in its seat.

'Mind if I ask you a couple of questions?'

Immediately suspicious, the woman started to push her
child away, but Frankie showed her ID and her manner thawed.

'Have you lived here long?'

'Nearly six months. My boyfriend and I broke up. I needed to
find somewhere. It's nearly impossible to get a first-hand contract
in the city, and with this little guy on the way I was just happy
to find a roof. We've got a new place over there.' She pointed in
the general direction of the apartment where Frankie had found
Dahlberg's corpse. The odds of it being the same place were next
to none, but she wouldn't put anything beyond the gods of fate
and real estate.

'Nice,' Frankie said.

'Not sure I'd go that far, but it's mine, and I won't have to
worry about the lease running out.'

'I hope it works out for you.'

'Thanks.'

'Do you know if there are any other basement flats available around here? Only recently rented, but it's come available again?'

'Maybe number 75,' the woman said, pointing along the street. 'It was empty for a while. Then I started seeing lights on in there. Didn't see a moving van, though. Haven't noticed any lights for the last week. Not that I'm looking all the time, you know? It's just that the little one keeps me up at night and we like to go out for a walk, don't we?' She said the last bit to the baby in the buggy, who gurgled like he actually understood.

'I don't suppose you actually saw the guy?'

'Sorry, no. You know how it is.'

'It's fine, thanks. Have a good day.'

'You too.'

Frankie watched the woman walk away, slowing every now and then to talk to her baby.

She was going to need a warrant before she could check out the man's hideaway. It didn't matter that the place was empty again, or that the killer would most probably have bleached the place clean, it *felt* like she was one step closer to catching him.

She crossed the street and she started down the dozen stairs to the basement courtyard, intending to peer in through the window, when she saw a small sign declaring the apartment was available to let, and offering a number to call.

She tried the doorbell and waited.

There was no response.

She tried again, this time pressing her ear to the door. There was no answering ring from the buzzer inside. She gave three hard raps on the door instead, banging loudly enough to wake any day sleeper.

She dialled the mobile number on the To Let sign.

There was no business name, so it fitted the profile she'd expected, a small private lease, no doubt undeclared income. A nice little side-earner.

That would make things easier at least, sparing her the backwards and forwards trying to get approval for entry. All she had to do was convince the letting agent to show her around. Easy.

He answered straight away.

'Good afternoon, my name is Francesca Varg. I work with the Eurocrimes Division of the European Union. I am currently standing outside one of your properties in Stockholm. I need you to get yourself down here.'

'Do you now? Why the hell should I do that?'

'Because I have reason to believe that there has been a serious crime committed inside.'

'This is a wind-up, right? Who put you up to this?'

'No one.'

'Then if you're serious, get a fucking warrant.'

'I can have a warrant here in thirty minutes. But if I do that, we break the door down. It's your choice, of course, but I thought I would do you the courtesy of informing you so that you didn't have to pay for a new door and locks.'

'This is shit,' he said, obviously unhappy with having his day ruined.

'I only need a few minutes inside,' she assured him.

'I really don't care, it's bullshit. You have no right.'

'Look, I'm not interested in you, or who you let your properties to, in general. I'm not with the tax office, and I'm not about to make life shit for you, I just want a few minutes inside this apartment. That's all. It's better this way, believe me. The last thing you want is a couple of marked cars with blue flashing lights pulling up outside the block, am I right?'

She gave him the address.

'Ground floor or basement? They're both vacant. Same guy rented them.'

'Basement,' she said, realizing the vacant ground-floor flat offered insulation against Anglemark's screams.

'I'll be there in a couple of minutes.'

He ended the call.

Frankie couldn't help but smile as she pressed her face up against the window. She used her hand to shield her eyes from the sunlight that caught the window. The curtains were closed but there was a narrow gap that offered a glimpse of the inside.

She could see a dining chair on its side in the middle of the room. As far as she could tell it was the only furniture in the room.

It felt right.

It felt like the kind of place the Memory Man could have holed up in for a week without anyone really noticing him, allowing him to come and go at will. There was no obvious view into the apartment from street level. Little in the way of foot traffic, but enough that him coming and going wouldn't stand out as unusual. Everything about it fitted the ideal needs of a man looking to hold someone prisoner. The fact that the tenant had taken the flat directly above, air-gapping the basement from the next set of tenants, convinced her she was right.

It was the kind of place where a man could scream and keep screaming long after his tormentor had cut his tongue out while the world walked by past his window none the wiser.

FORTY-THREE

A red-veined fat man waddled around the corner. He huffed and puffed, but there was no way he had the lung capacity to blow anyone's house down.

Frankie knew that this was who she had been waiting for; everything about him screamed slum landlord. She despised the sort. A roll of pale flesh hung over a belt that had no right reaching around his middle.

She perched on the low wall in front of the building. Her evidence bag was on the floor between her feet.

The man looked like he was trying to hurry, arms and legs moving frantically but with very little in the way of forward motion going on. He covered the distance slowly. She watched him every step of the way.

By the time he reached her his face was beetroot-red and coated with a sheen of sweat. He leaned on the wall for a moment, struggling to catch his breath before he spoke. In the end he didn't bother with wasting words, and instead held up a key like it was the Holy Grail.

'Stay outside,' she said, not asking permission.

He nodded and waved her away, rubbing the palm of his meaty hand across his face.

She opened the door and knew without setting foot over the threshold the place was empty. There was something about places that weren't lived in, they had a sound and a smell all of their own.

The air was stale.

Breathing deeply, it was immediately obvious no doors or windows had been opened in a long time. The door led into a cramped area where people could kick off their shoes, before opening into the room she'd been able to see through the curtain. There were no shoes or coats on the rack, though she noticed plenty of scuff marks along the woodwork.

This was the right place.

Anglemark had been tied to the wooden chair in the middle

of the room. The wood was stained where the blood had pooled around the chair legs. It was a lot of blood. The kind of blood she'd expect from someone having their tongue cut out of their mouth.

The mixture of odours was unmistakable.

She'd been around enough corpses for it to be imprinted on her brain – the twin reeks of bladder and bowels spilled. They were smells that lingered.

The three together, blood, piss, and shit, turned it into a death room.

She didn't walk deeper into the room, not wanting to contaminate the scene. There was no life to be saved here, only trace evidence of the lost.

She took her phone out and put in a call to the dispatcher to get a forensics team on site.

She put the evidence bag down on the floor just inside the door and retrieved a pair of blue plastic shoe covers, slipping them over her shoes before skirting the room so that she could check out the rest of the apartment.

She kept close to the wall.

The kitchen was spotless. It reeked of ammonia. Every surface had been bleached. There was not so much as a cup on the draining board. She checked the fridge. It was empty, the door ajar, the power off. There was no food in any of the cupboards, either.

Likewise, the bathroom smelled of bleach.

There were no towels, no soaps or toiletries in the shower.

The bedroom was positively monastic. There was a single bed stripped to the blue mattress. There was a built-in wardrobe, which held a couple of misshapen wire coat hangers.

The place had been scrubbed top to bottom.

Everywhere apart from the lounge where the politician's blood had been left to crust and soak into the floor until the last of his life was absorbed.

She heard the front door open.

She headed back to see the fat man on the threshold.

'What the fuck is that smell?'

'Out, now,' she demanded. No please. No polite request.

But it was too late.

He wasn't hearing her.

He had pushed passed her into the room and was staring at the blood on the floorboards. At the broken zip ties. At the dark shape of the torturer's chair deeper into the room. He started to heave.

Frankie couldn't get him outside before he vomited.

FORTY-FOUR

'Looks like we've hit pay dirt,' Laura said when she called him back. 'The car's registered to one Pietro Danilo. Cross-referenced the photo on his driver's licence and passport. He's aged hard over the last few years, but it's your guy. The STA hit turned up his home address. He's going nowhere, so enjoy the Roman traffic jam.'

'I'd enjoy it more with air conditioning,' Ash said. 'What do we know about Danilo?'

'Well, for one, he was already on my list. He managed a group home in Romania funded by the first incarnation of EuropaChild during the turmoil of the Ceauşescu regime.'

'Hallelujah.'

'Let's keep an open mind, but one thing we *can* be sure of is that Danilo has reasons to be afraid. Maybe he's next on the list, and would have received part of Maffrici, maybe he's already received something. You need to make contact.'

'Makes sense.'

'I'll text you his address.'

'Thanks. And make sure Frankie knows about the link. We're getting there.'

'I should charge you a membership fee.'

'What for?'

'My dating site services.'

She hung up before he could get his response in.

It was good that she was getting back to normal, too. That was the thing she hadn't realized, or maybe she had and just faked it better than he did, but Mitch Greer's death had messed with her, too. She used to be this sarcastic, humorous flirt on the end of the phone, always giving them crap over their crappy love lives, always teasing them about the dumb things the boys did, but always with so much affection. And that had changed with Mitch's death. She treated him with kid gloves. Probably because she was frightened he'd break – with good reason – but not realizing that those kid gloves made things so much weirder than they needed to be. He just wanted to get back to normal. Whatever the new normal was.

His phone pinged.

He keyed it into the satnav and spent another few minutes wrestling with the settings to change the language to English.

'Twenty-eight minutes to destination,' a woman's voice that sounded like it doubled as a phone-sex operator told him.

Ash leaned out of the window, peering down the line of unmoving traffic and told her, 'That's a bit optimistic.'

He killed the engine, no choice but to sit it out.

His phone rang again.

It was Frankie this time.

'I thought you'd like to know we've had a breakthrough this end. I'm waiting for forensics to arrive, but we've found the place where Anglemark was held. It's a rented basement apartment not far from his love nest. The landlord managed to puke his guts up all over the scene, so that's fun, fun, fun.'

'Nice. I think.'

'I'm taking him over the road for a coffee and a chat to calm his nerves when forensics get here. See what he knows about the guy who rented the place.'

'This is good. Really good.'

'Call when you've spoken to your orphanage guy. We'll talk properly.'

'Will do.'

The traffic up ahead started to move again, one by one the cars coming to life and edging forward until finally it was his turn to gun the engine.

FORTY-FIVE

'We got off to a bad start,' Frankie said, as she steered the fat man towards a threadbare armchair in what passed for a boho chic cafe where the lights were far too dim and the coffee was far too expensive. It was only a couple of minutes' walk from the apartment, and a lot more comfortable than trying to interrogate the guy in the street. After the vomit he no longer saw her as the enemy. He couldn't have been more effusive or happier to get absolutely everything he knew about his tenant off his enormous chest. 'I didn't get your name.'

She had no idea how long it would take for forensics to go over the place thoroughly beyond a basic concept of hours. So they had plenty of time. The lead investigator had promised to call her with his findings as soon as they were through.

'Galanos. Belen Galanos.'

'Greek?'

'My father was, but the name is all I ever got from him. It means arrow.' There was an unmistakable bitterness in his voice, a raw nerve even after all these years. Apologizing wouldn't help, and might make things worse.

'Do you own any other properties?'

'Three buildings on this street, all of them divided into eight to twelve apartments. I turned two of them over to the social to house asylum seekers. They rent well, but the building is basically destroyed in the process. It isn't worth it. Still, I've been lucky. Not like the poor bastards who've seen their places burned down.' He shook his head. 'I'm a good man, officer. I swear. I don't charge inflated rents. I look after my people. I have another building around the corner. We're changing the pipes. New bathrooms. New kitchens. If I was a bastard, do you think I'd do that?'

'I saw it,' she said. 'Expensive business?'

Galanos shrugged. 'The rent covers the mortgage as long as

the apartments are occupied. This country isn't set up for property tycoons.' He offered a bitter laugh. 'But in twenty years I sell up, move out to the islands, get older, get fatter, and die happy. It's not so bad.'

Frankie suspected that it paid a lot more than he was letting on, but that was between him and the tax man. She didn't care who he screwed to make a buck. 'So, what can you tell me about the man who rented the apartments?'

Galanos fidgeted in his seat, still sweating, but his breathing had at least moved out of the danger zone. He smiled up at the barista when their coffee arrived. He added a lot more sugar than was good for anyone, and stirred slowly, watching the granules dissolve into the black.

Frankie maintained her silence. The best way to get someone to talk was simply to allow them to fill the silence.

'The thing is . . .' he started.

'I'm not going to arrest you, Mr Galanos, and I'm not going to turn you over to the tax man for whatever scheme you've got going on with those apartments. I'm not interested in *any* of that. You understand that, don't you? I'm *only* interested in the man who died in that room and finding the person who killed him. I need to know everything you can tell me about the man who rented the property.'

He nodded. 'I want to. Honestly. I just don't know what I *can* tell you.'

'How about you start with what he looks like?'

This time Galanos shook his head and looked miserable doing so. 'I never met him. He paid by first and last month, told me he would be out of town a lot, needed to move in at night, late, so I left a key for him. The place is basically unfurnished, so it's not like there's anything to steal.'

'What about the lease agreement?'

'Didn't sign one.'

'And your books show that the place was empty the whole time he was there, I assume?'

He nodded, clearly guilty, but more embarrassed by the fact that he had been caught than the fact he'd done anything wrong.

'So how was all this arranged if you didn't meet him?'

'It was all over the phone.'

'Any sort of accent?'

'I don't know. I'm not good with that sort of thing. Eastern European. Maybe. I can't be certain. I know it sounds terrible, but they all sound the same to me.'

And their money is as good as anyone's, she guessed. 'OK, can I take a look at your phone?'

He hesitated for a moment, but fished it out of his pocket, used his thumbprint to unlock it and handed it over.

'When did he call you?'

'A couple of weeks ago. It was on a Sunday I think, but it was a blocked number.'

Of course it was.

She didn't look up as she continued to scroll through his call history.

Blocking the number didn't mean there was no record of it on the mobile provider's servers, only that the caller ID didn't screen it immediately.

She found dozens of calls from blocked and unknown numbers, but only one on the day. She made a note of the time, intending to get the source number from the phone company. Galanos tried to read what she'd written even though it was upside down. She showed him the time stamp and the blocked number on the display.

She gave him the phone back.

'What name did he give?'

'Yashin.'

'Sounds Russian.'

The man shrugged again. 'It sounded familiar to me. A footballer or something. Before my time though.'

'Then it's almost certainly not his real name,' Frankie said, but she would pass it on to Ash in case the name appeared in his investigation.

'I had no reason to doubt him. He only wanted a short stay. It was easy money. Plus he paid up front.'

'How did he pay?' She half-expected the fat man to tell her he'd left an envelope full of used banknotes into a dead drop.

She was pleasantly surprised when he said, 'Bank transfer.'

'You have BankID on your phone?'

'I'm not sure.'

'About the app or about letting me see your account?' He
made an uncomfortable face. 'I told you, I don't give a shit who
you are ripping off. I can call someone to run your financials,
we don't need a warrant in an active investigation. They'll dig
through everything. All I want is to see the details of one transaction. I'd say the smart thing to do was just let me do it, Belen.
I'm not after your secrets.'

His fingers trembled and twice he input the wrong number,
but eventually he turned the phone around to show her.

Frankie reached out for it, but he pulled back a fraction. There
was obviously something on there he didn't want her to see.

Instead of trying to take it off him, she just copied down the
details of the transaction.

The amount surprised her. It was considerably more than she'd
have guessed the place rented at. No doubt the black-market
contracts Galanos ran changed hands for substantially above
what should have been market value. But that was part of the no
questions asked aspect of it.

The transfer listed the sender as Lev Yashin. There was a
routing number and series of reference numbers that meant
nothing to Frankie but would help locate the sender's bank
through the IBAN system.

It was a direct line between her and Anglemark's killer.

Galanos's account number and sort code were at the top
of the screen.

'Thanks,' she said as soon as she had written everything down,
then flipped the notebook closed.

'So, do you know who was killed there?' Galanos asked.

'Yes.'

'You're not going to tell me?'

'Why do you want to know?'

He shook his head. 'I don't know. It just seems so . . . weird.
That's my place. Someone died in one of my houses. I don't
know what I'm supposed to do with that.'

'They didn't just die,' she corrected him. 'They were murdered.
That's different.'

'Yes. Of course it is. I just meant . . . who wants to live in a
place where someone was murdered?'

'There's always someone,' she assured him.

FORTY-SIX

A sh saw the Renault in the driveway before the satnav tried to seduce him with the promise he'd hit the spot.

The house was by no means a mansion, but it was far too big for an old man living alone. He didn't have any sort of point of reference in terms of value, but it looked more than the manager of an orphanage ought to have been able to afford. Of course, in Italy that meant little because family homes were handed down from generation to generation, and there was no telling how old the money was that was used to buy the place. But the upkeep couldn't be cheap.

He pulled the Fiat up across the drive, making sure the old man couldn't easily flee before he'd the chance to talk to him. Not that he could force him to cooperate.

Despite the cloying heat inside, Ash waited for a moment before getting out. He saw shadows move across the windows. He imagined Danilo frantically packing his life into a bag, desperate to run, but not sure what he needed to survive. It wasn't easy, running for your life. Not if you didn't want to get caught at the first road block, either metaphorical or literal.

He waited five full minutes.

There was no guard this time, and the gate was wide open. Ash walked down the driveway, straight to the front door. He rang the bell and waited. Not that he expected Danilo to answer. He couldn't imagine a scenario where the old guy opened the door and welcomed him in. He was expecting things to get physical; a chase as Danilo bolted from the back door. The alternative was that the old man would simply hunker down and hope he went away. But running was the more likely option, especially given the fact he was spooked.

Ash tried the bell again. No answer.

He tried the handle.

Locked.

He glanced back towards the road and noticed a woman at the

bottom of the drive, a small dog on a lead, tugging at her. Despite the heat, or perhaps because of it, she wore a headscarf and big shades. She stared at him. He knew she was memorizing both him and his car. She was being a good neighbour without actually putting herself in harm's way.

He heard movement around the side of the house. A scuff of feet across the small stones that surfaced the drive.

Ash stepped out from under the shade of the porch roof, and into the man's path.

Danilo struggled with a heavy bag.

He dropped it the moment he saw Ash.

'What do you want?'

'Pietro Danilo,' he said. It was a statement, not a question. Danilo couldn't mask his fear. His eyes darted from Ash to the Renault to the crappy rust-bucket of a Fiat blocking his escape.

'Who are you?'

Ash reached inside his pocket for his identification. The man took a step backwards. 'My name is Peter Ash,' Ash said. 'I'm here to help you. I'm with Eurocrimes Division, a joint European Union initiative.'

'Police?'

He nodded. 'Close enough.'

'You're English. You can't help me. This is Italy. You have no jurisdiction here.'

Ash took another step forward, closing the gap between them. 'Call the judge. He can confirm who I am.'

'Judge?' He was a terrible liar. In that one-word question he was trying to buy time and work out a second way out of the mess he was in, but nothing was going to move that Fiat, and there wasn't a hope in Hell of the old man outrunning him in this heat, so his feigned ignorance wasn't buying him anything.

'Maffrici. You can lie all you want, but I saw you together earlier, so you might as well be straight with me.'

'You followed me?'

'I did. And I know you're afraid.' Ash looked pointedly at the old man's go-bag. 'And now you're running for your life.'

Danilo didn't follow the direction of his gaze. He knew what was in that bag, and he knew Ash was right, but that didn't stop him from saying, 'I have no idea what you are talking about. Now I would appreciate it if you could move your car.'

'No,' Ash said.

'You have no right to detain me.'

'Who said I'm detaining you? I might have broken down there, you have no way of proving otherwise. Unless you'd like me to call the police? I'm sure they could help us out. It'd be what, an hour for them to respond? Something like that. It'd slow your escape down a lot. Or you can give me five minutes of your time. If you don't like what I have to say then I'll leave you in peace.'

The man hesitated. Ash knew that he had won the first battle at least.

Danilo hefted his bag and carried it across to the Renault, triggering the boot lock with a key press, and bundled the bag inside.

'Five minutes,' he said, and headed back towards the rear of the house.

Ash followed him to a door that led into the kitchen.

'Five minutes, then I would like you to leave.'

'That's all I want. I'm not here to hurt you. You have my word.'

Ash waited for the man to invite him to sit, but the invitation never came. He pulled out a chair from under the oak refectory table. Danilo sighed and scraped the opposite chair out and sat down.

'Did Maffrici tell you to get out of town?'

He shook his head. 'It was just two old friends catching up.'

'You're a terrible liar, Pietro, which is a good thing in life, but a terrible thing when you're trying to con a man who deals with liars every day of his life.

The man betrayed no reaction.

'Did you reach out to him, or did he contact you?'

'We just bumped into each other. It wasn't planned. Four minutes.'

'See, I think you're lying. I think you contacted him because you received a package urging you to remember Bonn?'

This time the man's eyes twitched, tiny micro-emotions there if you knew what you were looking for. They were as obvious as beads of perspiration.

Ash leaned back in his chair. 'Why don't we cut the bullshit, Pietro, and talk one Peter to another. I think you contacted the judge because someone sent you human flesh in the mail. I don't know what because every victim has been sent something different. That's what I think. Of course, the judge might have reached out to warn you because you were meant to get a piece of him. But one way or the other you're on a list, and everyone else on that list has managed to turn up dead.'

Danilo was doing his damnedest not to show it, but he was rattled. Silence seemed to be his only defence.

'Then there's the note that came along with the meat. "Remember Bonn," and a summons, a time and a place. So far everyone we know of who went to that meeting has turned up dead, or gone missing.'

'Jonas Anglemark and Jacques Tournard.'

He nodded.

'Maffrici told me.'

'Did you know them?'

'I've heard of Anglemark. Not the Frenchman.'

Ash knew that the man was lying.

'Have you heard what happened to them?'

'I heard Jonas washed up dead.'

'He had his tongue cut out.'

The man blanched. 'I wasn't sent a tongue.'

'I never said you were. That was sent to Tournard. What did you get?'

'A toe.'

'Does that mean anything to you? Anything specific about Bonn and a toe?'

Danilo got to his feet and retrieved a bottle of water from the refrigerator. His had betrayed the slightest tremor as he emptied it into a glass. He was still shaking while he drank.

He didn't answer the question directly, instead he said, 'What happened to Tournard?'

'I don't know for sure. I think he's lying dead somewhere just waiting for some poor bastard to stumble across his body. Maffrici was smart enough not to go to the meeting. But that doesn't mean he's safe. Our killer is determined. He's killed others, a guy called Ramirez in Seville. I think you and the judge are next.'

'Then you'd better stop him.'

'Where are you supposed to meet him?'

He didn't deny it this time, simply confessed, 'There's a bar, Caligula's, I'm supposed to meet him at eleven tonight. Feel free to take my place.'

'That won't help. He knows who you are. He follows his victims to the meet. If we send a body double he'll walk and we'll have lost him.'

'What do you expect me to do about it?'

'I'd like you to go.'

That stopped him cold. He put the glass down on the table. 'Are you fucking kidding me?'

'No.'

'You just said that Maffrici was smart enough not to go. You said that was why he was still alive. Why do you think I would be stupid enough to go?'

'Because whoever is doing this knows you and knows something that you need to stay secret. He won't stop until he's made you all remember Bonn. I can help you. If you trust me. I can keep you alive.'

Ash gave Danilo a moment to fill in the gaps if he wanted to, but the old man wasn't about to spill his guts. What he couldn't do was push too hard.

'He doesn't know me. I'll go in before you. I'll be in place. I'll draft in my Italian counterparts, we'll stake out Caligula's. We'll have eyes on you inside and out. We won't let you get hurt.'

'No police. If we do this, and right now it's a big if, it's you and me. The moment he shows up, I'm out of there. That's the only way I'm doing this.'

Ash was quite happy to let Danilo feel like he was dictating the terms, but the reality was if it didn't work for him, he wasn't doing it. He'd seen what doing it half-arsed had done for Mitch Greer. He'd gone into a set-up and hadn't walked out again. Fool us once. 'OK.'

Danilo shook his head. 'I don't know why I'm doing this. It's suicide. I should be getting as far away from here as I possibly can. I could be out of the country even before he even knows I'm gone.'

'But you know he'd just come looking for you, and eventually he'd find you, because like the old line goes: you can run, but you can't hide. And you can't. You're not some criminal mastermind. You used to run a kids' home. You don't have the skill set to survive a life on the run with a man like this looking for you.'

'Just me and you,' the man said again, like he was trying to convince himself it wasn't suicide. 'I'll park near the club, it's already got my bags in it. There's a full tank. Once he sets foot inside, you take him and I'm out of there.'

'Whatever you say.'

'Then I'll see you there.'

'I'll get there early. At least an hour,' Ash said. 'Don't look around for me. Chances are he'll be watching you. I'll be there, you have my word.'

The man nodded.

Ash wasn't even half-convinced that Danilo would show. The man was a flight risk. But what choice did he have? He couldn't babysit him all the way to Caligula's. Not with the killer watching.

FORTY-SEVEN

Ash had time to kill.

He went back to his hotel room for the three S's – shit, shower, and shave – and changed into a non-sweat-soaked shirt. He ordered a meal on room service and thought about dipping into the minibar but decided against it, given he'd need to buy a beer in the club to not stand out.

He sent an email to Laura, updating her on what he had been doing, including the proposed meet and the sting he'd set up with Danilo.

He remembered his promise to call Frankie.

He pulled up her number.

'Peter,' she said, even before the ring signal had had a chance to cycle back to him. 'How did things go?'

'I followed Danilo – the man the judge met – to his home outside the city. He's received a package. A toe.'

'A toe. Same note?'

'Same message. The meet isn't until tonight. A bar in Rome at eleven. He's agreed to let me use him like bait to draw the killer out.'

'How about backup? You bringing the Italian office in?'

'Nope. Just me.'

'That's stupid.'

'You don't need to tell me,' he said.

'Then don't be stupid. Make sure you have backup in place. That's what Division's for. Use our resources.'

'It was the only way that Danilo would agree to do the sit down. No police, his own car close by so he can make good his escape the moment I've got my hands on the killer.'

'Then don't tell him. Lie. Tell him it's just the two of you. It's not like he's skilled enough in tradecraft to pick backup out of a crowded bar.'

She was right, of course.

'I've been in touch with the Carabinieri so they know we've

got an op going down, and requesting transport to bring our boy in when we've got him.'

'Bet they loved that idea.'

'They weren't too keen, especially when I wouldn't give them any details.'

'You do realize the only reason Danilo wants his escape route clear is so he can run, right? Which means he's worried the Carabinieri will want to hold him. He's not some innocent victim in all of this. He's up to his neck in it. You don't end up on a grudge list like this without having done something very, very wrong.'

'My first priority is making sure no one else gets killed. After that, I'm happy to solve the mystery. But right now it's all about keeping everyone alive. So, how is it your end?'

He listened while Frankie filled him in.

Maybe the killer wasn't as infallible as they'd feared. There were mistakes in there. Uncharacteristic, based on everything they'd seen so far. He didn't know whether that meant they were good, or he was getting careless.

Or they were being led down a particularly shady garden path.

'Laura's running the financials from the bank account used to wire the cash to Galanos. The account name doesn't appear on any of the documents she's found so far relating to the charity.'

'False identity. Makes sense. So, what name did he use?'

'Lev Yashin,' she said.

Ash tried not to laugh, but for once appreciated their quarry's sense of humour. 'Eastern European accent?'

'That's right.'

'Lev Yashin.'

'You say that like you know him. Have you come across him before?'

'Bit before my time. I'm more of a Clemence and Shilton kind of guy. Hand of God and all that.'

'Is that supposed to mean something to me?'

He smiled despite himself. 'I can tell you're not a football fan.'

'More of an ice-hockey girl,' she said.

'Lev Yashin was probably the greatest goalkeeper in the history of the game. Certainly up there with Gordon Banks and Bert Trautman.'

'So, Laura is wasting her time.'

'Not at all. We'd expected a fake name, just because he picked a famous one doesn't mean we won't learn something from it.'

'But it suggests he expected us to find it,' she argued. 'And that means he is still controlling what we know about him, even down to playing games with his fake name. He's still steps ahead of us, and knows how we're following him, not just that we're following him. These aren't mistakes. He's the guy shooting at our feet cackling: *Dance, motherfucker, dance.*'

He couldn't disagree with that.

FORTY-EIGHT

The bar wasn't remotely what Ash had expected.

The night air was clammy but clear. He felt it tight in his lungs. As he walked down the narrow Roman street towards Caligula's he saw six girls, probably in their late teens, dressed in varieties of white: jeans, T-shirts, shirts, linen trousers, skirts – all laughing at something he couldn't see. Two sat on a low wall, one wolf-whistled at a lad on his Vespa, reversing traditional gender-harassment roles. One of the girls, with raven-black hair that reached all the way down to the hollow at the base of her spine, was busy rolling her own smoke. Ash saw her sprinkle a little something extra into the tobacco strands. She licked the paper and closed the straggly coffin nail. These weren't exactly Vesta's usual crowd.

A couple of them said something to him; he assumed they were mocking the old man and his poor fashion sense. He had never been the kind of man arrogant enough to think women would look twice at him, regardless of their daddy issues, low self-esteem or any of the other clichés that supposedly gave average guys a better than average shot at punching well above their weight. In point of fact he was generally useless with women and always had been. For a man who spent most of his life trusting the instincts and emotions that underscored investigative technique he was a poor judge of a woman's interest when it was in him.

Despite the warm evening the two doormen wore leather jackets, but no shirts. Every single muscle on their incredible physiques was defined, the skin glistening where it had been oiled. Now he realized why the girls were hanging around. The doormen weren't there to keep any sort of order, they were eye-candy meant to draw the punters in.

The sign above them, neon red against the night, said Caligula's. Together with the oiled abs and pecs, the promise of the kinds of temptation waiting inside were obvious.

He headed in.

Ash nodded to one of the two men as they smiled his way. The guy's teeth were too white. 'I'll be inside later,' the man said. 'I'll let you buy me a drink if you're lucky.'

Ash matched his smile with one of his own, but his mind was racing. The choice of venue, given the number of bars, restaurants, clubs, and public spaces in the city that would have functioned just fine for the killer's needs, couldn't be anything other than a message. It wasn't just that he'd picked a gay bar, but one so overtly Tom of Finland in its street presence made it a statement.

Of course, he only had Danilo's word that this was the right place. The old man claimed to have destroyed the note.

Inside was dark but far from dingy.

He walked down a series of stone steps into what might have once been a wine cellar but had been converted into a bar. The music was pulsing. He didn't know the tune this time even though the words, few though they were, were definitely in English. The speakers were huge for the relatively small space, covering all angles of the dance floor.

There were maybe twenty people in the dimly lit chamber, half of them at the bar, the other half at tables clustered around the empty dance floor. The one thing they all had in common was that they were fit, well-dressed, and attractive. There wasn't a bookish boy amongst the twinks, Muscle Mary's, and other friends of Dorothy. A door on the far side opened and a couple of bears walked out of what was obviously the playroom, wearing leather bandoliers over their hairy torsos. They were the closest thing he'd seen to fat men since he took the short walk down into Caligula's.

It was aptly named.

Despite the fact it was still obviously early and would get busier as the night wore on, there was already a vibe to the joint. It was another world. He couldn't imagine a place like this in London, but then, London was repressed enough that just about every flat around King's Cross was basically a brothel, not that anyone wanted to admit it.

One of the most beautiful women he'd seen in his life worked the bar. She stood maybe an inch taller than Ash, in heels, with eyes like sin and lips that promised damnation. She saw him and smiled as he approached the bar. He couldn't take his eyes off her, even after he realized she was a he, and she leaned towards him to ask, 'What's your pleasure, stranger?' Her voice was as husky as a sixty-a-day habit, which only made her appeal more magnetic.

'Una birra,' he said, pointing at a bottle of Nastro Azzuro.

He pushed the money across the counter as she uncapped the green bottle.

It was easier to pretend to drink with a bottle, so he declined the glass as she offered it.

He scanned the faces in the bar to be sure Danilo hadn't ignored his instructions and arrived early. There was no sign of him. Of course, now the issue was would he show at all.

There were a number of booths along one side of the room, only one of which was occupied. The couple in there were deep in conversation, their heads close together, hands locked like they were about to arm wrestle. It was obviously a deep and mean-ingful moment for the pair. Pity they couldn't hear themselves think for the relentless drum and bass, Ash thought, crossing the dance floor to take one of the empty booths. He picked the third one, as it gave him a clear view of both the doorway and the bar area, meaning he'd be able to see Danilo arrive, and the meet at the bar when it went down.

He checked his watch.

He still had twenty minutes to kill.

A few more people arrived; all men, all veering towards the twink stereotype, though one stood out because he was consider-ably older than the rest. He maybe had a year or two on Danilo, but he was in much better physical shape.

A buzz cut and a hairless boy came in next, and danced their way across the floor, popping and locking, or whatever it was called. Ash couldn't help but follow their exaggerated dance, taking his eye off the door.

He turned his attention back to the older man.

A couple of the younger guys drifted towards him, preening and posing like peacocks – or meat on display, no doubt hoping he liked what he saw. Ash had no idea what the gay version of a sugar daddy was, but could well imagine a good-looking, fit, rich guy was the white whale for some of these boys. No doubt Danilo enjoyed the attention. He noticed the girl at the bar waved a hello to him. A regular then. Known to the staff, and probably the punters.

Frankie had suggested that the killer had scouted out the place before he'd met Anglemark, choosing a place without security cameras. This place, Ash was sure, would have some form of security, but once it got busy it would be hard to make out faces through the strobing neon and the wild kinetic dance, though there was no knowing what was through that door and if it really was a playroom, or the safe space or whatever, but if this was that kind of club, gloryholes in the toilets, and a happy little cottage industry going on back there, maybe there were no cameras at all? Plenty of guys would be down to fuck, but not so down if they knew it wasn't anonymous. There were still plenty of guys who kept their sexuality secret from the outside world. Even in places like this. Or maybe especially in places like this.

People kept coming in. Now it wasn't just twinks, there were muscle boys and daddies and every other kink imaginable.

And they kept on coming, two by two, down the stairs into Caligula's.

Two bears with huge bellies spilling over their leather trousers put on a show in the middle of the dance floor, one pulling off his belt and using it to whip the other who crawled on his hands and knees, much to the delight of those gathered around the edge of the dance floor.

He raised the bottle to his lips, tipped it, but put his tongue into the mouth as he did so, so that there was nothing for him to swallow.

He put the bottle back on the table and made a show of wiping his lips with the back of his hand.

He was thinking. The problem was it was hard to think straight given the sheer volume and sheer volume of distractions.

Assuming the killer had used the same criteria when he'd chosen Caligula's, that meant he had a place close by. Somewhere he could take Danilo to torture him to his heart's content before he sliced a bit of him off to send to the next victim.

Something niggled away at the back of his mind.

Why do that?

Why add to the risk?

Why not just drug them, bundle them into a car, and be gone,

as far and as fast as possible, kill, mutilate, and dump the corpse
and move on?

Why rent a place for a month?

Was it just so he had a quiet place to do his worst? Or was it
something else?

He felt the urge to ring Frankie. He had something he wanted
to run past her, but there was no way he could call from inside
Caligula's, and a quick look at his watch said he was out of time.
Danilo could arrive at any moment. And there was no way he
could make a call in here.

Another couple came down the stairs.

He saw their silhouettes in the doorway before they stepped
inside. The stepped under the fluorescent lights, all smiles,
white teeth glowing like the Cheshire cat's. A couple of the
younger men propping up the bar cried out a greeting as
the music changed.

It was getting considerably hotter as more and more revellers
came down the stairs.

There were more people on the dance floor now, not just the
two leather-clad daddies.

In the last twenty minutes maybe two hundred people had
come in. It was so much louder now, and not just because of the
music. People crowded around the bar. Two more girls came out
to join the barmaid, though these two were sissies rather than
transsexuals. Their make-up was good, but it was obvious they
were cross-dressing, even in the flashing strobe lights and the
weird halo-effect of the neons.

Ash couldn't help but think that the emperor would have
been proud.

He caught sight of the older man as he emerged from the crush
around the bar. He balanced two drinks as he moved gracefully
through the revellers, until he reached a boy who looked barely
old enough to drink it, and handed it over with a stroke of the
cheek and an almost coy shrug. The old queen seemed content.
Ash couldn't imagine that the killer was already inside; no one
else was sitting alone, watching, removed from the fun. He was
a loner. He thrived on anonymity. He didn't put himself in the
middle of something like this. It was too much, too loud, too
many variables and room for something to go wrong. The only

thing in its favour was the fact it was dark, and offered darker
shadows off away from the main excitement, and no one would
be surprised to see one queer leading another out, under the
influence, after he'd been roofed. That was part of the play.
Part of the fun. Everyone knew everyone else. This was a
community.

Ash was the only stranger here.

Another couple of dozen good-time guys entered over the next
ten minutes before Danilo arrived.

Ash saw the man give the slightest glance in his direction,
nothing enough to sell him out to the casual observer, but enough
perhaps to give him away if he was being watched less casually.
Danilo caught himself, realizing what he had done, and continued
to scan the room, deliberately lingering on a few other faces,
just in case.

With ten minutes to the scheduled meet Ash still hadn't made
an obvious killer in the crowd, and assumed he was still outside,
giving the old man time to sweat it out before he descended into
this Caligulan fever dream. The bottle in front of him was empty,
but that didn't stop him from lifting it to his lips and pretending
to drink.

A couple of bar-hangers gave him the eye. One chewed on
his lower lip like some sort of come on. It was peculiar being
on this side of the mating ritual. Men, he realized, were pretty
basic when it came right down to it. None more so that the
twentysomething who walked up to him and asked outright if he
wanted to fuck. Ash said sorry. The guy didn't seem to mind.
He went on to the next booth and asked the same question,
playing the numbers game. Someone would say yes. They always
did.

Ash made a show of waiting for someone and glanced
regularly at his watch. It wasn't the most convincing charade;
he was hardly Tom Cruise. But he sold it because it wasn't a
total lie, after all.

He was so intent on watching the stairs that he missed the
arrival of a butch bearded guy who slid into the booth opposite
him. The bear put a bottle of Peroni in front of Ash and took a
deep swallow from his own.

'First time?'

It took him a second to place where he'd seen the guy before; it was the eye-candy doorman who'd flashed him that smile on the way in, only he'd changed the leather jacket for a tight-fitting white T-shirt.

'I'm meeting someone,' he said, trying not to sound rude but trying to move him on just the same.

'You keep looking at your watch. He's late. Being late is just rude. It's like saying, "Hey your time isn't as valuable as mine." Show a little respect, huh? You make a date, you show up on time. It's the least you can do.'

'I'm sure he'll be here soon.'

'Maybe he will. But you're still left sitting alone, which is no fun. So how about I give you a little company while you wait?'

'It's OK, I'm fine, honestly.'

'Well, if he's a no show, you come and find me, eh? You can buy me that drink back.' The man stood up.

Ash raised the empty bottle in salute. 'You never know, I might just do that. And hey, thanks for the drink.'

'It's not from me, I was just the delivery boy. There's a guy at the bar who bought it. Thought you looked like you needed company. Or a drink. Or both. I guess he was wrong.'

'Which guy?' Ash asked. The eye candy was blocking his view of the bar. By the time he'd moved, Ash realized that Danilo was no longer there.

FORTY-NINE

'OK, what did he look like?' Ash demanded, but the eye candy just held his hand out in apology.

'I'm sorry, man, I didn't get that good a look at him. Normal-looking guy. Nothing to write home about. Didn't stand out in the crowd. He's not a regular, though, I would have recognized him. There was a crowd at the bar, he bought maybe a dozen beers, handed me a couple and nodded your way, saying he'd seen me look.'

'How can you not remember what he looked like? It was seconds ago.'

The man shrugged and suddenly looked vulnerable. 'You know what it's like, everyone's a face, but you're not really looking at any of them. You're talking to them, sure, but you're scanning the room looking for something better. You looked a little lost, so I thought, why not?'

'Lost? Yeah maybe,' Ash said, thinking that was pretty much the perfect word to describe him on all levels right now. 'Anything you remember about him? Anything at all? Maybe his clothes? Anything?'

The guy shook his head. 'I feel like an idiot. I'm sorry.'

'I'm the idiot,' Ash said, and was already heading for the door before the eye candy could apologize again.

He scanned the faces, looking for Danilo, but knew he wasn't there. He kicked himself. He'd convinced the old guy to trust him, and all it had taken was a guy with a bottle of beer to get him to take his eye off the ball. Ash pushed his way to the stairs, working against the press of the flesh as more revellers came down to enjoy the sins of the Emperor. There was smiles and laughter, and enough cologne to sear away the fine hairs lining his nostrils.

He made it to the door and stepped out into the night.

In the time he'd been down there it had grown cold.

He felt someone grab at his arm and he spun around, ready

to let fly with a clenched fist, and only just managed to stop himself when he realized that it was the eye candy. The man had followed him outside.

'Look, I'm sorry. I'm really sorry. But there's no need to run away.'

Ash didn't have time to explain. He scanned the street, left and right, looking for any sign of Danilo. 'I'm not running away. I fucked up. Now I'm putting it right.'

'What's wrong?'

'Did you see the older man who came in maybe ten minutes ago? Skinny guy, losing his hair?'

'Pietro? Sure, he's a regular. He likes the younger boys. Got a thing for the innocent look. But he's OK.'

'Younger guys?' The way he said it, despite the fact he was maybe mid-twenties at the most, sent a shiver down the ladder of Ash's spine that had nothing to do with the cold night air. 'How young are we talking?'

'I should go back inside. I've got to help Trixie out behind the bar.' The fact he wouldn't answer the question answered the question.

'Did you see him leave?'

There were dozens of people out now, tourists and club-goers. A group had gathered around a street performer who seemed to be doing some weird kind of puppet show in the middle of the square. Delighted laughter rippled out. A moment later another entertainer appeared, this time on stilts and making a show of breathing fire. Even if they kept this up all night they'd be lucky to pocket minimum wage from the most generous tourist crowd.

He couldn't see Danilo anywhere.

It couldn't have been more than two minutes since he left.

Two fucking minutes.

'Not me,' the man said then spoke rapidly with the current doorman who pointed down the street. 'He's already gone. That way.' He pointed in the direction of the performers. 'Left with a guy, maybe in his late forties, early fifties.'

'Cheers,' Ash said, and started running in the direction the bouncer had pointed. He was forced into the road to avoid another group of girls walking arm in arm and taking up the entirety of the pavement. They were singing. Drunk already, or at least buzzed. They moved into the road to try and block him, laughing as they did so. Ash, forced out wide, didn't slow down.

There was no sign of Danilo, either alone or with another man.

Even as he crossed the street to where the crowds were thinner, there was nothing.

He stopped running and cursed himself.

He'd fucked it up.

He'd fucked it up and now Danilo was going to die.

This was all his fault.

He shouldn't have encouraged the old man to act as bait. He should have told him to run, as far away and as fast as he could. But oh no, he'd convinced a frightened man the only way he was getting out of this was by playing along the Peter Ash way.

There were any number of doorways in the couple of hundred metres he'd covered since leaving the club, huge oak doors, small unassuming painted ones, iron-banded relics and modern uPVC security ones. None of them looked alike. The street spiralled away from him, feeling vast. A thousand windows looked out onto the world – or at least that was how it felt as he turned and turned and turned, faster and faster, praying to a god he didn't believe in for a glance of Pietro Danilo's scruffy mop of thinning hair being ushered into one of the doors.

Patterns of behaviour. The other guys had gone with the killer willingly. Had Danilo done the same thing? Or had he tried to catch Ash's eye while he had been distracted by the eye candy and panicked that he couldn't?

Maybe he'd run?

He'd parked his Renault around here. Maybe he'd managed to give the killer the slip in the tide of people and made it to the car?

Any hope of that died almost as soon as the thought occurred to him, as Ash spotted the racing-green Renault parked on the other side of the road.

He had a choice to make now. He could call Division, get them to reach out via the Italian office to the Carabinieri and get them on board, go door to door and hope they rattled the guy's cage. Or he could start asking people, like a crazy man, up in their faces, 'Have you seen this old guy, skinny, losing his hair, he's with a fortysomething-year-old guy?' Someone would have seen them. But in a numbers game he was dealing with shit numbers; there were too many people milling around, too many bodies to work through, too many doors to knock on and buildings to check. It was an impossible task, because in the minutes it would take to convince the Carabinieri to get on board with the murder hunt the killer was going to walk.

And even if he asked everyone, that didn't mean he'd get the answer he was looking for. Maybe Frankie was wrong. Maybe that local bolthole was only something he'd done in Stockholm. There was no guarantee he'd repeated the pattern here, or even if he had tried, what was the likelihood he'd found a place that met his needs so close to the city centre? Maybe this time he'd got a car waiting?

Patterns of behaviour.

Comfort.

Habit.

Ash stood in the middle of the street, hands on his hips, knowing he'd blown it. All he could do now was go back to Caligula's and try and get a proper description of the killer from the doorman and anyone else in there who might have seen him.

He started to walk back the way he'd come.

He crossed under a streetlight, and glanced back towards Danilo's abandoned car.

Too late, he realized that there was someone sitting in the front seat. He hadn't seen them before because of the shadows and the distance, and because he hadn't really been looking for them. Now a security light had come on, casting the interior of the car into stark relief. He couldn't see who was in there. It was just a dark shape behind the wheel.

The engine roared into life and pulled away from the roadside.

At this time of night the traffic was non-existent. The biggest problem was pedestrians in the street, and they got out of the way fast as the engine roared and the Renault raced towards them.

Ash felt a surge of relief.

One shadow.

There was only one shadow.

Danilo was running.

The car hurtled past him, and in that moment all hope was lost. Danilo was not alone in the car. There was a second man, in the back seat.

Without thinking, he ran into the road, stopping the first car in a screech of brakes as it tried to avoid mowing him down. He didn't so much as flinch. He ran along the line of windows to the fourth car, a taxi, and pressed his ID up against the window even as the other drivers blared their horns at him. He ignored them. And the taxi driver ignored him, giving Ash the finger and pulling away.

Danilo's car was already starting to gain speed and would be out of sight soon and away into the labyrinthine Roman streets.

He had no choice but to run.

The racing-green Renault was three hundred metres ahead of him. There was no way he could possibly close the gap, even if traffic lights intervened, but that didn't stop him from summoning a burst of speed and running furiously, arms and legs pumping as he tried to force every ounce of energy out of his body, but it was futile. The Renault disappeared.

Ash fell to his knees in the middle of the road, trying to suck in air while drivers queueing up behind him leaned on their horns and gesticulated wildly through their open windows.

One of the Vestal Virgins stepped into the road and helped him to his feet. 'You OK?' she asked, in English. Her friends at the side of the road were very pointedly telling her to leave the mad man alone and not to get involved.

Ash brushed her concern away. 'Just out of shape,' he said, angry with himself.

'Did he steal your wallet?'

He heard what she was saying, but the words didn't seem to be making a lot of sense. He stood there, in a landscape of confusion.

'The man in the car? Did he steal your wallet? There's usually a couple of motorcycle cops down by the fountain at this time of night. You should tell them.'

More horns blared. Ash nodded and stumbled out of the way, allowing the cars to move past him. The drivers stared at him like he was the scum of the earth. One yelled a stream of obscenities in his direction. 'Doesn't matter,' Ash said, 'but thanks.'

'I hope you manage to enjoy the rest of your holiday,' the girl said. 'Rome really isn't that bad, I promise.'

She returned to her impatient friends. Maybe in the morning they'd hear about the killer's arrest and realize they were in the middle of it. Or maybe not.

He walked towards the quieter end of the street and made a call to Division, explaining he wasn't going to need that vehicular backup after all. He gave them the Renault's plate and they promised to put a trace on it. It wasn't much, neither help or hindrance really. They were all supposed to be working together, but it always felt like they were pulling in different directions these days. He'd lost count of how many times he'd been told not to get in the way by local agencies objecting to his presence on their patch.

The only person he could think of to turn to was Ernesto Donatti, and right now he trusted the Vatican fixer about as far as he could throw him.

FIFTY

'Remember me?' Two words to send a chill into Danilo's soul. They were all the man had needed to say when he approached him at the bar.

The man hadn't even looked at him, he'd simply leaned forward on the bar and ordered a dozen bottles of beer from Trixie and told her to line them up on the bar. He paid cash, then proceeded to share the bottles out around the coterie of young men who swarmed around him.

Danilo didn't recognize him, but there was an undeniable familiarity about the man.

He glanced across at Peter Ash, only to see that his so-called protector was deep in conversation with Luca, the good-looking door bait paid to lure the horny suckers in.

'I thought your friend would appreciate a refill, given his bottle has been empty quite a while now,' he said.

'How . . .' Danilo started to ask but the rest of the question would not form in his mouth. The man took him by the arm and gently steered him away from the young men and their free drinks. It was too loud for conversation. Words were replaced by subtle gestures and little touches. They were deep in that kind of conversation with each other.

'How did I get you alone? Ask yourself, Pietro, what, really, do you know about this hero of yours? What proof did he give you of who he was? How do you know I didn't tell him to get you here? In fact, ask yourself this, how can you believe anything he has told you? I know what you are thinking. You are thinking you should have run when you had the chance.'

His head started to spin, the flashing lights, the heat and the noise suddenly becoming too much for him. He reached out a hand to steady himself, knowing that something was wrong.

'I need some air,' he said and tried to stand.

The man caught him under the elbow and stopped him from slumping down before he'd even half-stood.

He shouldn't have come here.

The man was right, he should have run.

And he should never have stopped running.

If he had done that he could have disappeared. He could have been out of the country by now, on his way to a new life where no one knew him.

He struggled to think straight; there would be people outside, people who could help, groups he could hide in. Outside was better than in.

'I just want to talk,' the man said.

Which was a lie. It had to be. All the evidence in the world said it wasn't about talking.

'Don't insult my intelligence. I'm not like the others. I know what's going to happen to me.'

'The others?'

'Anglemark for a start.'

'He was different, and you know it.'

'I don't know anything,' Danilo said. But he did. He knew plenty. He knew that the worst lies were the ones you told yourself. He might not have done what the rest of them did, but he was complicit. He was part of it.

'You really don't remember me, do you?'

Danilo shook his head. 'I'm sorry.'

'I'm sure you are. Now. But it hardly matters. It was a long time ago. A very long time ago. But believe me, all I want to do is talk. You can spare me a few minutes, can't you?'

'Just talk?'

'If you help me we can get justice. And maybe, if there is a god, some peace.'

'What do you want me to do?'

'Tell me what you can remember. Everything you can remember about that place. In case I have missed anyone. Then I will leave you to your own conscience. I won't force you to do anything. You decide what happens to you. Will you help me?'

Danilo hesitated.

He wanted to believe the man.

And what harm could there be in talking?

'Confession is good for the soul,' the man said.

'Do you want the truth? Is that it?'

'I already know the truth,' the man said. Perhaps that was it, he wanted to hear his confession in his own words, then expose him and the rest of them. Most of the others were already dead. What did they have to lose if the truth came out now? No one would remember who they were in a month. But he was still alive and being implicated would ruin him. And that was a different kind of torture, wasn't it? Leaving your victim alive, stripping him of his dignity and his pride, stripping him of his name and undoing all the good things he'd done with his life and leaving a naked abuser there to face the lacerations of public opinion.

Sometimes dead was better.

Even as the thought entered his head Danilo saw his car. It was parked across the street, ready for the escape he'd never make now. 'You want me to drive us somewhere?' He indicated the car. His mind was working overtime. He was older than the man, and he kept himself in decent shape. Nobody liked an old queen who had let himself go to seed. The other man wasn't big, but size wasn't important. In this case it was all about power. And he had the power in the dynamic. But Danilo was older and kept a wheel brace in the boot of the car. That, around the side of the head, could be a great leveller.

The only thing Pietro Danilo knew for sure and certain as he walked across the road towards the Renault was that he had far too much to lose to let this man destroy him.

He needed to take control of the situation.

That meant he couldn't allow himself to be afraid.

The man followed him across the street and slid into the rear passenger-side seat without another word.

'There's a cafe not too far from here,' Danilo said. 'It's open all night. We can talk there. They have some of the best pastries in Rome.'

The man didn't say no, so he took that as being as good as a yes.

As he pulled away from the kerbside Danilo saw Ash walking towards them. He didn't think about it. He put his foot down and accelerated smoothly. The old Renault had a big engine. They gained speed quickly.

He made it three hundred metres before the traffic ground to a halt, red lights blocking the way. He glanced back in the rear-view mirror and saw Ash running like a madman down the middle of the road, fast. He was actually closing the gap. His eyes darted from Ash to the red light back to Ash back to the red light, willing it to change. He drummed his fingers on the steering wheel. The man in the back seat simply stared eyes front, utterly uninterested in Ash's futile chase.

Danilo cursed under his breath, unleashing a stream of invective that would have made the Pope blush, and then smiled as the divine chose to intervene and turned red to green, leaving Ash on his knees in the middle of the road.

'How far is it?' the man asked.

'Not far,' Danilo promised.

In truth he had no idea where he was taking the other man. He was still trying to think of a quiet place, somewhere he could pull over and retrieve the brace from the boot without his passenger being any the wiser.

He had mentioned a cafe because it was the first thing that had popped into his head.

'Up front, there's one open over there,' the man said, pointing towards a lit window. 'Park here.'

It was hard to think of a reason to refuse, especially when he saw a couple of spaces kerbside.

It was at least public. There were other guests inside. He was safe as long as he was around people.

The man did not move to open his door until Danilo was already climbing out.

Danilo took a deep breath, promising himself he was master of his own fate here.

Turn about. Go from prey to predator. Kill the man, carve away a body part to make it appear he was the intended victim all along. It wasn't brilliant, but it would lead them to the conclusion he needed them to make. And that was all that mattered.

He could kill.

He knew that much about himself.

A single barista worked the counter. Half a dozen customers were hunched over cups of coffee. It was far too late to be drinking caffeine, but that didn't stop them. 'I'll get them, shall I? Least I can do,' the man said as Danilo slid onto one of the bench seats. 'Due caffé,' he told the barista, who turned away and started to grind the beans.

A couple of minutes later the man who had killed Jonas Anglemark brought two small single shots to the table and took his place on the other side.

'So, what do I call you?' Danilo asked.

'Call me?'

'You know, a name? It feels wrong. You obviously know me.'

'You can call me Michael.'

'Michael? Is that your real name?'

'It doesn't matter what my name is if you can't remember me, does it?'

'I suppose not.'

'You still don't know who your hero really is, do you?'

Danilo looked at Michael, then reached into his pocket for a packet of cigarillos. He tapped one out and lit up. 'I still have no idea what you're talking about.'

'You should trust me,' Michael said and took a sip of his coffee. 'I'm the only one who won't lie to you.'

Danilo chose not to respond. Instead he drew on the cigarillo, blowing out a thin stream of smoke that rose between them like a curtain. 'So, you wanted to talk? About what?'

'The past.'

'That covers a multitude of sins. Do you want to be more specific?'

'The time when you were running the Romanian orphanage.'

'Now that is ancient history.'

'Not for me. It's like it was only yesterday.'

'You were there?'

'That's why I'm here.'

He looked at the man properly, into his eyes, trying to read them as he took another sucking drag on the cigarillo. 'Were you one of the orphans?'

'I was one of the unfortunate kids abandoned there.'

Danilo nodded. He half-smiled, like he was glad to see the boy all grown up and making his way in the world. 'Your English is very good for someone who came through that system.' That system. He knew that he was condemning himself with every word that came out of his mouth, every syllable a reminder, an accusation of the things he had been involved with back then.

'I guess I have you to thank for that.'

'Me?'

'Weren't you the one who insisted we all learned to speak English? You said it would be the global language, that the world was changing and that without it we would be left behind.'

'And look at you now,' he said, feeling stupid, like he was praising a serial killer because he had good grammar. He barely held in the nervous laughter that accompanied that thought.

'I'm not stupid, Pietro. The only reason you wanted us to learn English was that it made us more valuable. All of the visitors spoke English.'

'Visitors?'

The man sighed, tiring of the game. 'We're both men of the world, there's very little to be gained from keeping up the pretence. You know what I'm talking about. We both know what kind of people visited the house. People like Jonas Anglemark.'

'I don't know who you thought Anglemark was,' Danilo said, 'but he worked with the foundation that ran the orphanage. He was a good man.'

'A good man? I am not sure those are the words I would have picked. Good men didn't come to visit us. We both know that. They came for a particular kind of pleasure. I have the names of some. You are going to tell me the names of others.'

Danilo nodded. 'I could do that. If you think it would help you? But do you really want to go back there, if it was so bad?'

Michael reached into his pocket. He took out a single piece of paper. He unfolded it and laid it out flat on the table between them.

Danilo looked at the list of names.

He recognized them all, each and every last one of them. It didn't matter that he hadn't thought about them in decades, or that he wouldn't have known them from Adam if they met. One notable name was missing. 'I don't see Maffrici's name here.'

'The judge? Indeed not. But that is because his crime is a very different one.'

'Ah,' Danilo said, as if that made perfect sense.

'There is still a price for him to pay.'

He continued to read through the names, and realized there were two or three more he could remember that weren't on the list.

It took him a moment more to realize his own name was missing.

But there was one name that should have been at the top of the list, scrawled out in a mad spidery scratch of large letters, underlined, that was nowhere to be seen: the child who didn't keep his promises.

Remember.

He did.

He remembered it all, vividly. It was there, inside him. It lived under his skin.

He remembered all of it.

And until today thought that he had at least made peace with it.

He remembered Bonn.

'There's a lot of familiar names on there,' he said. 'I can't think of anyone you've missed. Though, I'll be honest, it's a relief not to see my name.'

'Why would your name be there? You were a witness. You did not add to our pain.'

'I'm so sorry,' he said.

Michael nodded. 'Can you think of anyone else? Anyone I've missed? It's so hard, sometimes, to let my mind go back there, but it feels like there is a dark shadow I'm missing. Another name.'

It was a trap. Michael knew what name was missing.

He wanted him to say it aloud, as though speaking it would conjure up the devil himself.

He left the name unspoken.

'I think we're done here, Michael,' he said. 'Can I give you a lift anywhere?' Danilo stubbed his cigarillo out, as though to signify their little chat was over.

FIFTY-ONE

Ash gave up and headed back to his hotel.

He'd driven around in circles for the best part of two hours looking for the racing-green Renault. It was a pointless exercise but he felt like he needed to be doing something. There was plenty of traffic, most of it comprising taxis and scooters, their drivers weaving in and out of each other's paths with suicidal abandon. He saw lovers walking hand in hand down the streets eating gelato, and fighters brawling as they spilled out of the bars. What he didn't see was the damned car.

There was a message on his room's voicemail. It was Donatti asking for an update.

He had nothing to tell the Vatican's fixer. What was he supposed to say? 'Oh, I convinced our best hope of finding the killer to hang out in a gay sex club, and lost him'? He looked at himself in the mirror above the desk. He looked like shit. He looked like a man who had just been told he had a week to live, and the bad news was they should have given him his results a week ago. He scratched at the stubble there. There was a good three days' worth of shadow now.

He was dog tired and just wanted to sleep.

He was so conflicted about Donatti. They were friends. Had been friends. Would be friends again. Probably. But the trust was damaged, and the lines between the good guys and the bad had blurred to the point he really didn't know on which side Donatti was operating this time. And until he knew his only option was to leave the Vatican man in the dark. At least until he proved he was working on the side of the angels.

If he was working on the side of the angels.

He packed his bag before he took a shower, and stayed in there nearly forty-five minutes, hands pressed against the wall, letting the heating flense his skin in a ritual flagellation. He was utterly spent when he final collapsed naked on the bed. He didn't even bother climbing beneath the covers.

His knees ached from where he'd fallen onto them. He was getting too old for the abuse the job put his body through, but he'd been *so* close to catching the killer. He'd seen him. Or his silhouette, at least. That was so much more than they'd managed until now. Frankie Varg had said the noose was closing around him. But he'd missed him. Was that it, their one shot?

Maybe.

He didn't want to think that way, but what were the chances of the guy screwing up again, or them getting the jump on him before he picked off his next victim? And what if Pietro Danilo was it, the bottom of the list, the last name? Because he wasn't a mass-murderer, he was a grudge-killer. He was exacting retribution. It was about vengeance. But when he was done, then that was it. He wouldn't be out looking for a fresh victim, he would simply disappear into the ether.

Maybe.

As in maybe they'd get lucky and Laura would be able to pull up a usable CCTV shot of the killer. It was only a couple of years since Rome had embraced the whole Big Brother thing, installing hundreds of cameras across the city, and on all of the famous landmarks, in an attempt to combat the escalating drug crisis they faced, and to deter prostitution. But the system was still new, and he had no idea if she'd be able to use it the same way she could use London's, following the Renault's route across the cameras, or if she'd have to comb through every camera's footage in search of the car, and then have to play a game of time stamps and a process of elimination to piece together a route. That wasn't his problem, but he wasn't holding out much hope, either.

He lay awake staring at the ceiling fan as it turned lazily above his head, wondering if he should just get a flight home first thing in the morning and regroup.

Every time it felt like they were getting somewhere something happened to set them back, and they found themselves without a suspect pool to trawl. By rights, by now, they should have been able to identify at least a small group of suspects, not just Lev Yashin.

The fan had a slight wobble to its rotation on every third revolution. It must have been a loose washer or something. It gave the blades a faint creak.

He couldn't close his eyes.

What did they know?

The EuropaChild Foundation funded orphanages in Eastern Europe. Danilo ran one in Romania. Tournard, Ramirez, and the other victims all had spent time volunteering in the EuropaChild orphanages, and Anglemark was some sort of patron of the foundation.

The foundation had to be the point around which all else pivoted, but how did Bonn fit in? Neither incarnation of the charity had any business in Germany, Maffrici claimed he'd never visited the city.

Any investigation was like building a house of cards, as piece by piece the foundations to support it were put into place, taking the weight, until finally it was there, complete. But all it ever took was one misstep and the whole thing came tumbling down. Bonn was that card that didn't fit, and it undermined the integrity of everything else they thought about what was happening.

But, discount Bonn for a second, that could be something as simple as a conference, something that took them out of the orphanage and into the city, if it was all connected, then it was connected to the orphanage Danilo managed, wasn't it? Romania in the time of Nicolae Ceaușescu was a strange, strange place. The was no way of knowing the kind of horrors hidden beneath that regime.

The ceiling fan wobbled again.

He stood naked on the bed and pulled the plastic chain that sent it revolving in the other direction.

Coming at it from the other direction, if the victims were linked to that Romanian orphanage, then the killer was linked to it, too.

And that meant his name had to be on the list Laura had compiled when she was cross-referencing the victims for a link. A vast number of people had been employed by the foundation, and record-keeping wasn't great, much of the paperwork had seemingly been destroyed in the revolution. Even so, the Ceaușescu regime had fallen in '89, meaning thirty years ago. Anyone working at the orphanage then would almost certainly be retired now, and anyone in their forties or fifties at the time would almost certainly be dead by now, in prison, or getting on for ninety and far too old to fit the profile of an intercontinental serial killer. Even someone in the thirties would be retired by now. Reducing that by another decade whittled down the numbers, but it didn't add up. To do what he was doing, they had to be looking for someone who had been a child. They didn't have to be a long-term resident, just someone who had been there for a few weeks or months, it was enough. And that list included hundreds upon hundreds of undocumented and vulnerable souls.

And how did you go about ruling them out?

One at a time was the answer, but without the proper paperwork surviving it was impossible.

Ash lay awake for half the night, turning it over in his head and getting nowhere. Every now and then he used the voice recorder on his phone to record his thoughts for Laura and Frankie.

The process of talking it through helped clarify his thoughts, even if there wasn't an actual answer there to be found. But that was just it, wasn't it? The answer *had* to be in there somewhere, hiding in plain sight.

The one thing he kept coming back to, as the hours moved from one to two to three, was that along with Maffrici, Danilo had to be up to his neck in it. And Maffrici was connected to Donatti. And Donatti was connected to Tournard. And the ankle bone connected to the shin bone and the shin bone connected to the knee bone – only as he said it he called it in a sing-song voice into the recording, the sin bone, and realized that was more apt than anything he'd said all night.

At five he decided that he'd added as much to the recording as he could, and probably more than he should have, but with his mind purged of the thoughts that had been fighting for his attention he finally closed his eyes and sank back into the pillow, dreaming of a couple of hours' sleep.

FIFTY-TWO

D anilo felt queasy as they emerged from the all-night cafe, but put the weirdness down to the cool night air and the coffee. He reached out for the support of an iron railing and then as he seemed to stumble from one side of the street to the other, the roof of a parked car. He struggled to keep his wits about him, but even as the thought surfaced it was gone, lost in the oncoming daze. He felt nauseous. Michael had dosed him with something; he was sure of it. But how, he hadn't let his drink out of his sight. Caligula's, he realized, his eyelids drooping. He forced himself upright.

He hadn't been on the list.

He was safe.

But what about the missing man?

'I should go,' he said, or slurred. The words sounded elongated inside his head.

Michael held out a steadying hand as they walked to the car. The streetlights blurred like rain across the street as his vision lost clarity and sharpness. The people and cars took on a peculiar haze, losing definition as he tried to focus on them. He blinked back what he thought were tears but couldn't understand why he'd be crying.

He reached into his pocket for his car keys and fumbled them. They hit the road, a timpani chorus in his own tragedy.

'Are you all right?' Michael asked, full of concern. The younger man let Danilo lean on him, support his weight. All the strength seemed to have fled his legs. All he wanted to do was sit. To go down. His mind cackled manically at the double entendre. He didn't find it funny at all. The only sober part of Pietro Danilo's mind was locked in horror, battling for control of his body against whatever had laid siege to his system.

'I'm . . . no . . . it's . . . OK . . . fine.' He tried to say the words but all that emerged was an incoherent mumble.

'Why don't I drive? I don't mind. You look like you need to

sit. We can open the windows. Maybe the fresh air will help? Here,' he knelt to gather the fallen keys, 'let me help you. Let's get you somewhere you can sleep it off.'

Danilo managed another mumble, trying to protest as Michael steered him around to the passenger side. The other man opened the door. He slumped inside, fumbling at the seatbelt. He hands wouldn't obey him. Michael leaned over him and clicked the belt into place. 'Don't worry. I've got you,' he said.

Michael got into the driver's seat beside him, and fired up the engine. They moved away from the kerb, driving well within the speed limit as they left the cafe behind.

That locked-in part of Danilo's consciousness knew what was happening around him but was helpless to exert any sort of control on the rest of his mind. All he wanted to do was close his eyes. There was no plan now. He couldn't run.

Michael talked, but he couldn't concentrate on his words. The dissociative fog filled him mind. He felt the blood in his veins. He felt the hairs along the backs of his arms. His was horribly aware of the churning tumble-dryer nausea churning up his guts. He had no strength to fight whatever was happening to him.

And then he was gone.

FIFTY-THREE

When he came to, all sense of movement had stopped. His eyes were gummed shut. His bones felt impossibly heavy.

'Welcome back, Pietro.'

He grunted. It was barely a sound.

'Don't worry, your head should start to clear soon, though it will hurt for a while. I'm told it feels like a hangover.' It was Michael's voice . . . wasn't it? No. Yes. No. He tried to claw on to what little sense he could find, but he was sure suddenly he was listening to a ghost.

The words of the past.

No.

A voice of from the past.

The accent had changed, but there was something within it that couldn't change. Something that refused to be abandoned, that clung on tenaciously.

He tried to say something, but his lips felt bloated and numb.

'Drink?' he managed, though he could have been asking if the drink had been drugged or if he could have precious water now.

His captor smiled. 'Ah, Pietro, far too trusting, too gullible. It was no fun at all. You thought you'd kill me? Really? Would you really go that far to keep your dirty little secret?' Michael laughed, bitterly. The sound echoed around him.

It wasn't until that moment that Danilo realized he couldn't move his arms or legs. At first he thought it was some residual effect of the drugs in his blood, but then he saw that he was restrained.

He was sitting on a chair, bound in place with electrical tape wrapped round his wrists and the armrests, his ankles, and the chair legs.

'Where am I?'

'Of all the questions you could have asked, that is not the first one I would have expected. Open your eyes, Pietro. Take a look around. Think. Cast your mind back. You might recognize it.'

The only light came from a small table lamp perched on a packing case. The electrical cable snaked away into the shadows beyond the bare bulb's reach.

Danilo blinked again, trying to clear the crust matting his eyelashes. It hurt to look into the light. He began to make sense of what he was seeing around him. How could he not? He was in his own home. The basement.

'You have to love technology. I simply set the satellite navigation to take you home and here we are.'

'What do you want from me?'

'See, now, that's a much better question than where am I. In your place it would have been much higher up my list. But then I'm not you. Like I told you, I don't want *anything* from you. Well, that's not strictly true. I want you to recognize what you did and then to pray, truly and repentantly, for forgiveness.'

'Forgiveness? But I did nothing. You know that. You said so. So said I wasn't on your list.'

'I did, didn't I? But you're right. You did nothing. You did nothing to stop them. You accommodated them, you turned a blind eye to the pleas and begging for help. You were complicit. And maybe you were worse than that? I look at this house and wonder how you could possibly afford it on the money you made at the group home, and I know. I know where your money came from, Pietro. You sold us. One by one. You sold us.'

'That's not true. I worked hard all my life,' Danilo said. 'Everything I have, I earned.'

'I'm sure you did, but the things you learn from dying men . . . they talk because they think you might spare them some ounce of pain. You sold us, and that makes you no better than Anglemark. You might not have fucked us, but you fucked us.'

Danilo strained against the tape, but there was no give in it. The fibres dug into his flesh as he struggled against his bonds, but they weren't breaking.

'It's horrible being helpless, isn't it?'

He said nothing.

'It's the worst feeling in the world, knowing that you're next, that the next time the door opens they're coming for you. Knowing what happens when you try and fight back. They enjoy that. They enjoy breaking your body and your spirit. It adds to their pleasure.'

'I die because I didn't stop them? Is that my punishment?'

'Ah, Pietro, I already told you what was going to happen. Don't you listen? I'm going to give you the chance to repent your sins. I am going to give you time for reflection. To see if you can find clarity. I suggest you use it to make peace with God. Who knows, perhaps it will help you remember people you had thought long forgotten?'

Michael reached out and turned off the lamp, leaving the cellar in total darkness.

He turned on the torch in his mobile phone and made his way to the stairs. Danilo heard his footsteps on the wooden stairs followed by the closing door.

Danilo was alone in the dark.

FIFTY-FOUR

I t was barely 6 a.m. when Frankie picked up the voice memo from Peter Ash.

She saw the time stamp on it, and realized he must have been up most of the night running this stuff over and over. Given his last words, less than an hour ago, were, 'Now I'm going to try and get some sleep,' she didn't call back.

Even if she was an early bird it would still be a couple of hours before Laura got in to River House.

Ash had made a mistake and he knew that.

What happened next would define him; right now he was in the crucible of grief and anger and either it shattered him or he came out, tempered, like steel. She couldn't do it for him, but that didn't mean he was alone.

Despite the fact they'd never met they were in this together, so the question was: what could she do to make things right? She might not be able to carry the guilt or unburden him of the grief, but there were still practical things she could do to take the weight. She thought about heading down to Rome, but his message seemed to indicate he was heading back to London. He'd hit on something in his rambling night-long memo: they should be looking at the children, not just the adults. It made sense. The chronology was such that anyone who had been a child then would be in their thirties or forties now, young enough and fit enough to exact this sort of elaborate scheme. The problem, as far as she could discern, was that Laura was having trouble getting a comprehensive list of children who had passed through the system. The Romanians had burned a lot of the records they'd kept and hadn't kept great records in the first place.

She had convinced herself a lot of them had been destroyed to hide the ugly truth of what went on in those places.

She showered, had a breakfast of hard bread and cheese, and was out of the door half an hour later when her phone rang.

Henrik Frys.

'Francesca? I was hoping you might have some progress to report?'

Frankie sketched out where her enquiries had taken her, confirming that the tongue had turned up in Paris, and what she'd turned up with the secret apartment, all of which she knew he already knew. What he didn't know was that she'd found the basement room where Anglemark had been tortured. And then, to fill in the silence, she explained about Ramirez in Seville.

'You think his death is connected to others? That it is a grand conspiracy?'

'If we just look at the facts, we have Dooley, a suicide just outside of London, Ramirez, a heart attack in Spain, Tournard, an abduction in Paris, Maffrici, a judge in protective custody in Rome, and Pietro Danilo, currently missing. All of these men have received body parts in the mail along with the same warning Anglemark did. These men are all linked, and it is our working hypothesis that they were involved in a charitable trust that operated orphanages in Eastern Europe, notably Romania during the fall of the Ceauşescu regime, and that something must have happened there.'

'All well and good, but your priority has to be closing the Anglemark aspect of this, and as quickly and quietly as possible.'

'With all due respect, sir, that's not the priority. The priority is to stop the killer before he can claim any more lives.'

'Well, yes, of course. I am just thinking about Anglemark's family. He was a good man. The world doesn't benefit from raking over the fine details of his personal life. Secret apartments, dead lovers. It's all very salacious, but all it serves to do is detract from his legacy.'

'Sir, can I just clarify, are you *telling* me to brush this under the carpet?'

'No. I'm asking you to make it go away. Find the killer. We cannot allow this to become another Palme. And do it without destroying a good man's reputation.'

'What if he wasn't a good man?'

'I'm going to pretend I didn't hear that, Miss Varg. And I suggest very strongly you don't repeat it. I would hate for *anything* to impact on your very promising career.'

'Why call me in? In the first place, I mean, if you didn't want me investigating it properly?'

'No one has said that, have they? I most certainly haven't.'

The only reason she could think of, which she wasn't about to give voice to, was that someone higher up the chain had decided she was disposable. It was always good to have a sacrifice to hand.

'I hope we understand each other,' Frys said.

'Oh, I understand you, sir.'

'Good. Very good. Well, that's all. I do wish you the very best of luck, officer. I look forward to your call telling me you've got your man and we can all rest well in our beds.'

'I'm glad you can sleep at night, sir,' she said, and hung up on him.

FIFTY-FIVE

Ash woke to his phone ringing.

He didn't answer it. Eventually it stopped. He gave it another minute or so before he reached over to check who had been trying to call him.

The display said 8:59.

He'd missed three calls from Laura and one from Frankie.

He listened to the voicemails. Frankie's was only two words, 'Call me.' Laura's were a little longer and grew more insistent with each one.

He called Laura first.

'When I call you pick up your fucking phone,' Laura said, no hello. 'I thought . . . I . . . don't do that to me again.'

'Do what? Sorry.'

'Where the hell have you been?'

'Asleep.'

'I've been trying to get hold of you for over an hour and you were asleep? I thought you were in trouble. I was about to call Division and then get the Italian stallions dispatched to check on you. I know what you've been like. I know what losing Mitch did to you . . .' She didn't finish the thought. She didn't need to.

'Sorry,' he said, and he meant it. 'I didn't think.'

'Famous last words. Well, as long as you're all right I guess there's no harm done.'

'I'm fine. So, what have you got for me?'

'I found Danilo's car.'

'Where?'

'The most obvious place. It's in the driveway outside his house.'

'You're shitting me.'

'Nope. Satellite imagery confirmed it was still there as of five minutes ago. I can tell you that you were right, there were two men in the car, but because the Memory Man was in the back seat we haven't got a decent facial image.'

'The who?'

'That's what Frankie's been calling him, the Memory Man. I
kinda like it.'

'I don't. It sounds like something the *Sun* would dream up.'

It didn't make sense. If Danilo had given the guy the slip there
was no way he'd go home. He would have run for the seven hills
around Rome and then kept on running.

He said as much.

'And yet there he is – or at least his car,' Laura said.

'Have you spoken to Frankie?'

'Next on my To Do list.'

'She called me when she couldn't get hold of you. She
has some ideas about breaking down the list. We've started
working on it.'

'Excellent.'

'Go and check out the house. I'll let Frankie know that you're
actually alive.'

'I'll check in later.'

Her heard the start of her making another joke at his expense
but ended the call before she had the chance to finish it.

It was only as he headed down to his hire car that Ash realized what the killer's presence here in Rome meant: Tournard
was dead.

FIFTY-SIX

Time lost all meaning.

Pietro Danilo was consumed by the darkness.

At first, he had actually thought about his sins, and felt guilt, then anger and frustration that he was the one suffering. He wasn't part of this. He hadn't touched the children. He was a good man. He had tried to help them. That was where the money had come from. He hadn't sold access to their bodies, he'd taken payments to facilitate adoptions. But he'd only ever taken money from good homes. He was helping those children to get a new life. A better life. He wasn't the monster here, he was the hero.

He heard something scuttling not far away from him, claws scratching against the concrete floor.

Mouse or rat. It didn't matter.

There was no point wasting his breath crying out for help. The only person who would be able to hear him was the liar who called himself Michael.

He tried to reconstruct the layout of the cellar in his mind's eye, picturing the boxes and shelves scattered around the room, and once he had a very basic memory of the layout, tried to remember what was inside each of them.

Not that he'd be able to wriggle or squirm his way out of the tape that secured him, but it gave his mind something to cling on to.

Perhaps Michael would make a mistake.

It was possible, wasn't it?

There had to be a chance.

It couldn't end like this.

Eventually he heard the door open as Michael returned. The other man walked slowly down the wooden steps, shining the way with the torch from his phone once more.

'There's a light switch just inside the door,' Danilo said. He wasn't sure why he said it. He was already forgetting what

Michael looked like; the features he thought had been burned on his brain during their time in the cafe had become indistinct, the face he remembered now had been moulded and remoulded by fat fingers in Plasticine because of the drugs.

'The darkness is better for you,' Michael assured him. 'You don't want to remember my face when Ash asks you to describe me. It would be a pity if you did. For you.'

'You think he'll come here?'

'Oh yes. He should already be on his way. The car in the driveway is a nice touch. He might even think you've escaped.'

'Then what? He knocks on the door, do you kill him? He's not part of this. Let me talk to him. I can tell him everything's fine. He has no idea who you are. You can still walk out of here.'

'Have you repented yet?'

'You know I'm sorry.'

'I am here to take your confession. Don't you remember how you made us do that?'

'You were one of the children at the orphanage?' He seemed so clear, so rational, and yet he was obviously broken.

He could almost hear the curl of Michael's lips as he told him, 'You made us go into the confessional with one damned priest after another, do you remember? The problem was we didn't have anything to confess, and they didn't want to hear anything but the sucking slurp of our lips on them.'

'But I had no idea . . . I swear. I didn't know until later. If I could go back . . . If I could change things . . .'

'Then what? You'd save us somehow? Please don't insult me. You knew what you were doing when you led us down into the cellar. You knew exactly what was waiting for us as you pushed us stumbling forward into the darkness. You knew about the links, shadows and pain, darkness and light. You knew that and denied us the light, giving us up to the shadows. It didn't matter if we begged. I know, because I did. I begged you as you closed that door and left me alone in the freezing cold with no light, no food, no water, and no idea of how long I would be down there. Do you remember me now?'

Danilo hung his head, not in shame, not in regret. The weight of his actions was coming back to haunt him and he couldn't shoulder the burden.

The children had been difficult. They had behaved like wild animals. They deserved what they got. They needed to be broken, for their own good, or no good family would want to save them. But how could he make Michael understand that everything he had done to them he had done *for* them? He hadn't made them scream. Not when they down there. The darkness broke them, but only so he could put them back together again, like the nursery rhyme.

Was that what Michael was trying to do now? Break him so he could put him back together again?

He wasn't a child. He was a survivor. There was a cockroach's heart beating in his chest. He would do whatever he had to, say whatever he had to, to survive.

Michael produced a bottle of water.

He unscrewed the cap and offered it to Danilo, holding it close to his mouth.

He kept his lips closed, even as a little liquid dribbled down his chin.

He turned his head away.

'You don't want it? I'm being generous, Pietro, more generous than you ever were. Or are you frightened I will drug you again? I don't want to poison you. I don't want to kill you. You saw me break the seal. It's clean. You can drink it. But it's your choice.'

Michael screwed the cap back on and put the bottle down beside the lamp. He wasn't about to let the man know just how much he did want it. 'It's there if you want it,' Michael said, shaking his head as though he couldn't quite believe how stubbornly stupid his prisoner was. He turned the lamp off again. 'Now, I think you should take the next few hours to reflect,' he said. 'If nothing else, it is good for the soul. Isn't that what you used to tell us, Pietro?'

FIFTY-SEVEN

Ash saw the racing-green Renault parked alongside Danilo's house. He parked across the street and watched for a moment. A few hundred metres away a man was walking towards him with a newspaper tucked under his arm. He saw a boy and his dog, and a girl bouncing a tennis ball off the kerb while her mother plucked apples from the trees in the garden. On the other side of the street another man trimmed his hedge. It was a postcard scene. It was a moment of Italian life captured through his car window.

It was hard to imagine anything truly evil flourishing in such a banal landscape of normal suburban life.

But then it was hard to imagine someone receiving a tongue through the mail, or a toe, or a finger or an eye.

He got out of the car just as the same woman that he had encountered the day before walked past with her dog. This time she at least gave him a slight smile before walking on. The dog didn't even pay him that much attention. Perhaps after even one visit he was no longer thought of as a stranger. He smiled to himself and headed up the driveway.

He walked up to the door and hammered on the wood.

No response from inside.

He hammered on the door again, using the side of his fist. He rang the bell, too, then beat on the door a third time.

No answer.

He didn't like it.

The car was wrong. The silence was wrong. Every instinct screamed danger.

He backed away from the door, peering up at the windows for signs of life inside. He couldn't see any. Ash was about to go around the back when the man with the newspaper under his arm appeared at the gate and called out to him.

'Are you looking for Pietro?'

Ash shielded his eyes from the sun. 'Yes,' he said, walking

towards the stranger. He produced his Division ID. The man barely looked at it, accepting the fact it looked official.

'You've missed him. He left a couple of hours ago. Took a taxi. We had a chat. I live a couple of doors down the street. He told me he was leaving town for a few days. Going to visit his sister. He had a lot of luggage for a couple of days.'

'I don't suppose you know where she lives?' Ash asked, knowing the answer was going to be no. Danilo was running. He'd left the Renault because it identified him. The fact Ash had used it to track him had spooked the guy enough. His mobile phone and anything else that might be used in this modern interconnected world to hunt him down was probably on the kitchen table, abandoned.

The man shrugged. 'Sorry. Maybe Milan? I'm sure he mentioned Milan once.'

'Thanks anyway,' Ash said, cursing himself as he walked back to the car.

Leaning against the side of the Fiat he called Laura.

'Do me a favour, Law.'

'I shall use my copious amounts of free time to do your bidding, master.'

'Ha. Just get me an address for Danilo's sister.'

'You got a name?'

'Nope. Honestly, I'm not even sure she exists. I think he's made a break for it. He took a taxi from home, so either the station or the airport. I figure he just told the neighbour he was visiting family to shut him up.'

Twenty minutes later he was driving back towards his hotel, frustrated. The phone rang.

'I'm not sure you're going to want to hear this,' she said.

FIFTY-EIGHT

'He's quite the trusting soul,' Michael said when he turned on the lamp again.

It felt as though he had been gone for hours. The darkness lied like that. It could just as easily have been twenty minutes. Time passed differently in the dark. Danilo had no idea whether it was day or night, never mind what time it was.

His mouth was parched, his tongue furred and swollen. All he could think about was the bottle of water on the table, inches away from where he sat. It might as well have been a mile away. Without the use of his hands he couldn't take it.

'Who?'

'Your friend, Peter Ash.'

'Ash? I've told you, he's no friend of mine.'

'I just had a nice little chat with him. He seems quite concerned about your wellbeing. Of course, he now believes you are visiting your sister.'

'I haven't got a sister.'

'You learn something new every day,' Michael smirked.

'He'll find out, he'll check. He'll work it out.'

'Oh, I do hope so.'

He didn't say anything for fear that panic would creep into his voice. Once you showed fear you were beaten. The weak always gave in. They didn't have the backbone. But he *was* afraid.

'You still think I'm going to kill you? I'm disappointed by just how banal your mind is, Pietro. If I wanted you dead I could have poisoned you in the bar, or in the cafe. I could have slit your throat from the back seat of your car or opened an artery after I taped your wrists to the arms of the chair. I could just stand behind you now, reach around to grip your jaw and break your neck. I don't need to do all of this.'

'But that's not you, is it?' he said, finding courage he didn't know was there. 'That's not what you did to Anglemark though. There is no easy death here.'

'Very good,' Michael said. 'You are right, there is no easy death here. But we are both men of the world, Pietro. We have done things,' and the way he said it made it absolutely clear that in his mind their crimes were far from equal. 'I am neither judge, jury, nor executioner.' Michael laughed. 'I chose this name for a reason. Did you ever think that? Michael. I am the avenging angel.'

The man was crazy.

There was no reasoning with a mad man.

And there was no way of getting free of bonds tying him to the chair. He was helpless; completely helpless.

And that frightened him more than anything.

More than the dark.

More than the memories that lurked there, waiting for him.

Michael produced a packing knife and a hypodermic needle.

Danilo strained against the electrical tape, muscles trembling as the edges rolled and thickened, tearing the hairs form his forearms.

He screamed, not caring that it would only be heard by the avenging angel.

And he prayed.

He prayed that whatever was in the needle would work before Michael began to use the knife.

FIFTY-NINE

'**Y**ou were right.'

'And you didn't think I'd want to hear that?'

'No sister. I've gone through everything. There isn't a single reference to a sister. There was a brother but he's dead.'

'Sister-in-law?'

'Nope. The brother died in his teens. So, like I said, you were right. He's laying down a false trail.'

'Is he though?' Ash said, realizing that he might just have fucked up more spectacularly than he had last night.

'What do you mean?'

'Why tell a lie that can't possibly be true? He knows it'll take two minutes to check on his family and realize that there isn't one. Why not say he's off to visit an old friend, or say anything? Play the conversation through in your own head, "Hey, going somewhere nice?" asks the neighbour, it doesn't need any specifics, does it? You answer, "Just taking a break," or "Oh yes, beach here I come. Do me a favour, keep an eye on the house, would you?" and that's it. You can run the conversation a hundred ways without needing to add lies.'

'Maybe the neighbour got creative? Told you something you wanted to hear?'

'Or maybe the neighbour doesn't know Danilo has no family. Maybe the lie wasn't to protect Danilo. Maybe he's lying to protect himself.'

'You've lost me, Pete.'

He was kicking himself. He should have seen it, but because the guy came from the opposite direction, playing nosy neighbour, he just took him at face value. 'I think I might have just had a cosy chat with Frankie's Memory Man.'

'Jesus, that's a leap.'

'I dunno. Stick with me. He left Danilo in the house, alive or dead, while he went for a walk. He knew we'd be coming. He parked the car out front to lure us there. We took the bait.'

'It's still a stretch,' Laura said. 'But that doesn't mean you're wrong.'

He fell silent for a moment, the implications filtering through his brain.

The signs had been there.

It was obvious in retrospect.

The guy had played him for a fool.

He'd walked right up to him, let him have a good look at his identification, and the man hadn't blinked at the obscure division or questioned what trouble Danilo might be in or ticked any of the usual nosy neighbour boxes. All he'd done was spun Ash a line and he had swallowed it whole.

'He spoke to me in English,' he said. 'Fucker. Spoke to me in English and I didn't get it. Christ.'

'That's not unusual is it, even in Italy?'

'It is when you don't know someone. You don't call out in a foreign language. Fucker knew who I was. He made me in Caligula's so he knew my face. And he knows I'm English because he knows I'm hunting him. I fucked up, Law.'

'But so did he, you got a look at his face.'

He thought about it. He hadn't locked in the guy's features, thinking he'd be doing that to Ash from the end of the driveway. But he could sit down with a sketch artist, they'd get something.

He slammed the steering wheel hard, but it didn't make him feel any better. Danilo was no innocent, but he had let him down twice now. He had a hard time believing there would be a third.

Ash turned on the radio to the first song he'd recognized in this country; AC/DC's 'Night Prowler'. The song thundered in the compact car. Ash caught himself driving to the rhythm of the lead guitar, pushing the little Fiat as fast as it would go.

The drive back to the house took less than half the time.

But it was still more than half an hour since he had driven away. Danilo's racing-green Renault was still parked in the driveway. There was no sign of the neighbour, or the girl with the ball or the mum picking apples. There wasn't a soul to be seen.

Cities have souls, he'd read that somewhere, some philosopher or other. If it was true, then this little place on the outskirts of

Rome *knew*. It knew what was waiting in Danilo's house. It knew
the evil that had walked casually up to Ash with a newspaper
tucked under his arm and lied a man's life away. It knew. And
it had hidden from the moment of discovery, not wanting to
witness it.

Ash walked back up to the door but didn't waste time knocking.
He tried the handle. Locked. He headed around the side of the
property, peering in through the side windows first. There was
nothing immediately wrong inside that he could see. He reached
the side door.

It was wide open.

Ash went in.

He moved cautiously, keeping his steps light, so as not to make
a sound. The house was silent as the grave, save for the single
steady drip, drip, drip of water.

He followed the sound to a downstairs shower room. The air
inside was still moist and a couple of damp towels had been
discarded on the tiled floor.

That wasn't Danilo.

The man was a fastidious prick.

Beads of water dripped from the head into the tiled shower
tray. They added to the sheen of pink-stained water.

Blood.

He moved back into the hallway.

The downstairs was silent.

The killer had moved on, the blood in the shower meaning
he'd done what he came here to do. The doorways led into a
dining room, a lounge with a large wall-mounted television, and
a smaller study with an antique desk. Everything was neatly
arranged, scrupulously tidy. There wasn't a single thing out of
place save for those two towels. He walked through the entire
downstairs, the only sound that of his own breathing.

Another door opened beneath the stairs, he thought it was
going to be a toilet, but instead was to another flight of stairs,
leading down.

The descent was cramped, and the space below shrouded in
complete darkness. He fumbled with his left hand and found a
switch, flooding the stairwell with light from the bare bulb
hanging from the ceiling.

He was only halfway down when he realized there was someone down there, sitting in a chair. Bound and the ankles and wrists. Naked.

Danilo.

Blood pooled around the dead man's feet.

Ash saw the look of abject terror on his face. He'd never seen a death's rictus like it, and with good reason.

Between his flaccid thighs there was a bloody hole where his penis should have been.

Ash felt his gorge rise, but stopped himself from vomiting. He was about to walk away with the meaning of the faint dribble of blood registered. Blood only pumped out when there was a pulse to drive it.

He stepped forward into the blood and reached for the Danilo's neck, feeling the faintest flutter of a heartbeat fading. But for a moment longer at least it was still there.

Danilo's eyes flickered open. There was no sense in them. No clarity. He was blind to the world, lost in pain. But his lips twitched, a sound barely coming from them.

Ash recognized the word even though he still had no idea what it signified.

Bonn.

SIXTY

A sh spent far too many hours in a police station until someone finally made the right call.

He'd radioed in for an ambulance, knowing it couldn't possibly make it because even with the damp towels from the bathroom and the improvised tourniquet he fashioned with his belt, Pietro Danilo was done. Even if he'd wanted to fight on, his body couldn't stand the shock of blood loss and went into cardiac arrest long before it arrived. And it was a mercy that he did.

Ash had seen some truly horrible things, but the Memory Man had stripped Danilo naked and cut off his genitals while he was conscious. It was a level of sickness that was well across the border of psychotic. He'd taken the time to have a shower to remove the blood before calmly walking out of the back door. Who could do that?

Reading the scene, the discarded hypodermic at least suggested Danilo had been out of it on morphine or some other opiate pain med, but not enough to render him unconscious. The killer wanted him awake enough to know what was being done to him.

He'd told the Italian boys in Division, who had liaised with the Carabinieri to ensure the forensic team were there with the first responders. He admitted to his own prints in the middle of the blood, and had taken his shoes off to prevent spreading more tracks around the house and waited for them to bring him in. He played it all by the book, though at one point he did feel like they were treating him like a suspect, which in their place he might have. But finally, Division dispatched their men to vouch for him and he was released, with the proviso that he wasn't to leave the country. He made no such promises.

It was mid-afternoon by the time he returned to his hotel to check out, and almost midnight before he was back in his flat in London, breaking the promise he hadn't made almost immediately.

He kicked off his blood-stained shoes on the doormat and went through to the lounge to put on some music. He was old school, or had reverted to old school, to be more honest about it, and preferred vinyl over CD, so sat in front of the album collection for a moment looking for something to suit his frame of mind. He ended up settling on R.E.M.'s *Eponymous*. He sat in the chair and listened through the first side before he did anything else. The music helped him disconnect, and that dissociative state helped him think. The fact that the first side was only twenty-one minutes long meant he couldn't get lost down that rabbit hole, either.

The killer moved quickly from country to country.

There was no telling where he was now. Not Italy. He'd moved from Spain to Scandinavia and on to Paris and then England before Italy. He didn't stay in one place long.

They didn't even have a name they could use to try to track him; it wasn't as if the airlines would be able to pull up a search for the Memory Man. Though he must have had official paper-work, or at least a convincing enough forgery to open an account in the name of a dead footballer. It felt like they knew less about the guy than when they started, but that wasn't true. He'd looked into his eyes. He'd heard his voice.

He went back through to the hall to pick up the mail that had gathered while he was away.

Bills and junk mail. No one sent real letters any more.

Ash put on side two before he stepped out of his clothes. He could just hear the music above the spray of the water as he scrubbed the Memory Man out of his skin, then towelled himself off, and went back through for a nightcap.

He poured two fingers of decent whisky, and sat on the couch. He didn't want to sit in silence, so, remembering the only song he'd recognized in Italy, decided to sit back and listen to the soundtrack of his future, 'Highway to Hell'.

Bon Scott's vocal was as blistering as it had ever been. There was so much prophecy in it. When the needle followed the groove into 'Night Prowler', a song about one of the US's most famous serial killers, it hit him. Bonn. It didn't have to be the German city, did it? Bon Scott wasn't born Bon, his name was Ronald. It could be a nickname, couldn't it?

He fell asleep in the chair, wrestling with his demons.

His sleep that night was fitful.

His dreams were punctuated by glimpses of Danilo bleeding to death in the chair. Mitch visited him, too, standing behind the cockless man, saying in that laconic way of his that Ash should have saved him, though whether his guilt meant Danilo or his partner his dream state mind couldn't decipher.

It was almost nine when he woke to a knock at the door.

He couldn't remember the last time anyone had done that.

Anyone not living in the block needed to use the buzzer downstairs.

He opened the door a fraction, half-expecting it to be Ethel, his septuagenarian neighbour, bearing leftover lasagne and tutting about how he'd never get a nice lady if he didn't put some meat on his bones.

There was no one there.

He opened the door wider. The landing was empty. He assumed it was the kids from upstairs playing knock-down ginger, then wondered if kids still played that.

He was about to close the door when he saw the package on the floor outside his door.

He knew what it was before he opened.

The package was identical to the one Jacques Tournard had received in Paris, Jonas Anglemark in Stockholm, Dooley, Maffrici, and Danilo. His heart raced, blood surging through his temples as he reached down with trembling hands.

No.

He stopped himself, and ran down the stairs and out of the front door into the street, trying to see where his mysterious mail man had gone. There were half a dozen people out there, heads down as they hustled towards bus stops and the Underground station four streets away. A dozen more came around both corners and others queued at the lights waiting for the green man.

He couldn't see anyone out there who didn't look like they belonged.

He gave up and went back inside.

He picked up the package and carried it into the flat.

Why him? Why send one of the trophies to him? Was the Memory Man telling him that he'd made himself a target? Or was it a parting gift to say it was done now, ended with Danilo, and Ash had failed?

The temptation was to tear it open.

The smart thing to do was bag it and take it to River House and get someone to test it.

He rang Laura and told her he was coming in, and what he was bringing with him.

SIXTY-ONE

Frankie had been at her desk for a couple of hours.

She hated this kind of grunt work. It wasn't why she became a cop.

She wanted to be out there, hunting the killer, not in here hunting a name.

Laura had set up a database, names along with whatever information they had on them, but no matter how she tried to sort and re-sort the stuff into any sort of order she couldn't see anything that the other woman hadn't already flagged and dismissed.

All she could think was that they were both looking at the list in the wrong way. Not that she knew what the right way was.

One thing that niggled Frankie was that one of the names on that far smaller list had died before they'd even realized that there was anything happening. And what that made her think was that it was possible that the Memory Man had been on the hunt for much longer than they thought. Just because they hadn't found other victims didn't mean there weren't other victims.

They'd discounted the dead, because they were looking for future victims.

But couldn't there be other victims within the deceased?

Was it unreasonable to think that way?

Or entirely reasonable?

She was going out of her mind, going round and round in logical circles.

Frankie stood up and stretched, working the muscles in her lower back and shoulders. It was possible, wasn't it?

She collected a mug of coffee from the pot on the hot plate in the break room and returned to her desk.

She called up the list of connections Laura had already identified as deceased. There were a lot of them.

She eliminated anyone who had died more than a year before. That narrowed it down.

Only three people on the list had died within the last twelve months.

One of them had been almost eighty. Laura's two-word note alongside her name was BREAST CANCER.

The second name on the list lacked any concrete detail. There was nothing about the cause of death. She made a note to check with Laura to see what avenues were still to be explored.

The third and final name on the list felt strangely familiar, but for the moment she couldn't place it. The detail that Laura had entered beside it listed cause of death as AUTOMOTIVE DEATH. He hadn't been a young man and could easily have been contacted by the killer in the lead up to the accident.

She needed to know more about the accident.

The name gnawed at the back of her mind.

It didn't take long to realize that the dead man had lived in the southern suburbs of Stockholm, close to her.

The date of the deaths had only been recorded with the month and year, but Frankie was sure that she knew exactly what date he had died on. And she knew where it had happened, because it had been no accident, she was sure of that.

She'd seen it.

The guy in that car had burned alive.

She needed to see the post-mortem report, but she remembered the raging heat inside the burning car as she'd tried to get to Stefan Karius. Would the coroner even be able to tell there was a missing body part, or would the man's corpse have been so badly charred it was basically incinerated?

She filed a request in the system, asking for a copy of Karius's post-mortem, but then grabbed her jacket from the back of the chair.

This was something she needed to check out for herself.

SIXTY-TWO

'What the hell is that?' Laura asked, as the forensic technician teased open the package.

Ash didn't need to ask.

He knew.

The forensics man was painstakingly methodical in his work, doing everything possible to retain the integrity of the packaging and not compromise any potential evidence inside. It wasn't exactly pass-the-parcel, but Ash wished the guy would just rip the packaging off and get down to the meat of it.

Meat.

'Did you go to a convent?' the technician asked.

'Is that—?'

'It's Danilo's penis,' Ash said.

But it was not Danilo's severed genitals that interested him, it was the note that came with the shrivelled meat.

Everyone else had got a note.

'Is there anything else in there?'

The technician nodded, teasing out a small card with a pair of tweezers that he slipped into a plastic evidence bag.

Ash read it.

'*Si vis veritatem cognoscere Bonn*' followed by the name of a bar in Paris.

Ash only had a smattering of Latin, most of it gleaned from movies, like Carpe Diem, but he knew what it meant: *If you want to know the truth about Bonn.* The only reason he had any idea what it meant was because Veritatem cognoscere was the motto of the CIA.

'I can make it if I leave now.'

'I'll call Etienne Reynard, get you some backup in place.' She was already reaching for the phone. She saw the look on his face and cut him off. 'I don't want to hear you say you can handle it on your own.'

'I have an advantage, though. I know what he looks like.'

'Big help that is,' she said.

'Book me on the next Eurostar.' He didn't wait around to argue. He was already on his way for the door. 'I'm not going to take any risks.'

'That's what Mitch always used to say.' She cut him down with those seven words. He stopped in the doorway.

'I'm coming back. I promise.'

'You better,' she said.

A ping on his phone confirmed receipt of his booking before he pulled away.

The killer had allowed him enough time to get to Paris, barely. He was going to be travelling for the best part of six hours. A flight would be quicker in theory, but with travel to Heathrow, sitting around a couple of hours before take-off, and all the rigmarole of passport control and security, the train was just easier.

SIXTY-THREE

Frankie had probably driven along this street a thousand times. More. She'd even looked at an apartment around there when she first moved to the city.

They had been a little out of her price range then and were more than three times that now. Property prices inside the city had exploded over the last decade or so. Older people who'd bought into the area before the turn of the millennium were sitting on a gold mine.

The address that Laura had entered in the log was a maisonette in a house that had been divided between the five floors. His was the penthouse, top floor and attic. The developer had gone upwards rather than down in terms of trying to squeeze value out of the property.

Unlike Anglemark's bolthole this place was beautifully maintained, the gardens outside the door manicured, the interior freshly painted. It was a proper character place. The penthouse apartment had flower boxes that brimmed over the top of what looked like a large terrace.

Each of the apartments had a separate entrance off the main hallway, and there was a wire-caged elevator that ran up to the top floor. Even that looked well maintained. She didn't go inside. Instead she went around the side. She knew what she was looking for. The rear of the building took her out of the view of the street, but there were still central gardens overlooking the courtyard.

Frankie climbed the fire escape up the side of the building, intending to go in through the terrace.

It was a long climb, meaning plenty of time for someone to see her. At the top, more than fifteen metres from the ground, she clambered over the flower boxes and dropped down onto the terrace. There was a large plate-glass window, and a door. The entire length of the terrace was looked out on by that window, meaning she could see into the whole of the apartment from out here.

It reeked of money.

Serious money.

Frankie tried the handle tentatively, knowing it would be locked. The window was a single sheet of plate glass, triple-thick. She wasn't going to be able to break it.

She took her jacket off, wrapping it around her fist, then punched out the glass around the door handle. It made a terrible racket that echoed what felt like miles because of the height, but the reality was even if someone heard it on the street they wouldn't have been able to place it.

She opened the door, breaking into the dead man's house.

Beyond looking for next of kin, there was no reason for the beat cops to come traipsing through the place. The place was a huge open-plan area with iron stairs that curled up towards bedrooms in the eaves. The place must have been worth ten million kroner, easily. More. The furniture was styled, designer. The art cost more than a year's salary. There was no television, she realized, then saw the recessed projector in the ceiling which, she assumed, would turn one entire wall into a cinema screen for viewing. Nothing about the place looked lived in.

The only phone was actually for the intercom system. This was the modern life. People didn't have landlines any more, it was all cellular. It also meant the owner was unlikely to have a physical address book for them to go through for points of inter-section with Laura's list.

Upstairs she found a wet room and a vast bedroom.

There was one other door up on this level. She pushed it open. It held a single unmade bed pushed up against the wall, and a small bedside cabinet with a lamp on it.

Behind the door was a cheap desk and chair, the kind she'd expect to find in a kid's bedroom. It was completely at odds with the lavish decor of the rest of the apartment.

There was a whiteboard on the wall above it.

It took a moment for her to realize what she was looking at, a moment for her brain to take it in and make sense of it all.

What she saw changed *everything*.

Frankie felt a mixture of anger, shock, and elation at her discovery as she fumbled in her pocket for her phone.

She was taking a picture of the board when she heard the groan of floorboards and turned to face the barrel of the gun aimed squarely at her face.

SIXTY-FOUR

Before he arrived in Paris the call came through that Tournard's corpse had been fished out of the Seine.

There was symmetry in that. Like Anglemark. The killer liked to dump his bodies in water.

Ash didn't know if that was going to help him, but every little detail helped build an understanding of the man he was going to meet.

He reached the bar with barely twenty minutes to spare.

He had had a moment of clarity on the Eurostar; the killer knew where he lived and must have known who he was even before he set foot in Caligula's, looking to trap him.

But how could that be?

The bar was dimly lit, most of the tables occupied by couples. It was an intimate environment for the killer to choose.

Patterns of behaviour.

Did that mean he had access to a place nearby?

Was he expecting Ash to willingly walk out of here with him and sit there happily whilst he cut his cock off?

'Not happening,' Ash said to himself.

He'd parked the hire car in a multi-storey car park five minutes away. He had considered getting a taxi, but he didn't want to be stuck chasing the guy if he bolted.

Only three of the tables had single occupants.

Ash walked straight up to the third table as the man pushed out the chair opposite him with his foot.

'Peter Ash.'

'You have me at a disadvantage,' Ash said as he sat down. He took a good look at the man this time, locking in everything about him. The lines of skin around his mouth and eyes said sixties, but he had the muscular physique of someone much younger. He was tanned. With dark, close-cropped hair.

'You can call me Michael if you like,' the man said and pushed one of the two glasses of beer already on the table in his direction.

Ash had no intention of drinking it.

He called a waiter over and ordered a bottle of Evian.

'The beer not to your taste?'

'I'm on duty,' he said.

The man shrugged and took a long draw on his own then pulled the other towards him. 'Waste not, want not.'

'So, Michael, what's so important that you had to drag me over here rather than just meet in London? It can't be the beer.'

'What I need to show you is here, not in London.'

'Why not just tell me in Rome? I could have saved some air miles.'

Michael laughed. 'So perhaps you aren't useless, after all. I wasn't sure you would remember me.'

'So, you're not denying that you killed Danilo?'

The man took another drink. 'Why would I deny anything? If you're half as good at your job as you seem to think you are I'm sure that you have a wealth of evidence – more than enough to arrest me. But I don't think that's why you are here.'

'Why not?'

'If you wanted to arrest me you would have turned up here with a posse in tow.'

'How do you know that I didn't?'

'I know people.'

'That's a big risk to be taking, Michael. Because right now there's so much shit going on inside my head I don't even know what I'm going to do next.'

'And yet you still came alone.'

'I did. So, in your head, what happens next? When you've showed me whatever you need me to see, what happens then?'

'Then I'll just slip away and you never hear from me again.'

'What makes you think I won't stop you?'

'It doesn't matter if you do, Peter. There's nothing you can do to me that God hasn't already. I'm dying. I'll be long gone before any trial.'

'Sucks to be you,' Ash said, not sure if he believed him. Maybe it was true. Using your remaining time to exact revenge on people who had crossed you was a strong motivation. As strong as any.

His phone rang.

'It could be important,' he said, but didn't reach for it.

'Not more important than talking to me,' Michael said.

'I guess not. So, how about you show me yours, Michael.'

SIXTY-FIVE

Frankie stared at the screen of her phone for a moment. Her call had rung through to voicemail.

It had taken her a good sixty seconds of fast talking to steady the trigger finger of the nervous young cop who'd found her inside Karius's apartment. She explained, and explained again, telling him she was taking out her ID, showing him it, telling him he could call into Division, or contact Henrik Frys, he would explain, and eventually he'd lowered the weapon.

He took her identification from her and called through to dispatch on his radio.

A second officer stepped into the room and watched her as she made her own call. He didn't stop her. His sole role was to make sure that she didn't bolt.

'How did you know I was here?'

'A neighbour called it in. She knew the place was empty because the owner died recently. You shouldn't have broken in. Not without a warrant. The law has to apply to all of us.'

'Good in theory,' she said, 'shit in practice. Sometimes you do what you have to do. Believe me, if I could tell you more, I would, and you'd understand.'

'Try me.'

But before she could, the other officer returned and handed her badge and ID back. 'We're to help you with whatever you need.' The sudden acquiescence earned him a quizzical look from his partner. 'That's all they said.'

The two men waited for her to tell them what she wanted them to do.

'What are we looking at?' the first officer said, joining her to look at the whiteboard.

'Looks like a list of dates, times, and places,' the other said. 'What does at all mean?'

Frankie told them. 'These dates match the dates of a number

of disappearances. Two of them,' she pointed at the corresponding dates on the board, 'have already turned up dead.'

'Maybe he was just following the case in the news? Plenty of weirdos do that. Get obsessed with true-crime stories.'

His partner didn't disagree with him.

Frankie didn't want to make these two men feel stupid, but it looked like she was going to have to. She didn't have to. His partner saw the discrepancy.

'Hold on, Jens. Look at that one, and that one. Some of these dates, the guy who owned this place was dead by then.'

'Then how could he have known? Psychic? I don't fucking think so.'

The answer was obvious, because there was only one answer it could be. When you come right down to it, the obvious answer was always the best. Strip away convoluted theories about accomplices and psychics and you got the only reasonable solution. Whoever she'd seen burn in that car hadn't been Stefan Karius.

Karius wasn't dead.

'I want you to tear this place apart. You're looking for proof. Anything at all. Computer, notebook, diary, anything. Got that?'

They nodded.

They couldn't all search this small room, so she sent one to the master bedroom and the other back downstairs.

An hour later she was beginning to doubt herself.

Half an hour after that she was resigned to the point of giving up when it hit her:

Why hadn't he wiped the whiteboard clean?

He'd left proof right there in plain sight.

That was unlike the Memory Man in every other regard.

That was his mistake. It linked him to this place, this name.

They'd pulled open the drawers and turned them out to check the liners, they'd rifled the wardrobes and everything else. They'd double- and triple-checked them.

It was only when she went around behind them, putting things back in their places, that she found she couldn't close one of the small drawers. Something was stopping it from closing flush, which left the front protruding by a few extra millimetres, but in an apartment so immaculately designed this singular lack of attention to the perfection in the details was jarring.

Instead of trying to force it closed, Frankie pulled the drawer all the way out.

And there it was, stuffed into the back; a loose-leaf binder.

She flicked through pages of handwritten notes, photographs, schedules, and itineraries.

When she saw Jonas Anglemark in one of the pictures she knew that she'd got him.

The two officers came into the room and saw her on her knees, going through the file.

'We've got him,' she said.

She needed to speak to Ash and she needed to do it quickly.

His phone went straight to voicemail again.

SIXTY-SIX

Ash had walked out of there willingly with Michael.

Michael had been insistent that he drive. His car. Not Ash's. He went along with it. He wasn't happy about it. But he still felt in control, though he heard Laura's voice nagging away at the back of his mind reminding him that that was how Danilo and Tournard and everyone else had felt, too.

'What I'm going to show you, the evidence I'm going to show you, is bigger than any crime you've faced in your career. It deserves the attention of the world. The understanding. And that only happens with you, because of who you are. Otherwise it will just be cleaned up.'

'What makes you think that?'

'Because that's what they do. All of them.'

'Who is "all" supposed to be, Michael? I want to understand.'

'Politicians, judges, the Church. They all watch each other's back. Everything gets cleaned up. Sanitized. They live a life of lies.'

'So, tell me about it, you can trust me.'

'Can I? Or are you trying to control the situation? What do they call it, hostage management? If you had realized who I was when we met in Rome you would have arrested me, wouldn't you? You would have chosen to save Danilo over exposing the true crimes of him and his kind, even if I had told you. You wouldn't have listened. Because it doesn't fit your narrative. And then they would have made me disappear to make absolutely sure the truth didn't come out.'

'How much further?' Ash said.

The light was starting to fade.

'Not far. Once upon a time you would have been able to see it from here.'

'See it? See what?'

'The orphanage where I grew up.'

'And these people, the ones you killed, they were all connected with it?'

'Yes.'

'Not Romania?'

'No. Not Romania. The foundation grew considerably over a relatively short period of time. Romania was Danilo's reward for running such a profitable institution here.'

The car slowed and came to a halt in front of a sign that warned people to keep out.

In the fading light Ash could just make out the outlines of a large building's foundation in the overgrown landscape, where weeds ran riot, nature reclaiming the place for its own. He had the weirdest sense of déjà vu upon seeing the place.

'This is it,' Michael said, killing the engine. 'Come on.' He climbed out of the car. Ash did likewise.

'What happened to it?'

'Demolished. To hide the secrets that they wanted to keep hidden.'

'And this is what you wanted to show me?' He gesticulated towards the dark outline of what might have been a scullery wall or a bedroom or the refectory, or just about anywhere else within the huge orphanage when it had still been standing.

Michael moved to the rear of the car and opened the boot. 'You'll need these,' he said, nodded toward the spade and torch that were inside. 'It's going to be dark before you've seen enough.'

Ash didn't ask any more questions.

Michael slammed the boot and led the way though a gap in the wire fence. There were lights on in a house further up the road, more than half a mile distant. There were no other lights to be seen. They had well and truly left the city behind. And he'd been so wrapped up in trying to unravel the conflicting threads in his head that he'd barely noticed it.

Flickers of long-buried memories struggled to the surface of his mind.

He had no idea of where he was.

'Why not wait until morning?' he called, following Michael, deeper into the wasteland.

'The ghosts deserve to be at peace,' Michael said. It wasn't any kind of answer. Ash followed in the man's wake, allowing him to stay a few steps ahead of him. The was an eerie familiarity about the shadows. Michael paused every now and then to check his bearings. Remembering. 'It has changed a lot since I was last here. The trees are so much bigger now. It is as though the land has tried to purge the evil, swallowing it whole. It is barely recognizable.'

'How long since you were last here?'

'Almost fifty years.'

'It's hardly surprising that things have changed, then. Why come back now?'

'A chat with an old friend and his son.'

He stopped walking and turned, looking back at the building to get his bearings, before he pointed at one of the trees. It was a great oak, dominating the garden. Pete had seen that tree before. He was sure he had. But that made no sense.

'It was much smaller in my memory, but this is the place,' Michael said

'Are you going to tell me what I'm looking for?'

'Just dig, you'll know when you find it.'

'And you're sure this is the right place?'

'All around here is the right place, trust me.'

'And I'm not just digging my own grave?'

'Just dig,' Michael said again. He shone the torch at a patch of dark ground. 'There will do.'

The quickest way to find the truth was to do as he was told. It was also the quickest way to ending up six feet under. Still, Ash took his jacket off and handed it to Michael before he used the spade to mark out a shape in the grass. He lifted the turf to expose a patch of worm-filled earth a metre square.

'Here?'

Michael nodded.

He dug, driving the blade of the spade into the black earth, and worked it free, tossing it aside. He repeated the motion again, and again. It took him two minutes to dig down deep enough that he hit something hard. His first thought was that it was a stone, but Michael shone the torch into the hole.

'Look,' he said.

Ash crouched down, reaching to the hole with his hands to scrape away some of the earth that had fallen from the sides to backfill the hole.

He was wrong.

It wasn't a stone, it was a bone.

He clawed away at the earth, scooping handfuls out of the hole as he widened it, to expose more. A clavicle. A pelvis. Both under-developed; a child's bones. He scrambled frantically, digging out more and more of the earth with his bare hands, tearing at his fingernails as he clawed up fistfuls of the stuff. Within five minutes he'd exposed three more skulls.

Michael shone the torchlight across the patch of land. 'They're all along here.'

'Who are they?' Ash asked, though he already knew the answer.

'Keep digging, you need to see.'

'I need to call this in. We need a full forensics team here to take this place apart. With every handful of earth I'm destroying the scene.'

'Not yet. They've been here all this time, that can wait until morning for their justice. I need you to dig. You will understand. I promise. I need you to see what happened here so that you believe me.'

'I don't need any more convincing,' Ash said.

'You do,' Michael contradicted him.

There was no way he'd stumbled upon the only bones here, not from memory over fifty years old. Michael had already told him, they were everywhere. All around here was the right place.

He believed him.

Ash bent his back and started to clear another patch of damp earth.

He found another bone, and another.

Michael shone the light down on them. Like he needed to see them. All of them. Two could never be enough. He needed to shine a light upon them all.

'There,' Michael said, pointing at another patch of dark earth. 'Dig there now.'

Ash did as he was told.

It took longer this time find strike the first bone, the body was buried deeper.

It was backbreaking work. But it was necessary. Good, even. These poor children. They needed someone to speak for them.

He could understand what had driven Michael to such extremes.

He could see himself doing the same thing, and that placed a chill deep in his gut, because, but for the grace of God, there went Peter Ash.

He straightened up, kneading the small of his back.

He ached.

A sudden sharp pain lanced through his shoulder.

Ash reached up, caught more by the surprise than actual pain, and found the hypodermic still sticking in his flesh.

He fumbled, trying to pull it out, but the plunger was already depressed, the drug working its way into his system. The fine motor control fled from his fingers as the world turned black.

He fell.

SIXTY-SEVEN

Frankie sat in her car and flicked through the file, willing Peter to either pick up the phone or return her call.

She'd called him twelve times and stopped herself from calling a thirteenth. Not out of any sort of superstition, more because she felt like a fool.

He'd call her back.

His phone was off. It rang straight through to voicemail. His battery was probably dead. For all the good these new smartphones delivered, the sheer lack of battery life was a constant frustration.

She recognized several of the names in there, but there were many more that weren't on Laura's list.

Each page had a photograph or a cutting from a newspaper pasted to it, an address, a telephone number, a proposed meeting place, like a twisted scrapbook. It was a dossier on the foundation, the orphanages it ran, and so much more. It was Karius's hit list. It detailed all manner of details about the targets, intimate stuff that demanded surveillance and time.

She worked through the pages, seeing Tournard and Danilo and Anglemark and others she didn't recognize. Men who had means, men who supported the charity with substantial donations. Men, she realized sickly, who paid for access to those vulnerable children.

One of them, she realized, was the face of the man she'd watched burn.

She brought up the photograph of the whiteboard she'd taken, checked the name and date against those in the dossier, and took a photograph that she attached to an email for the coroner, along with a two-line explanation to run his details against the corpse they'd assumed was Karius.

Frankie turned the final page and saw a much younger face staring at her. The man in the photograph must have been twenty or thirty years younger than anyone else in the dossier. The name written out painstakingly in neat block capitals was PETER ASH. Beside it was all sorts of personal information. It was all there, job, address, even down to habits like his preferred coffee shop along the Thames, his routine walk to work, his dead partner, even details about a one-night stand including where the woman had picked him up and his drink of habit. The inference was obvious, not only had Karius been watching Ash, he had been interfering with his life for months.

She needed to talk to Ash. To warn him. This was personal for the killer, and it ended with Ash. She had no idea why, but he was right in the middle of this.

She did the only thing she could: she rang Laura.

'Have you talked to Ash? I can't reach him.'

'He's in Paris,' Laura replied.

'Paris?'

She listened as Laura told her about the package and the rendezvous.

'And he went? You didn't stop him?'

'There was no stopping him.'

'He's in trouble,' she said.

'All I've got is the address for the meet.'

'When is it supposed to happen?'

There was a moment's pause before Laura replied. 'An hour ago.'

Frankie's mind raced. There was no way they were still in the bar, but that was the only reference point they had. 'Give me the number, I need to call the bar. If he's there he can't leave. Not with the man.'

'What's going on?'

Frankie told her about the dossier, and the last target. She took photographs of each page and sent them through to Division, including the link to Karius, the man she'd thought she'd seen burn to death. Laura's fingers were already flying across the keyboard as she ran all sorts of searches around that name.

'Why Peter?'

'I don't know,' Frankie said.

'I can't lose him, too,' the other woman said. Frankie understood. She knew what she needed to say, but she wasn't in the habit of making promises she couldn't keep.

'Contact Reynard. Pull every resource we have. He's not alone.'

'Already on it,' Laura said.

She hung up and called the bar. It took a while for anyone to answer. It was loud and hard to hear.

'I need to talk to a customer,' she said.

'Impossible. Sorry.'

'It's not. You're going to make it happen. This is a matter of urgency. I am with the Eurocrimes Division of the European Union, you're going to find out if there is an Englishman in your bar. His name is Peter Ash. I don't care if you have to walk around every single table and ask each man their name, you're going to find out if Ash is still there.'

'Is this some kind of joke?'

'No. I don't have time to argue with you. Just do it, unless you want to face charges of aiding and abetting in the act of murder.'

That one word did it.

The woman on the other end of the line cupped her hand over the phone as she lowered the music. Frankie heard her ask in French if there was a Peter Ash in the bar, and then again in English. The babble of voices returned, the music right behind them.

'You heard me ask,' the girl said. 'There's no one here by that name.'

She hung up before Frankie could ask if anyone remembered seeing Ash or anyone who matched his description.

She had the photograph of Peter Ash staring back at her.

'I won't let you down,' she told it.

She was banking on Laura coming through with everything she could find on Karius, and fast. She needed to see his photograph, either via the Passport Office records or from the driver's licence.

Why Ash?

Why was he in that dossier?

What had he done to Karius? All of the men in there had failed the Memory Man in some way or other. How had Ash failed him? How had he earned his place on Karius's grudge list?

Her only hope lay in the fact that he had an established pattern. He wouldn't just kill Peter. He'd hold him somewhere first, like Anglemark and Tournard. He'd held Danilo, even if only for twelve hours. There was something he wanted from Peter. There had to be. That was the only thing that could account for the time the others spent in captivity. The longer they held out, refusing to give Karius whatever it was he wanted, the longer they lived.

He was English. That had to count for something, didn't it? Every Englishman she'd ever met had been a stubborn bastard.

She prayed that he didn't break the rule.

'Where are you? Where would he take you?' she asked the photograph, then started flicking back through the pages of the dossier, hoping there might be something in there that would give her a clue.

SIXTY-EIGHT

A sh woke in agony.
His shoulders screamed with a pain his brain could not understand.

He remembered the needle.

He remembered trying to pull it out of the muscle and his legs betraying him. He remembered very little after that. Fragments of sound. The sensation of hands on him. That was it.

He opened his eyes.

Coloured rays of light streamed in through a stained-glass window. Meaning it was morning. He didn't recognize the place, but it had to be a church or a chapel. It smelled cold and damp. Unused.

Somehow, he was upright. How could he be standing? The angles were wrong. He was higher than the pulpit, looking down. He realized why his shoulders burned so desperately; his arms were outstretched and his ankles were tied together with electrical tape. Symbolically at least, he was being crucified.

'Ah, Peter, you are awake, good,' Michael said, rising from one of the pews. 'I was beginning to worry that I had given you too much of the sedative and that you might never wake. That would have been a pity.'

'You could have just killed me and saved yourself a lot of waiting,' he said.

'No, no, no. You still don't get it, do you? I promised that you would learn the truth.'

'I thought you showed me that last night.'

'Dear boy, that was only a fraction of it.'

'Then tell me, unburden yourself, and we can get this over with. I don't feel like hanging around,' Ash said.

'You're a funny man, Peter. I didn't expect that. I did expect the death wish though. So few people can face so much personal tragedy and hold themselves together. They put on a mask to face the day, but underneath that mask, that's where their pain lives. I understand you. I know you. Better than you know yourself.'

'You talk a lot for a man who isn't saying much,' Ash said, goading Michael. It was the exact opposite of the hostage-negotiation playbook. He should have been placating the man, listening to him, making deals.

But if he was going to die, he was damned if he was going to go meekly into that endless winter. Fuck it, rage, and all that. No one was going to save him. No one even knew where he was to do any white-knight saving.

'You are very predictable, Peter. There's so much anger in you. You should let it out. Cleanse yourself. Go to your final meeting with your namesake pure,' Michael said.

'Hate to break it to you, Michael, but there is no God.'

'You say that too easily. But you are right. And this place and what happened here is proof of it. You must know that already.'

'I've seen the bones of children in the grounds. You tell me it was an orphanage. How do I know it wasn't some alms hospice or a battle ground, or hell the scene of some horrible Nazi war crime? I don't *know* anything.'

'We lived in fear, all of us, boys and girls. It didn't matter. They didn't care. They didn't differentiate. We were meat. We knew what happened to the kids who didn't do what they were told, and we were promised that the good kids, the ones who did, they were adopted. They found new families. Some were reunited with long-lost relatives. We were told they were getting the fairy tale. They were being saved. But we knew the truth.'

'Are you telling me they were, what, charging people to experience the thrill of killing a child? Profiting from death?'

'They said that the devil was in us. They told us they had to drive him out.' Michael was lost to the memories now, earning the crude nickname Frankie had given him. 'They made us beat ourselves over and over, until we bled down the lengths of our spines from deep lacerations. It was the only way we could prove that we loved God. That we gave ourselves to Him. What kind of god demands a child does that, Peter? What kind of god?' He didn't wait for an answer. 'And they punished us. There's a lake. It's not far away. Eight hundred metres from the main building. They made us run naked to the far side, swim across, and then run back inside again while all the other kids were forced to watch. I saw one boy drown trying to swim it in the middle of winter. The shock of the icy water was too much for his weak body. This wasn't to *prove* anything, you see. This was a warning to everyone watching. Do what you are told. Obey.'

'And did you?'

'Not always. There would be new children arriving all the time. Two or three a week. We told them what happened, we warned them, but they didn't believe us. Why would they? No one wanted to believe that their salvation could be so twisted. They thought we were making up stories, that we were trying to scare them. They learned the hard way. Believe me. They were locked in the cellar and left there. Sometimes they were down there for a day or two, alone in the dark, no food, only a little water. Other times it was as though they had been completely forgotten about. But then one of the priests would come with a story about their new family.'

'But you knew different?'

'There would always be a new mound in the garden. Black earth that had been freshly dug. So many of them. And nothing to mark where they lay.'

'I'm sorry,' Ash said.

'Your apology means nothing to me. That isn't why I brought you here. And I have no need for your pity.'

'Was Danilo one of them? One of the men who gave out the punishments?'

'He was the worst. And they rewarded him for it. Giving him a new hell to rule over in Romania, where he was protected. Imagine this, Peter, they would beat any boy they found touching themselves. Whip them with the metal edge of the belt buckle. There was one boy, William, who couldn't stop himself. He was simple, that was the word they used for it back then. Simple. Simple William. He was the politician's favourite. He taught him to pleasure himself. Watched him. He never did any harm, he was the sweetest child, but he couldn't stop. He thought it would make them happy, like it made Anglemark happy, to watch him. They would catch him at night. Night after night, they would come for him.'

'And Danilo beat him because of it?'

'Oh no, Peter, Pietro Danilo was the devil. He did not resort to crude lashes when he could dispense true agony. Danilo cut his penis off in front of us. He used a bread knife. He heated the blade in a coal fire. Poor William. He didn't understand. He thought they were going to save him, because that's what they kept telling him. They offered him salvation. I can still hear his screams. Then they took him away. We never saw him again.'

'Jesus Christ.'

'He has nothing to do with this place. Danilo held the knife. He did that. And he did it with a smile on his face.'

'So, you took his penis in return. Justice. What about the others? The eye? The tongue? What had they done to deserve your punishment?'

'They used us any way they wanted. Danilo was a sadist, enjoying inflicting pain. Others came to satisfy their sexual predilections. They enjoyed the girls; they enjoyed the boys more. If we didn't do whatever they wanted, we were beaten until they broke us and we did it anyway. For some it would become too much. They would try to kill themselves. Sometimes they succeeded.'

Ash was struggling, his body was in torment, but it was nothing beside his mind. He believed every word no matter how much he didn't want to. He shook his head. 'How long have you been planning your punishment?'

'There are not many of us left, Peter, victim or abuser, but I've been planning this for most of my life in one way or another. It became a concrete plan a year ago when I realized I no longer had the luxury of time.'

As Michael spoke, Ash thought he caught a flicker of movement in his peripheral vision; at the back of the church, a shadow. The light was playing tricks on him. Or the pain. He was balanced on his toes, barely taking the strain from his shoulders, but he couldn't keep that precarious balance for ever. Sooner, rather than later, his feet were going to slip from the wooden block supporting them, and his arms would be torn from their sockets.

He gritted his teeth against the pain. There was one question he needed to ask. 'Why am I here? How have I failed you?'

'I did wonder when we would get to that. There was a boy, he was older than the rest of us. He saw what was going on, but to be painfully blunt he wasn't young enough or pretty enough for the visitors to want to pay for him. So he ingratiated himself with Danilo, making himself useful. You know the sort, the devil's right hand. The thing was, he was growing, and growing fast. He was a big lad, and only getting bigger. It wouldn't be long before he was big enough to fight back. That made him dangerous.'

'I can imagine,' Ash said.

'One night he came into our dormitory and asked for our help. He was going to escape. It was a grand thing. It filled us with hope. I hate hope. I can't begin to tell you how much I hate hope. He had it all figured out. He needed us to cover for him when Danilo did his rounds at curfew. He promised me, he looked me in the eye and promised he was going to tell the world what was happening to us. He was going to get help.'

'And that's how it was shut down? He saved you?'

'Oh for fuck's sake, you really are naive for a policeman, Peter. Saved? We never heard from him again. He got out and he ran. He made himself a new life. He forgot all about us. We waited. He never came. Some of us thought he'd been caught and was under one of the trees, food for the worms. Danilo made sure we paid for helping him escape. He lit a fire in the big hall. He had us suspended over the red-hot coals, burning the soles of our feet. One by one he brought us to the fire pit and hauled us up over the flames. One by one he broke us. We were children. Someone was always going to be weak enough to confess our part in the escape. We held out for six hours, Peter. Six hours of torture, to buy him the time to run. And he abandoned us.'

'Or you were right and they caught him,' Ash said. He did everything in his power not to look towards the back of the chapel as he caught another flicker of movement. He didn't want to look, for fear of drawing Michael's attention to it. He didn't want to hope, because waiting to be saved was a chilling parallel to the Memory Man's story.

Michael laughed, a short, bitter, mirthless bark. 'He didn't die. He escaped. He made it to England. I only found out a year ago, and he was already dead by then.'

'Too late to face him,' Ash said, feeling his balance go and struggling desperately to right himself before his weight pulled him forward.

'And that is why you are here, in his place. Because I cannot face him.'

Ash shook his head, still not grasping how he fitted into such an elaborate – and personal – revenge.

'But why me?'

'Because he was your father, Peter, and it is our curse to suffer for the sins of our fathers.'

SIXTY-NINE

'**N**o. You're wrong,' Ash said, but he knew he wasn't. It explained the birthday pilgrimage to orphanages to give presents. Survivor's guilt. It explained the memories of the sign and the tree. He'd been here before. His father had brought him here to show him his biggest regret without ever admitting he had failed the ones he'd left behind. It was a devastating truth. Christ, how could he have lived all those years with that inside him?

'I am not wrong, Peter. Believe me. My research is thorough.'

Ash shook his head in both refusal and denial, but Michael was no longer paying any attention to him. Instead, his tormentor set about gathering stacks of prayer books and casting them across the stone floor around Ash's feet.

Forty, fifty, one hundred, he gathered everything that would burn, and built what would become the pyre before the altar.

And there was nothing Ash could do about it.

He tested the restraints but couldn't pull his wrists clear of the crucifix holding him upright and couldn't break the bonds tying him to it. He mustered every ounce of strength he had, but without the leverage couldn't force so much as a creak out of the old wood. All that he succeeded in doing was losing his precarious footing, and put all his weight on his wrists, spread-eagled and in agony.

The sudden surge of pain tore a cry from him as he kicked out desperately trying to find his footing again.

'Save yourself the pain, Peter.' Michael threw another pile of prayer books onto the pyre. 'The cross might not be as strong as it was, but it's more than strong enough to hold you while the smoke eats into your lungs and the fire chars your skin.'

It didn't stop Ash trying. He tensed his muscles, testing the bonds again.

Beneath him, Michael went back to one of the pews where he had stashed a petrol can. He uncapped it and began to calmly splash petrol on the pile of books. The stench was incredible.

He needed time.

He felt the electrical tape bite into his wrists as he strained desperately against it. There was no give left in it. He couldn't rub it against the wood, trying to build up friction and saw through it. It wasn't about to snap.

He wanted to rage but could barely muster a whimper. 'You haven't told me about Bonn,' he said. 'What happened there? How does it factor in?'

'There?'

'Germany.'

Michael began to laugh. The acoustics of the chapel made it sound hysterical.

'What's so funny?'

'I have told you about Bonn. I've explained it all to you, Peter. You're just too slow to put it all together.'

'Then tell me again. Make me understand.'

'You've been looking for the wrong thing, Peter. Remember Bonn, poor sweet simple William Bonn, who had his cock cut off because he couldn't stop playing with himself. Do you know the worst of it? Some of them had forgotten. They'd blanked him from their memories. Turned him into nothing. He deserved better from his tormentors. He deserved to be remembered. Even when I faced them down they tried to pretend he never existed. Anglemark masturbated over him and had the gall to lie to my face, trying to convince me I was wrong, that he didn't know the boy or any of the boys like Bonn. Danilo at least didn't deny it. He owned his part in it at the end. Not that it saved his soul. The others, Dooley, Ramirez, Tournard, and Maffrici, they saw what was happening, they could have spoken out, they knew but they didn't value those children enough to save them. It wasn't a secret what was happening there. More deserve to die for what they did, but they escaped me, dying before I could reach them. I regret that. You have to understand, Peter, someone had to fight for them. For Bonn and all the children like him. Someone had to make them pay for what they did to them.'

'I can get justice for them,' Ash swore. He'd caught the

references, they saw, they didn't speak out. Eyes, tongue. He could piece it together now. In Michael's eyes they were all to blame, whether they were the judge who failed to prosecute, or the guardians who sold access to the boys to perverts like the politician. It was a fucking mess. And his own father had been carrying that inside him all these years? It was heart-breaking, and just proved how little he'd actually known the man. But then, like he'd said to Dooley's housekeeper and his father had said to him, 'every man deserved his secrets'. He wasn't sure he could believe that any more. More than anything he wished the old man was still around for him to talk to. That was a guilt he should never have had to bear, not to the grave. 'But not from up here. That is what we do. We speak for the dead. We get justice for those who can't get it for themselves. Let me help you.'

'There can never be justice, only vengeance.'

'You don't have to do this. Cut me down. It doesn't have to end this way.'

'Yes, it does. This is the thing that makes sense.'

'Please. Do you want me to beg, is that it? I'll beg. Because you're wrong about me, I don't have a death wish. I have seen far too much death.'

'Then think of this as a final release, Peter.'

'How do you know it's true? How do you know it was my father who betrayed you?'

'Because I told him,' said a voice from the shadows. 'But I never meant it to come to this. There has been far too much suffering because of me. It stops now, Stefan.'

Michael turned in the direction of the voice.

'Don't call me that, Stefan Karius is dead. I am Michael.'

He reached beneath his jacket while the new arrival stepped into the light.

Ernesto Donatti stood in the aisle, his hands held up to show that he meant no harm.

'I'm sorry, Peter. This is my fault,' the Vatican envoy said, walking slowly down the aisle, hands still raised.

'Don't flatter yourself,' Michael said.

'I am not. I am torn by guilt and sadness. You came to me for names, Stefan. I gave you them but I had no idea of what you were planning . . .' He shook his head.

'I am doing this for every child who survived that place. And for all of us who didn't. They deserve justice.'

'But you don't know what these men did after and what good they may have done. You didn't know Peter's dad. You never knew him, Stefan. Do you know what he did every year? He took Peter here on a pilgrimage of guilt to different orphanages. He delivered presents. He tried to bring a little happiness to their lives. And that was because he couldn't forget. Don't get me wrong, he wanted to. That was all he ever wanted to do. But those memories would never leave him. They were a part of the man he became. But the older he became the more distant they became, like a dream, and the horrors faded. He couldn't remember what was real and what was imagined by the end. But he never forgot what happened to you there. He came back after the fire. He thought you were all dead, and he bore that guilt heavily. You need to remember, he was just a child himself. He couldn't change things.'

'You lie.'

Donatti shook his head sadly. 'You should have let sleeping dogs lie, Stefan.'

'And let those men live?'

'They are all old. Spent. They pose no danger to anyone. They will face the Lord and face his judgement. Ours is not to exact His righteous fury. You should have told your story. You should have shone a light on the horrors of this place, and places like it, and brought some peace to the restless dead. But no. You wanted to be the hand of God. "For our God is a consuming fire." Hebrews 12:29, Stefan.' Donatti lowered his hands slowly. 'They made you into what you have become, and I understand that, I truly do. I see the path you have followed, and how far you have fallen from the light. But the great tragedy of this is that you are no better than they were.'

There was a blur of movement, a flash, and the chapel filled with furious noise for a moment – a single deafening shot – before Donatti fell to the ground. He no longer lay in the glorious technicoloured light of the stained-glass window but had fallen into the shadow.

Michael let his arm fall to his side, the smoking gun in his hand. He let it fall to the flagstones. 'He shouldn't have said that,' he said, unable to take his eyes off the body on the ground.

The blood began to pool around Donatti.

Ash felt betrayed. Bereft.

His friend had known all of it. Not just known, he was complicit. From that first note in Paris, the Monsignor's disappearance and the yellow-brick road that led all the way to Maffrici's parlour; he had known all of it.

He must have known Michael – Stefan as he'd called him – was responsible.

'You don't have to do this.'

'I have to. This is the path to salvation. I cannot stop until I have finished. You are the last of them that I can reach in this life.'

'Your confession, though, people need to know what happened here. There needs to be a reckoning.'

'I am that reckoning.'

'No. It needs to be more than that. More than a few corpses littering the street. People need to hear the truth.'

'I have written everything down. Everything I remember, everything they did to us, every crime.' With his free hand he slipped a notebook from his pocket. 'It is all in here. Who the people were, what they did, and who they did it to. Everything.'

And with that, he took a lighter from his pocket, thumbed the wheel into flame, and tossed it on top of the pile of petrol-soaked books.

The flames caught instantly and grew, voraciously consuming the paper as it fed the fire. Michael didn't stand idly by watching his handiwork. He dragged the remains of several broken chairs and pews up to the altar and fed them to the flames.

The flames grew, licking up at his feet. The stench of petrol rose.

The air was filled with heat and smoke.

Ash coughed, gagging on the smoke.

He had seconds. Any longer and the only way he was coming down from the cross was to become his name.

He strained for all he was worth to free one hand, twisting his back against the cross-brace of the crucifix.

The wood creaked and groaned.

The smoke stung his eyes, bring tears to them.

He blinked them back, but more came, turning the inside of the chapel into a blur of smoke and shadow.

He could have sworn in that moment he saw the silhouette of

a man in the doorway, waiting to guide him into the light. He doubled down, roaring a deep primal scream as he really gave into the rage, the anger, frustration, and fear that had hounded him since he heard the news of Mitch Greer's death. He was not ready to meet his old friend. Not yet.

'Go,' he rasped, banishing the familiar ghost.

And finally, the wood cracked.

The integrity of the crucifix was failing but not fast enough. He writhed about, trying to put all his weight into each desperate twist, as the flames rose up around him. In seconds he would burn.

But Mitch's ghost refused to abandon him.

Light hurt Ash's eyes as he tried to banish his friend one final time.

The black silhouette ran down the length of the aisle, charging into Michael and sending him sprawling across the flagstones.

He had never imagined that the spirit tasked with guiding him into the light would fight so desperately to take him.

The acrid smoke stung his eyes.

His lungs filled with the stuff. He could barely breathe, but then his hand was suddenly free.

'Am I dead?' he tried to ask, thinking his spirit had liberated itself from the bonds of flesh, as he fell forward.

He didn't fall all the way; he hung awkwardly by one wrist. The sudden searing agony that tore through his body convinced him he was very much alive. No matter how desperately he thrashed about, kicking furiously, the heat of the flame clawing its way up his body, he couldn't pull free of the worm-riddled wood.

And then he fell into the fire.

The burning prayer books scattered around him.

He felt the searing heat on his skin.

'I don't want to go,' he told Mitch Greer's ghost. 'I'm not ready.'

He felt hands close around his ankles and drag him clear of the blaze. Then felt the weight of someone smothering him with their body to put out the flames.

'Mitch?' he said, or tried to say. His voice wouldn't obey him. 'Leave me alone. Please.'

He saw a face through the smoke and tears.

It wasn't Mitch's.

There were no ghosts in the chapel save for those Stefan Karius had brought in with him.

It was a woman's face.

He only saw it for a moment, the silence in between heartbeats where hope lives, and then he was gone.

SEVENTY

Ash woke in a hospital bed.
His entire body felt as though he was still on fire.
He was alive.
He had no idea how.
He didn't care.
He was still alive.

A woman sat in the room's only chair. She read a magazine. She looked bone-tired. He tried to shift position in the bed, but the feel of the sheets against his skin only made the pain worse.

'Lucky boy,' she said.

He didn't feel it.

He knew the voice, but not the face.

'Frankie?'

'Peter.'

He shook his head, and immediately regretted it. 'What are you doing here?'

'Saving your life. Not that you wanted me to.' This time it was her turn to shake her head. 'Telling me to leave you alone. You don't know me very well, do you?' Her smile was gently mocking.

'It was you?'

'Who else did you think it was?'

'I don't know . . . I thought I saw . . .'

'Donatti,' she said for him, filling in the gaps. 'It would have been a lot harder without your friend's help.'

Ash started to say he was no friend, then remembered the man sprawled out on the chapel floor, his lifeblood leaking out of him.

'He was willing to give his life in return for yours.'

'How did you find me?'

'Laura. She was frightened you'd hit some kind of self-destruct button after your last conversation.'

'How,' he said again.

'She found Donatti. He confessed. I was already on my way to Paris. He met me at the airport. We went straight there.'

'I don't even know where "there" is. Michael took me to the remains of an orphanage, but then he hit me with some kind of sedative. The next thing I knew I was in that chapel.'

'It is in the grounds of the orphanage. It didn't burn down when the rest of the house did.'

'How did Donatti know we'd be there?'

'Patterns of behaviour,' she said. It was one of his favourite touchstones when it came to any investigation. Criminals fell back on patterns of behaviour. 'It was where it all began. It was where it had to end.'

Ash listened as Frankie told him about the discovery of the dossier in Karius's apartment, and the switch – how he'd burned one of his first victims and traded places with them, letting them be dead for him. She told him about the final page in Karius's dossier, and how he had been marked as the Memory Man's final victim.

'It was only when I said your name that Donatti understood what he had done. He was determined to put it right. He made me wait outside. He wanted to talk to Karius first, to convince him to see sense.'

'And we know how that worked out,' Ash said.

'I came in after the gun went off. I saw you hanging on that cross, the flames rising up around you. I didn't think I'd be able to get to you. But somehow you pulled yourself free. Then when I tried to drag you out of the fire, you started shouting at me, telling me to leave you alone, you didn't want to go.'

'I thought you were someone else,' he said, managing a wry smile.

'Well, I dragged you out of there, but the fire was out of control. The roof was collapsing. Everything was going up. He'd doused the entire place in petrol, not just the Bibles and hymn books. I didn't think I'd be able to get Donatti out of there, but I was damned if I was going to leave him to burn with that bastard. Karius carried him to the door, not me. I didn't realize it until we were away from there, in the ambulance, but he put a journal in Donatti's robes. His last act was actually a noble one. He saved the man, then turned and ran back into the chapel before I could stop him. The entire roof came down on top of him.'

'Donatti?'

'He's out of danger.'

'Good. I . . . he knew. He knew it all. And instead of saying something, making Maffrici confess, he let the judge hide his sins.'

'He didn't have a choice, Peter. A higher power told him what needed to be done.'

'God?'

She laughed at that. 'A little more mortal.'

'The Pope?'

'A few years ago, during an investigation into child abuse within the Catholic Church, a number of crimes of the priests and others came to light. The secrets of several of these Church-sponsored orphanages were exposed, and a prominent priest was implicated. The judge managed to help him avoid a trial. They were protecting the Church. Closing ranks. See No Evil. Hear No Evil. Speak No Evil. The motto of the holy men. The Father gave up his liberty. He lives basically under house arrest in the Vatican, dedicating his life to prayer. He can never leave the Holy See.'

Given everything Karius had told him in the derelict orphanage, being locked up in the luxury of the Vatican didn't seem like much of a punishment. He said as much. 'Maffrici was the judge?'

She nodded. 'Karius believed he was complicit, that at the time of their greatest need he had let the children down, taking the Church's coin.'

'Just like my dad.'

'He didn't take any money,' Frankie contradicted. 'He was a child running for his own life. He did nothing wrong. Did he never talk about it?'

'Never.' Ash shook his head. 'I knew that he had grown up in care, but he never let on. My father had a lot of secrets.'

'Don't we all? And like I said, you're a lucky boy. The doctors tell me most of the burns are superficial. There'll be some scarring, but you'll be fine. They're more concerned about any damage to your lungs.'

'Maybe I'll get that sexy sixty-cigarettes-a-day rasp all the ladies love.'

'Speaking of which, Laura sends her love and told me to tell you to get your arse back to London. It's all change.'

'What do you mean?'

'A decision's come down from Division, everything is centralizing. They're moving us into a custom-built complex. She's not happy because it means leaving London.'

'Where to?'

'You'll like this.'

'Where to?'

'Go on, guess.'

He shook his head.

'Bonn.'

He couldn't help himself, he burst out laughing. It felt good to laugh, right up to the moment he thought he was going to cough a lung up in the process.

'It gets worse,' Frankie said.

'Do I even want to know?'

'This wasn't my decision.'

'What wasn't?'

'Division don't want anyone working alone. The edict's come down from on high. Until the relocation's complete I'll be working out of River House.'

'How do you feel about that?'

'That depends.'

'On what?'

'How did you vote in the referendum?'

'Ah,' he said. 'That.'

'Yes. That. The elephant in the room.'

'I didn't vote.'

'You didn't vote?'

'I was too busy being shot at in Spain by rather pissed-off members of a drug cartel.'

'I can see why voting would slip your mind,' Frankie said.

'Do I pass the test, partner?'

'We'll see.'